THROUGH THE FIRE

FIRE COMPANY 143
BOOK 2

DANIELLE BROOKS

DEDICATION

This book is dedicated to the lovers who need the reminder that even the phoenix rose from the ashes. Keep believing that when the smoke dissipates, love will be on the other side.

Happy Reading!

Through the fire, to the limit, to the wall
    For a chance to be with you
    I'd gladly risk it all

— CHAKA KHAN

FALLON

A distant whistle sounded off in my mind, forcing it to wake before my body. My eyes twitched as I realized the whistling were actually birds in concert outside of my window. Peeling my lids open, I was met by the blinding pale, yellow beams of the sun's rays, quickly forcing them closed again.

I need to remember to order light-blocking curtains.

The thought drifted away quickly as I exhaled and squirmed under my sheet, readying myself to return to my slumber. I stilled and squinted one eye open as the bass of a groan rumbled from behind me, and then a stubbled chin brushed my bare shoulder, quickly cluing me that I was naked. This wasn't unusual as that was my favorite state to be in, but the strong, finely haired arm gently wrapping around my midsection had me questioning how exactly I came to this state last night and who the f—

"Good morning, gorgeous."

Slightly rotating the upper half of my body into a bouldering chest, I twisted my head further to the drawl of a Southern tenor. The deep crease in my forehead relaxed as my eyes met hazy light brown ones, and the puzzle that was my memory of the night pieced together in my mind. Heat began to radiate from between my thighs when I noticed the ring of grey in his retinas as his pupils dilated.

Oh shit, he's in love. Well, maybe not in love, but he's definitely feeling too much.

My alter ego, Hazel, entered the chat as my inner voice. She was me, and I was her, but when it came to my entertainment for the evening, I went by my middle name, Hazel, instead of my given first name, Fallon. It kept things impersonal, light, and fun. However, when my company for the night began to look at me like my current one is now—*I can literally see the hearts bouncing in his eyes; yes, he was definitely in love—*Hazel stepped in, hand on hip, with a traffic stop sign and whistle in tow.

A grin spread across my guest's face, revealing the pearly whites behind his beautiful pink lips. The man's identity came through clearly and concisely.

"Captain," I greeted with a soft smile, maintaining an even tone.

"At your service." His grin curled into a mischievous smirk as he moved to…snuggle me?

Flipping over to face him, I gently placed a hand on his chest. Softly chuckling, I reminded, "No snuggling."

He moved his arm from around my waist and put a surrendering hand in front of himself as he asked through a nervous titter, "Damn, you meant that, eh?"

The memory of us stumbling into my unpacked apartment as our hands stripped articles of clothing from each other's bodies while tangling liquored tongues came to the forefront. It had only been hours before that moment that I met Captain Langston Calloway. I remembered his name because he was the pilot of my flight from Damask to Lovey's Bay. Who could forget such a charming name for an even more enticing and gorgeous man?

Standing over six feet tall, with smooth skin, bright white teeth, and a muscular frame that suggested he spent time in the gym, Langston had a memorable presence, but that wasn't what initially made him unforgettable. It was the accidental bump of my backside brushed against his well-endowed member as I struggled to lift my carry-on luggage over the rickety metal plate separating the cabin from the cockpit. *That's* when I noticed his handsome face. Needless to say, we were both intrigued by one another and soon found ourselves engaged in flirty conversation over drinks at the airport bar, which led to us sharing a ride to my apartment.

So that's when our night really began, just barely in my apartment with me in nothing but a lace bra and panty set, and him in boxer briefs that were struggling to contain his mouth-watering bulge. I remembered Captain lifting me to his waist as I swung an arm behind me, drunkenly guiding him to my bedroom. But before I let him please me, I felt it was time to lay down the law.

"This is just sex, Captain," I remember panting out the beginnings of my rules as he nibbled on my neck. He soothed the mix of pain and pleasure with the warmth of his mouth to the spot. His large hands gripped the sides of my ass hungrily, and I could feel his erection teasing my center. "…and good sex, I suspect."

"*Very* good sex," he groaned as he stepped over the threshold of the dark bedroom. When he placed me on the bed with great care, I knew it was pertinent that I continued the rundown of my rules

"Good," I whimpered as he played with my nipples through my bra before skillfully popping the hook and freeing my breast. Like a hungry puppy, he took in a mouthful of my D-cup breast before flicking his tongue against my swollen peak while tweaking the other.

The intoxicated cloud I was on heightened my senses, and I remembered audibly expressing my enjoyment of his play with my breasts as I moved the mission forward by sliding his briefs over his hips. He broke from his suckle, and I creamed as I watched his third leg swing like a pendulum as he stepped out of the last article of clothing he wore. With the moon shining through the blinds of the window behind us, I could see Captain Calloway had the body of a god. Tight muscled chest and arms, rows of abs, and a dick that would make a woman fall in love. The rules were *definitely* necessary to lay out.

As Captain hovered over me, ready to plant a kiss, I placed a finger between our lips and instructed, "Fuck me good, Captain. Take me to the moon. This may be your first and last flight on Hazel Airlines."

Though it was a very sexy way to say it, I was telling him the truth. I had no plans to make this more than just a night of fun between adults, and I wanted to ensure I made that very clear. I remembered him smirking at me with lustful, liquor-laden eyes before he shifted his gaze to my manicured index finger. He pecked it, then swirled his tongue around the finger before teasing the tip as if it were my most sensitive spot. The sensation made my center pulse and tingle.

He looked up at me with that sexy ass grin still plastered on his face. "Sounds like you're the pilot of this flight, Captain Hazel Fine Ass."

I remember giggling and cringing inside at his corny joke and then finding my breath stolen at the feel of his hand covering the lace seat of my panties. It was the only barrier between his hand and my pussy, and he didn't let it stop his stroke and then pressed on my clit. He whispered in my ear, "Any other rules, Cap?"

I lifted up, helping him remove my panties, and then reached to pull open the drawer of my nightstand, pushing past my toy to the only other items littering it: condoms. I pulled one out and passed one to him between two fingers. I squirmed as I watched him sheath himself, my center pulsing at the thought of having him inside of me. He climbed onto the bed as I scooted to the middle and laid back. As he hovered, I spoke the most important rule:

"No cuddling."

I remember his thick eyebrows bunched as he held himself up by his fists, and then he huffed a laugh and parroted, "No cuddling?"

I licked my lips and raised an eyebrow. "Yeah. After this is all said and done, no cuddling. This is physical… not personal."

Langston looked down at me, his squinted eyes slightly widening as the realization that I was serious hit him. He stayed there for a moment, mouth half agape as if he was thinking. That moment was short-lived, and soon after, he was plunging in and fucking me like he had something to prove.

"Right, no cuddling…" Langston reminded himself before I could pull myself away from the memory of the previous night and remind him.

I looked at him with my eyebrows raised and a nod. I sucked my bottom lip between my teeth as I held myself up by my elbow. He took a hand to the strands of my touseled bob, grazing his thumb over my cheek and then my lip before cupping my face to lean in and kiss my lips. I stiffened, not returning the kiss as Hazel entered the inner chat again.

Abort the mission and him now!

Langston's head veered back slightly, realizing I failed to return the kiss. He did that nervous laugh again and then said, "You're stone cold, baby. But like a moth to a flame, I can't keep my eyes off of you. I kind of like that."

I threw my head back and cackled. Bringing my head forward again, I said, "And that, my friend, is why no snuggling is allowed."

A rumbling, howling laughter rolled from his lips as he fussed with the sheet and took position over me. Lowering into a push-up position, he whispered in my ear, "Well, can my cock make a pit stop before you kick me out?"

Internally, I cringed at the joke, remembering he had been full of these corny jokes last night. I wondered how and why I looked past that, but then I locked in on those eyes, his gorgeous caramel face and his ripped body. *Sigh* That was enough to cause the jokes to slip under the radar. He didn't wait for me to respond. Instead, he trailed kisses and licks down the center of my chest, to each nipple, down the center of my caved-in stomach, and then paused at the opening of my spread legs, peering up at me as if he was waiting for my approval.

He blew a soft and warm breath over my opening, sending a wave through my body and a quake between my legs. My lips parted slightly as a wanting breath escaped, and I rimmed the inside of my top lip with my tongue.

"Go ahead, Captain. You have control of this last flight—ah!"

As if knowing his time was almost up, Captain Langston Calloway showed why he held the first chair, taking hold of my legs and letting his tongue guide me to Cloud Nine.

———

It took Langston thirty minutes too long to leave. He tried. After a finale, he rolled over, attempting to go back to sleep. The way he laid it down and served it—long and hard—he deserved a nap; hell, even breakfast, but that would've felt too personal. So, I gently nudged him from his impending slumber and tapped on his strong shoulder, reminding him that he had a hotel room to check into.

"Get some rest and safe travels, Captain," I said, holding my apartment door open with a swing of my hips. I tugged at my robe's lapel, ensuring that it was secure around my naked body before crossing my arms over my chest.

Langston leaned down, aligning his face with my

5'6" height. His lips were mere inches from mine, so close that our breaths mingled. I was convinced he was going to attempt a goodbye kiss by the way his mouth twitched indecisively towards pucker. My heart began to race, thudding against my chest so loudly that I could hear it. I contemplated sending a quick, inaudible goodbye before slipping behind my door, but then he turned his head slightly to my right, leaving a sweet peck on my cheek. My chest hollowed as a discreet sigh of relief escaped me.

"See you again?" Langston asked. His drawl was less pronounced than before, and his voice now held a heavy crack of uncertainty.

Every imaginary siren within me went off, signaling for me to answer 'No.' We'd only known each other for 12 hours, and he already seemed like he wanted to ask me to be his lady. I didn't doubt that he was a great man; he had been a perfect gentleman throughout our entire encounter. But that was the issue.

Langston acted like he liked me, genuinely liked me enough to want to see me again and pursue me seriously, but serious dating was not on my Bingo card. The centerpiece of my Bingo card boldly proclaimed "Casual" in red letters, and everything that would make my card a winner had to be just that. I was in a new city, Lovey's Bay, and I left every inkling of seriousness down south in Damask. However, as I got lost in Cap's pleading, hypnotizing eyes and recalled how amazing sex had been between us, I considered that maybe I could entertain him again the next time he was in Lovey's Bay.

"Potentially," I said with a lazy shrug of my right shoulder. "Hit me next time you're in town."

A flirty smirk danced at the corner of my lips as I took his phone to enter my number. Before returning the phone, I added Hazel in the name section of my contact. No legal name, no attachments.

Tucking the phone into his trouser pocket, Langston grabbed the handle of his carry-on bag and donned his aviator hat. He took a few steps back, then winked and moved forward, his walk infused with a swagger he rightfully owned. Just as I turned to retreat into my apartment, I sensed eyes on me.

"Damn, girl, where'd you find that one?" My neighbor, Joni, stood at her door with a bag of trash by her side.

Her apartment was diagonal and across from mine, giving her the perfect view of Langston's exit. I twisted my mouth to the right, trying to hide the guilty smirk that longed to break free. Instead, it burst forth as a laugh I couldn't suppress any longer, thanks to the look of curiosity and nosiness plastered on Joni's face.

I didn't mind Joni's inquiry. She was cool, making her introduction to me during my first week at Bayside Apartments. She reminded me of Charmaine from A Different World — you know, the short, fast-talking freshman who joined as part of the newer generation of students. Joni was just like her in real life: fast-talking, witty, and seemed to notice everything that happened at the complex.

That being said, I only knew Joni from the brief meetings in the hallway over the past month, which wasn't enough for me to share all the details of my dating life. I shrugged apathetically and offered a vague truth, "Oh, he's just a guy I know."

"See, that's why I knew I'd like you," she replied, tapping the air with her index finger. "You're like a female Marcus Graham from Boomerang."

I scrunched my nose, considering her analogy. "Mm, I'd say more like Jacqueline. She had a bad reputation in Boomerang, but essentially, she did what Marcus did—only she was a woman… and she did it better."

"I know *that's* right!" Joni twisted her wrist in the air and snapped it down. I shared a quick giggle with her before waving goodbye and retreating into my apartment to prepare for my delayed morning start with a shower.

As the steaming shower water cascaded down my body, washing away the physical remnants of last night's adventure, I replayed the brief conversation with Joni in my mind. I stand firmly on the idea that I am the Jacqueline in my version of Boomerang. I was living my best single life without hesitation or regret. After years of being trapped in a suffocating controlling rela-tionship, it was my time to live on my own terms, and right now, those terms included freedom and fun—

safely, of course. Those terms are why I'm in Lovey's Bay now.

I left the vibrant and bustling city of Damask, Georgia, for sunny bayside living in Lovey's Bay about a month ago. Damask had been my home for most of my life, as I settled there during my early childhood after moving back to the States from London. I grew up there, graduated from high school there, and even began my first serious relationship in Damask. I suppose I could credit Damask for ending that same serious relationship there too, and with that realization, I knew it was time for a change of scenery. While I had the option to return to London, the thought of having my judgmental mother in my ear was not my idea of change. In fact, it would have trapped me back in a bubble, draining the life out of me again. So, I chose Lovey's Bay as my new home, a city just forty minutes from my brother's second home.

My older brother, Parris, made Stonecrest, Greenbrook, his home when he began dating superstar Tinsley McCoy, who is now his fiancée. Stonecrest was her hometown, so it made sense that they frequented it often, especially since their relationship was low-key in the beginning. He often spoke about how much he enjoyed Greenbrook and how diverse the state was, with its countryside living, a booming capital, and a sunny bayside. The mention of the sunny bayside caught my attention.

Living by the water piqued my interest and seemed like a great way to start over while being close to the one man who always had my best interests at heart, my brother. Don't tell him I said that, but the idea of living a free life and knowing he would be nearby every now and then felt reassuring, especially since I was leaving everything I knew behind in Damask, including my best friend, Zaria.

As if she knew I was thinking about her, my phone vibrated against my pelvic bone inside the pouch fastened around my waist. I had dressed in workout gear suitable for the early spring weather: leggings, a sports bra, and a cropped T-shirt. I paused my movement as I stepped onto the sidewalk outside my apartment complex and began jogging in place while looking at my watch displaying Zaria's face. I tapped my earbuds to connect the call.

"You're late."

"By ten minutes, damn!" I playfully argued Zaria's very true statement.

"Yeah, yeah. You leave Damask and leave your schedules and morals behind," Zaria continued to fuss. The chuckle that accompanied it gave away the lack of offense.

"Oh, hush, Z! I'm getting ready to start. What about you?"

"Already hitting the pavement. Again, you're late!"

"Ugh, I'm coming," I scoffed with enthusiasm before breaking into a light jog down the two blocks toward the boardwalk.

Just like when we were both in Damask, Zaria and I would go for a morning run together as long as our schedules aligned. When I was in Damask, those morning runs were our thing—our time to catch up and indulge in girl talk without the male species. In our line of work as firefighters, we were always surrounded by men, and our running time offered a chance to balance out the overload of testosterone. When I decided to leave Damask, we promised we'd still maintain this routine: getting up every morning we could to go for a run, no matter that we were hundreds of miles apart.

"So what was his name?" Zaria probed after a few minutes of nothing but measured breaths between us.

"What?"

"Don't play coy, Fallon. I know your 'hot in the pants' ass very well. You are never late for our run unless you were entertaining the night before."

"Damn, Z, you make me sound like a lady of the night!"

"You said it, not me," Zaria quipped and then cackled.

Unable to breathe and laugh at the same time, I stopped at the edge of the Lovey's Bay Beach boardwalk and doubled over with laughter. I placed my hands on my thighs and gasped, "Put some respect on my name!"

Zaria egged on. "You know I'm playing, but you also know I'm telling the truth. Spill it!"

I looked left and then right, surveying the scene. It

was just a little after nine in the morning, and the boardwalk, adorned with apartments and hotels, was sparsely populated with people either exercising or walking their pets, as today's sunny early spring weather made it a perfect day to enjoy the fresh, slightly crisp air. I decided to turn left and run along the boardwalk toward the Ferris wheel and a more residential area. With much less foot traffic, I felt a sense of privacy as I shared the details of my night with Zaria.

"Captain Calloway. Pilot."

"Bitttcchh. Tell me you didn't snag the pilot from your flight yesterday," she said, nearly winded.

In between gasps of air, I retorted, "I'd be lying if I said I didn't."

"Girl, teach me your ways!" I could hear Zara's high-pitched cackle on the other end, infectiously causing me to burst into laughter. An older gentleman power-walking past me caught the bug, smiling brightly at me and then quickly winking.

"There's nothing to teach," I said as I huffed a short laugh at the fleeting flirtation by the man. "I am a woman and free! You have the same superpower."

"Yeah, well, you must have some of that heart-shaped herb potion from Black Panther in your genes because your superpower is potent! You're meeting pilots; I'm meeting bus drivers. We are not the same."

I shook my head as if she could see me. "Girl, whatever. There's nothing wrong with a bus driver. They earn a good salary and have paid-off homes."

"Says the one pulling captains of whole planes!"

I cracked up again at her theatrics, which made me stop my run to catch my breath. I glanced down at my watch and noticed I had crossed the one-mile mark, so I decided to take a break. Leaning over a nearby railing that separated the boardwalk from the beach, I looked out at the smooth, gentle waves rolling in from a distance. I reflected on what Zaria said before answering, "I think the difference is, I'm not looking for anything. I'm just having fun, so I'm attracting fun, uncommitted men…who happen to be captains and stuff."

We both laughed at the unexpected twist to my very honest observation about my choices before Zaria settled down and spoke again. "I guess. Who would've thought…"

"Me. I thought about it and pursued it. A life I want," I interrupted, not allowing Zaria to finish her thought. I knew where she was headed, and I had no desire to follow her there. The past was my past, and it was staying there with my old life.

"Okay," Zaria murmured, clearly picking up on my hint to switch topics. "So, are you planning to return to Damask, or was this your last trip?"

"I won't be back unless I'm coming to visit you at this point. I just had to close out a few logistical and financial things during this last trip. Hopefully, I'll be hearing something about work in the next week or so."

"You're trying to go back to work already?" Zaria asked, her breath now sounding as if she was walking. This prompted me to push off the rail and continue my trek forward.

"Yeah," I sang. "I have bills to pay."

I did have bills to pay, but I wasn't hurting for money. I *wanted* to go back to work. I missed the rush of the firefighter life, and after being away from it for nearly six months, I was itching to get my adrenaline going again. I had much to prove.

"I hear you," Zaria said. "I'd still take another month off, though. Are you really ready to jump in there with another group of funky men?"

I snickered. "It's been six months, Z! I'm ready for the excitement of the job again. I'm ready to be back in the field and not just sitting on the sidelines. Heck, I wasn't even on the sidelines except in my relationship. Those days of playing small for a man are over."

"Okay, Fireball," Zaria teased. "Well, look, I have to go. I start my shift in a couple of hours."

I halted my run and gasped. "Z, you didn't have to do the run this morning if you are starting a shift."

"I know I didn't, but I did. I miss you, pooh!"

A content smile settled on my lips. "I miss you, too, Z. You have to come up here and visit one day."

"You're right," she agreed. "Because I need to sit and study your playbook."

I shook my head and let out an airy goodbye as I turned on my heels and started jogging back to my apartment. Zaria spoke just before hanging up the call.

"Oh, I heard you when you said you weren't settling for another man. You were never small, Fallon. You were just in love. Maybe with the wrong person… but still in love. There's nothing wrong with going through a little fire to find your way to love, whether that love is with someone else or with yourself. This one was for you. Be proud of your journey, pooh."

I slowed to a walk, biting my bottom lip as I took in Zaria's words. Zaria always knew how to strike me right in the chest out of nowhere, and I was struggling to maintain my composure after her encouraging words. I exhaled sharply, blinking away the tears gathering at my lash line, and resumed my jog.

"Thanks, Z. Now, get your sappy ass off my line!"

We shared another laugh before ending the call.

"Man, there's never a dull day here or a shortage of bizarre stories."

"Who you tellin'? A fisher damn near fry himself while trying to make fish and grits? Never in my days had I heard of anything like this until now!"

The fire station garage filled with laughter, the sound of heavy metal engine doors slamming, and the clunk of rubber work boots. It was the typical noise that filled the station after we'd finished a job more amusing than life-threatening, like this one. In the early morning hour of five, the crew and I were awakened by the alert of a fire on Lovey's Bay. The actual bay. When we arrived on the scene, there it was: a blazing bright orange fire on the still water. Quickly, the crew and I got the raft out and doused the flames.

The cause of the fire? A hot plate with an overcooked piece of fish. Why did this happen? Spilled bait oil. Thankfully, the fisherman thought to throw on a life jacket and jump out of his small boat before he ended up just as burnt as his whiting.

After stepping out of my smoky protective gear and leaving me in just one of my many company T-shirts, athletic shorts, and socks, I padded through the still lively crew, up the cement stairs of the garage, through the open space of our combined kitchen, dining room, and lounge area, and headed toward the locker room. My body felt heavy with exhaustion that seemed never-ending, and I was ready to get out of my gear and head home to do what I often did now: sleep.

I sat on the bench and looked up at the coal-grey steel locker, its surface etched with my name: Benjamin Deacon. One agonizing and repetitive thought that haunted the back of my mind surged to the forefront: *She didn't even want my last name anymore.*

I sighed, shaking my head to rid myself of the thought, and entered my passcode. Within seconds, I heard three beeps and a click signifying the lock releasing, and I opened my locker. My eyes fell on the picture of me and Vanessa taped to the back of the locker, allowing that annoying thought to circulate in my mind again.

She didn't even want my last name anymore.

A grunt settled in my throat as I reminded myself that, at some point, I needed to take that picture down.

"There's no better time than now," I said under my breath, peeling the picture from the wall. I diverted my eyes to my sneakers, grabbing them and dropping them to the floor before grabbing my keys and bookbag, stuffing the picture into the small zipper opening. As I shut the door to my locker, I noticed the shadow of a person replacing the locker door.

"Aye, man, you good?" Denzel asked, standing with his arms crossed over his chest, his mouth twisted, emphasizing his question about how I was doing.

With a heavy head, I lifted my gaze, half greeting him and half preparing the lie I was about to tell. "Yeah, I'm good."

His eyebrow arched toward his fresh hairline. "Mm, alright, man. You've been a bit distant lately. Usually, you're the ringleader of the jokes and the clowning out there."

"It's been a long ass week, man. I'm just ready to get home and enjoy my days off," I said, still partially telling the truth.

Honestly, I was tired. Working several 24-hour shifts back to back takes a toll on the body, and I was ready to get home and rest. What I wasn't ready to say out loud was that part of my apathy toward joking with the crew had a lot to do with the heaviness that still weighed on me from my failed engagement.

"How have you been holding up? You know, being in the new place and all?" Denzel asked, clearly seeing beyond my response. I groaned, the sound trapped in my throat. One thing Denzel does is probe until he gets the answer he wants. I knew he meant well, but damn.

"It's cool," I replied, ready to end the conversation right there, but Denzel didn't budge. He just stood there, waiting for me to elaborate. I knew he wouldn't let up until I gave him a real answer. "I mean, it's different. I haven't lived alone in three years, so…" I shrugged my shoulders instead of continuing about how incredibly lonely it was without Vanessa's presence.

I moved to Bayside Apartments four months ago after realizing I couldn't stay in the condo that Vanessa and I shared before she left me. There were too many memories there, and it reminded me that she made the choice to end our relationship. Hell, she even left Lovey's Bay. At first, I thought she was just trying to create space between us, but after a week of her being gone, she showed up with a moving truck and her brothers, both of them sporting mean mugs as they monstered through the apartment, clearing out all her belongings, including the sofa she contributed to our condo. I was flabbergasted, unable to believe what was happening. She left me standing in the middle of the sofa-less living room with nothing more than a "Goodbye."

Could I blame her? No, she'd been telling me how she wanted us to move forward and set a wedding date for two years before she left, and I either joked my way out of committing or buried myself in work. If "fuck around and find out' were a person, it would be me, right at the center.

"It's going to feel like home soon," Denzel said, giving me a reassuring pat on the back.

Going back to putting on my shoes, I grumbled, "Yeah, I hope so."

"You know what you need to do? Get your ass out of the house and *live*. Go meet you a new jank."

The unmistakable voice of Tevin chimed in over my shoulder. My inner jokester wanted to clown on him, but solemnity and exhaustion overshadowed that side of me.

Tevin continued yapping, "You should come with us to The Romance is Blind speed dating event at Rhythm and Brews. Women always say, "The best way to get over your old man is to get under a new one." Be like them. Get over your old jank with a new jank."

I glanced over my shoulder with narrowed eyes just in time to see Denzel elbowing Tevin in the side. Denzel bulged his eyes at him, then looked at me with a shoulder shrug and a furrowed brow. He somewhat agreed, saying, "Although that's not exactly how I would phrase it, he has a point. You should go out with them and dip your toes back into the dating pool."

Tevin stared and attempted to whisper as if I weren't sitting just inches away from them. "Same thing I said.

Why you always sugarcoating the shit with him? He needs to get his moping ass out."

Denzel continued the awkward whispering. "Because the man is going through it. Give him some grace."

Tevin clicked his tongue. "Fuck grace, unless the new jank name is Grace."

My bah-humbug mood couldn't resist the chuckle that fell from my lips. I shook my head and stood up, tossing my bag over my shoulder as the two guys continued to bicker like an old married couple. "Y'all know I'm right here, right? Y'all are a trip, but I'm outta here to catch some real Zs."

I heard Tevin behind me as I walked towards the exit, "Think about it, Deac! Rhythm and Brews…next week!"

Just as I rounded the corner to return to the community space, I heard heavy shoes jogging behind me. I looked over my shoulder to find Denzel slowing down beside me.

"You know Tevin ain't got no sense," Denzel said with an apologetic tone.

"He doesn't, but he might have a point," I admitted as we jogged down the steps into the fire station garage. The garage was now empty except for two crew members wiping down the engine we had just returned.

"Getting out may not be a bad idea," Denzel agreed. "Just because it didn't work out with Vanessa, it doesn't mean it can't work out with someone else."

I slowed to a stop at the open garage door, allowing

his words to stab into my heart. I took a deep, measured breath through my nose, pushing back my feelings while savoring the crisp spring air. The bay's water hung heavily in the air as the sun peeked through the sparse floating cumulus clouds.

"Somehow, your ass always knows what the fuck I'm thinking about," I mumbled, looking out to the morning traffic accumulating.

Denzel slapped my shoulder and then gave it a squeeze. "That's what friends are for: to pull out the shit out you don't want to be seen, so you're not stuck. You did it for me through my ups and downs with Nina… even though I dropped the ball a time or two."

I turned and raised an eyebrow. Snickering, I said, "More like you dropped your common sense when you didn't get your key back from Thandie."

"Yeah… you've got a point there," Denzel chuckled, scratching his head. His laughter faded into a chill smile as he looked over at me, seriousness cloaked in his expression and words. "But honestly, you're gonna be aight, man. You're a good dude, and you're gonna go the long way with the right one eventually. Just don't beat yourself up about it. Shit happens for a reason. Maybe The Big Man Upstairs has other plans for you. That sounds like something you would've said to us."

Denzel's mention of The Man Upstairs struck me to my core, reminding me how much I had lost touch with my Light. Here he was, preaching to me when I was usually the one keeping the crew centered in the midst of my jokes. Yet, none of that had come from me lately due to the dark cloud I had allowed to linger over my head, obscuring the possibility that perhaps this all happened for a reason.

I huffed a short laugh and looked back out to the street. "It was hard for me to believe The Big Guy would take away the woman that I believed to have been the blessing in my life."

"What's that thing you used to say? If you don't take care of the blessing, don't be surprised when it's taken away?"

I whipped my head toward Denzel, thrown off by him using my quotables against me. Beneath the surprise, the knife of truth was digging into my chest. I shifted my weight and adjusted my bag, brushing off his words. Dapping Denzel, I dismissed myself and set off on my ten-minute walk home. Five minutes in, I began regretting not driving as the spirit of sleep started knocking at the door of my body. Shifting my book bag from one shoulder to both straps, I picked up my pace to a light jog. I felt my eyes growing heavy as the cool air whipped against my slightly damp body and my adrenaline kicked in. Somehow, I felt some of the weight from the conversation with Denzel lifting with my momentum.

"Hey, watch out!"

"Oh, shit! My ba—"

My eyes popped open just before I collided with a

petite, pretty brown woman. She glared at me, surprisingly enhancing her gorgeous appeal, before dashing out of my way and nearly tripping over her own feet. I spun around to help her avoid hitting the pavement, but she was already several yards away, giving me the finger.

I winced, slowing my jog at the sentiment. Before rounding the corner to enter the entrance walkway of my apartment building, I mumbled, "Seems like the sentiment of every woman in my existence."

———

Steam and hot water seemed to be the remedy to everything. As soon as I stepped into my apartment, taking a shower was the first thing on my list to do to start my unwind. When I stepped under the rainfall showerhead, I felt the exhaustion of the work week wash away with the grime of the bay from my last work emergency. It was so draining, I fell back against the tiled wall and just let the water cascade over my frame, letting my thoughts float through my brain like clouds. Working 24-hour shifts straight is taxing on the body as it is, but having the weight of heartbreak on your shoulders made it even harder to maintain an energy level necessary to be focused in the moment of an emergency.

I really needed to shake it off, as Denzel and Tevin encouraged. It's been six months, and I haven't heard a word from Vanessa, not even a thumbs-up to the numerous messages I tried to send her after she moved out. She's moved on, so…I should, right?

Right. I should move on, but one question is keeping me stuck in my feelings and thoughts: What did I do wrong? I was the head of the household and took care of the bills, leaving her with only the responsibility of keeping our fridge stocked. Within a year of being together, I proposed to her and gave her the ring. Whatever she wanted, she got it.

"You gave me the ring and no commitment. We've been engaged for two years. Two years too long!"

Vanessa's words from the night she kicked me out of our apartment rang through my mind.

I remembered pacing the carpeted floor, my head throbbing, partially from exhaustion from just coming home from a week-long trip to fighting a wild fire in Robin's Bend. The other part was because Vanessa had a suitcase packed for me, waiting at the door.

"Nessa, can we talk about this later? I'm just getting home," I griped through a weary sigh.

"We're always pushing back the time to talk about this. You left here last week with the question of when hanging in the air!"

"I had to go. My job was calling me," I reminded through clenched teeth. My jaw was so tight I could feel the vein in my head pulsing.

"Tuh," Vanessa scoffed. "I don't have to worry about

another woman, because your job is the other woman. I'm tired of competing with her! Get out!"

I cringed at the memory of Vanessa telling me to "Get out." I remembered several things going through my head. The first was, I paid the bills, but I wouldn't dare speak that fact aloud. Although true, Vanessa played an equal role in keeping our household afloat. Our home felt like a home because of her, with the halls scented like flowers and vanilla all the time and a home-cooked meal always plated on the table for me, no matter what shift I was coming home from—except for that night. That night, the house still smelled like a garden of flowers but there was no aroma of a meal. The home was quiet besides Vanessa's wrath. That's how I knew, I fucked up, even though I didn't really understand how.

I was tired. I was confused. I was frustrated and I didn't want to argue with her anymore for the night. I figured I'd leave for the night and come back the next day, and I could stroke her walls of all her doubts about us getting married. Behind that thought, I remembered a tiny voice questioning, why was it taking me so long to set a date for us to get married?

The shock of the water from the shower abruptly shifting to icy cold felt like the shock I experienced when I returned to the apartment the next day to find Vanessa and her suitcase gone. A week later, she returned with her brothers to get the rest of her things, leaving me with only a good-bye. Cold, cold world, and so was the shower I still hadn't hastened my way through.

I made a quick quadruple egg and turkey bacon sandwich before I slumped down on my couch. I looked, my weary eyes going from my bare off white walls now painted with the sunlight from my unconcealed windows.

"I gotta remember to get some sun-blocking curtains," I mumbled before sighing and sinking into the couch, taking a big bite of my sandwich.

The aroma of the sandwich hit my nose, masking the scent of nothingness that usually filled the room. That's what my new apartment felt like: a rented space devoid of warmth, not a home. Gulping down the last morsel of my meal, I took a deep breath and puffed my cheeks out as I exhaled, mentally reminding myself that it was now my task to make the apartment feel like a home and that it was up to me to pull myself out of this stupor.

I clutched my phone from beside me and swiped through until I found Tevin's text thread.

Me: You think you can cop me a ticket to that speed dating thing? I'm good for it. Shoot me the cost and I'll drop you some Apple Cash.

One essential factor in my search for a place to live in Lovey's Bay was being close to a really good grocery store. I wanted a store that offered a decent variety of fresh produce, a fantastic selection of seasonings, and a wide range of products. I know, it sounds like normal requirements, but you'd be surprised at how many grocery stores lack access to quality food. When I learned about Lovey's Pure Foods Market, I did a web search and discovered they had a 4.5 rating and rave reviews. I knew then that I had to find an apartment nearby. I got lucky with Bayside Apartments, located just a few blocks away, making it easy to walk there if I wanted to get some extra steps in and only needed a few items.

Today's visit, however, required me to drive my BMW because I was in dire need of making my fridge look like I wasn't starving myself. In the last month, I've only made quick runs for small items or ordered takeout, which was another reason I needed to go grocery shopping. I've been eating through my savings on surprisingly tasty takeout like I wasn't still unemployed. This expense also made it necessary for me to run a few extra miles to offset the carbs I was indulging in.

Speaking of running, as I turned down the pasta aisle, I spotted the sidewalk bully who nearly caused me to meet the cement face-to-face the other day. I sneered, and at the same time, my eyes twitched with intrigue. Although it was a quick run-in, literally, I remembered him because, as he approached me for an impending head-on collision, I had a moment to take in that he was fione. Tall and milk chocolate with bouldering biceps bulging from what I thought was a police or fire department T-shirt. I didn't have time to figure it out because I was mere seconds away from colliding with his rock-solid body.

Although I could only see the side of his face and one bicep, I knew it was his inconsiderate ass. I had to admit, I might not have been the nicest either, flipping him off as I passed by. I had a feeling he noticed the gesture since his apology ended abruptly as I continued down the sidewalk that day. Maybe that wasn't the best way to greet a potential neighbor.

Feeling a little embarrassed by crassiness, I slowed down my pace, trying to figure out how I would get the box of penne pasta he stood in front of without him connecting the dots. It wasn't looking in my favor, because he appeared to be studying the rows of pasta like if he chose the wrong one it would cause him to lose some supermarket sweep or something. I felt myself holding my breath as I crept closer, knowing he'd be coming face to face with the woman who told him to fuck himself with no words.

The vibration of my phone in my crossbody purse drew my attention, and I hoped it was a call about a position I had applied for. Instead, my brother's name flashed across the screen. A smile spread across my face as I answered.

"Parris!"

"Little sis, how are you doing?"

"I'm doin'," I answered with a giggle. "What's up with you? In Damask or Stonecrest?"

Not caring about the collision with Sidewalk Bully, I stood beside him and reached between him and the shelf to grab the pasta I wanted. No excuse me or anything, and then continued pushing my cart down the aisle.

"Neither," Parris answered. "I'm actually in London. Tinsley had some work out there. I saw Mum."

"Oh, how nice. Mum got to see her favorite," I said, my voice swollen with sarcasm as it trailed off.

"Don't be like that, Tweety. You know that isn't true."

I scrunched my face like the defiant little sister I was

as I tossed some condiments into my cart. I hated when my brother called me that. It had been his nickname for me since we were little kids, his way of saying I was always "chirping" like a feisty little bird.

"Says the one that never gets chastised or has Mum trying to control your life," I argued. I felt a pout grow on my face. Parris sat quietly on the other end, proving that I was right.

My mother and I...we don't see eye to eye. The "illustrious" Audrey Lennox lived the perfect life with her pinky finger high and her nose even higher and tried her hand at controlling my destiny to be her replica. That wasn't me and she and my ex, Travis, almost had me pinned down, succumbing to their fight to control me before I woke up from the sunken place. Travis wanted me to be a Stepford wife and my mother seconded that notion, not once encouraging my desire to be my own woman.

To top it off, just as Travis almost persuaded me to live a life of luxury and control, I discovered that there was another woman who had been living luxuriously off him for two of the five years we were together. What did Mom think? Oh, she suggested I should sweep it under the rug along with his physical attempt to harm me. That was it for me. I packed away my past, including my relationship with my mother, while she called me a lunatic for leaving him and pursuing a new life—in another city.

"Mom was fucked up about how she handled things.

I get it," Parris admitted after a long pause. "But is there any way you two can at least be on a cordial note for my wedding? You and Mum duking it out is the last thing I want to have to keep an eye on not happening. We're already dealing with real security issues."

The thought about being cordial with our Mother felt like a mountain I didn't want to climb. A feat I didn't want to conquer. A mouth full of teeth to be pulled. But, Parris was my big brother and has always been there for me while I've been at odds with our mother. Besides that, he was marrying the biggest singer in the nation. I wasn't about to get kicked out of the wedding of the year because of Audrey.

"I wouldn't let my issues with Mom ruin your wedding, Parris," I said sincerely. I slowed to a halt in front of the ice cream fridge, debating if I would grab myself a jar or two of my favorite. "What security issues are you talking about, anyway? Tinsley still having issues?"

Parris sighed. "Somewhat. She hasn't gotten anything suspicious or weird lately, but we still don't know the level of threat to classify things. So, we are keeping location undisclosed for safety measures. I'll get you the details later. You know the deal. Keep it to yourself."

"Of course, bro," I agreed, also agreeing to myself that I could manage to spread out two jars of my favorite ice cream, Sea Salted Caramel, for two weeks.

"Enough about my stuff, how are you doing out there

in Lovey's Bay? You know you could've come to at least Regency if you didn't want to settle in the country."

"I definitely wasn't moving to the country," I gagged at the thought and then giggled. "And Regency would be way too close to you."

"Ha! I'm barely in Stonecrest. We're always on the road, between Damask and Stonecrest and wherever else.."

"Okay, and when you're in Stonecrest, I don't need you hawking over me. I've had enough of that in high school," I said, reminiscing about our years there. Parris and I were only two years apart, so we spent two years in high school together. During that time, he was my shadow, dimming the light of any guy who dared to approach me while he was around.

"It kept the dummies away," Parris argued and then scoffed. "If I was around when you met Travis, I would've blacked his eye when he tried to black yo—"

"Okay, enough," I interjected, my entire body tensing and bringing me to an abrupt stop in the middle of the grocery store. My hand shot up, almost reflexively in response to the memory. I shuddered, shaking off both the recollection and its grip on me. I exhaled and continued, shifting the topic. "Enough about him. I'm doing well in Lovey's Bay. I like my apartment based on what I've experienced over the last month I've been here. I'm still working on getting it set up. I've just been busy."

"Busy with what?" I could hear Parris's disbelief, and

I scoffed as if he were in front of me. "Are you working yet, or are you just out here losing all your morals?"

I scoffed once more, loudly enough to catch the attention of a passerby as I made my way to the register. "I'm enjoying my single life. A man does it and he gets a pat on the back. A woman does it and she's labeled a hoe."

"I didn't call you a hoe," Parris corrected.

"You may as well," I shot back, lifting my nose in the air.

"It's just, you're my sister, and every time I talk to you, you're on a date with another one of the Peanut Gallery and I know you're out here—"

"Backing it up?"

"Ugh…"

"Twerking dat ass?"

"Fallon…"

"Giving away some W.A.P.?"

"STOP! Ugh.." Parris barked, then grumbled.

I burst out into an echoing laugh at my victory in getting under his skin.

"See," Parris started. I could tell he was speaking through his teeth, tickling me even more. "This is why you need to be in Regency. So I can keep an eye on you."

Loading the conveyor belt, I protested, "I don't need anyone keeping an eye on me. I was under the watchful eye of a man and a doting mother for years. It's my time just to be free. To do what I want. Hopefully, I'll get that call from Fire Company 143 and I can live my best fire-woman life again. This time as a single woman with no strings or restraints. Wait…restraints might be fun…"

"Fallon!" Parris growled. I snickered at my last and final push at his buttons before he abruptly said good-bye and hung up.

What does one wear to a blind speed dating event?

The concept was foreign to me when Joni approached me about attending, describing it as speed dating without the sense of sight. It reminded me of a dating show on that popular streaming service. I've seen a handful of couples actually find success after the show, but a lasting relationship wasn't the prize I sought. It was all about the fun of it, a new experience in Lovey's Bay. So, why was I standing in front of my full-length mirror debating my choice of a rust-colored midi dress under a moto jacket with black booties?

"It's a blind date, Fallon," I muttered to myself. Giving myself a final once-over, I shrugged. "Fuck it."

I really didn't expect to make a connection with

anyone, but why not be cute behind the wall? *And smell good*, I thought as I went to my vanity and chose one of the three scents I frequently wore. This one was light and fun, soft and fresh at the same time and as I misted the fragrance behind my right and then left ear, the scent floating to my nostrils lifted my spirits a notch higher. I sprayed two more times, once to the underside of my right wrist and then the left. Just as I motioned to put the bottle back, I paused and then twisted my upper half of my body, bending at the knee to spritz behind one knee and then the other.

"Never know," I thought to myself, not knowing how the night would end.

Finally, I placed the bottle back on the stand and moved on to another task: finding out who was calling me. I strutted over to my nightstand, retrieving my phone, but I did not recognize the Lovey's Bay phone number. Usually, not being able to identify a number would automatically cause me to choose to let the call go to voicemail, but something was nudging me to answer this one.

"Hello?"

"Hi, I'm trying to reach Fallon Lennox."

"Uh..this is her," I announced, reluctantly. A low grumble settled in my throat as I began to think this was a call I should've let go to voicemail.

"Oh, good. This is Chief Denzel Payton from Fire Company 143."

My eyes perked, and a smile crept to my face as I released my reluctance. I stumbled, "Oh… Hi… how are you?"

"Good, good. I know it's a little late to be calling but you know how a firefighter's life is."

Chief's chuckle pulled one from me. "I do, very well, sir. Life and timing is unpredictable yet rewarding in the field."

"Very true," he answered insightfully. "So I won't hold you long, I just want to say that your transfer came across my desk from the station in Damask. Were you still interested in a position?"

"Of course!" I wanted to exclaim, but instead I cleared my throat and calmly said, "Yes, I'm still interested. Is it being offered?"

Chief Denzel chuckled once more. "Well, yes, Ms. Lennox. I'd like to extend an offer for you to join the crew at Fire Company 143."

Quietly, I let loose, shimmying my shoulders, wiggling my legs, and mouthing a resounding "YESS!" before returning to my calm. With a measured enthusiasm, I accepted, "I'd love to join your crew, Chief Payton."

"Great. It will be good to have another woman on the team, but that's not why I'm offering the position. Your transfer came in with glowing remarks from Chief Poplar."

My heart swelled with warmth at the thought of

Chief Danny Poplar. Chief was tall, dark brown-skinned, with a snow-white mustache that added flair to his always clean-cut face. He was my Chief while I served as a firefighter in Damask, having taken me under his wing after I graduated from Fire School. He was more than just a Chief; at times, he felt like a dad, looking after me and giving me a hard time. He's the reason I hold him in such high regard.

"I'll have to send my thanks to Chief Poplar," I said, coming out of my thoughts.

"And please let him know I said Thank You for giving up one of his best to us in Lovey's Bay," Chief Payton glowed. I lifted my chin as my smile grew bigger. "So, how about getting your first day set for two weeks from now? Oh, and we have a Crew Night coming up in about a week. You should come out, get to know the rest of the family before you start."

"Yes and yes," I responded, a giggle escaping from me. I bit down on my lip to keep the rest of my excitement at bay.

I could hear Chief's smile over the phone as he said, "Great. I'll touch base at the beginning of the week with details for your onboarding. I hope you enjoy your weekend."

I ended the call with Chief Payton with another thank you. As soon as I pressed the End button, I squealed with contained excitement and threw myself onto the bed, landing on my back. I kicked my feet and flailed my arms, fully allowing my joy to take over. Landing the job I wanted was more than just a financial gain; it felt like regaining a lost piece of myself, feeling reconnected to my source of fulfillment that I had set aside to fulfill someone else's desires. Those days were behind me, and now the days of serving myself had begun.

———

"Girl, I'm so glad you came out with me. Since my girl Nina moved with her boo, I've been without a good good Judy!"

"Well, I'm glad to be her replacement," I joked, snickering. Joni and I rounded the corner where our rideshare driver dropped us off, with our destination just half a block ahead. It was my assumption because there were groups of patrons entering the only brightly lit venue on the block. As we drew closer, a collapsible sign reading Rhythm and Brews appeared, confirming my assumption.

"Oh, don't say it like that," Joni said, throwing her hand. "She's still around, you're just a new good good Judy."

I nudged her as we kept walking. "I'm just playing. Thanks for inviting me out. It's nice to have someone show me around Lovey's Bay."

"Oh yes, it's so much to do here. You have the beach and then…"

It was great to have Joni around, even though she rambled on a mile a minute about all the sights of the city. She may be a talker, but she was good company—more than what I had when I moved to The Bay. Uprooting from Damask, where my best friend Zaria and my former life resided, wasn't easy; it was necessary. Lonely, but necessary. Lovey's Bay, a city five hundred miles from my hometown, was out of my comfort zone, and that's exactly what I needed. I craved an experience that would push me out of my comfort zone. A new path through the scorching hell I once lived in, leading me to a new life and a new me.

"…but Rhythm and Brews is the spot," Joni raved as the half block distance became a couple hundred feet from the large venue. "It's a nice bar with good food, music, and stuff like this…you know, speed dating and a weekly Karaoke Night. The men are always coming through here."

I smirked. "I like the sound of that."

Joni stilled me by placing a hand on my arm. She looked at me with mischievous eyes. "So you know you've got to fill me in on your game. I need the play-book because you've been snagging all the fine men since you got here!"

I chuckled, shaking my head at her charm. I turned fully toward her and crossed my arms.

"I'm not doing anything special—literally." Joni sucked her teeth. "No, seriously. I have two rules I follow: seek the fun and not the fall, and then keep a little mystery."

Joni sat in her hip and folded her arms. The look she gave me was between not believing me and confusion.

"Basically, I'm all about the fun of it all. I don't want to fall in love, I just want to have fun. That's what most of the men out here are doing anyway. Once I started doing that, the fun came out and here I am, having *big loads* of fun."

Joni squealed. "I like the sound of that. I mean, I was doing that until I met this young thang, Tevin. Good dick had me giving him all of my time and days."

"Ooo," I cooed. "I mean nothing's wrong with that. If you like it, I love it."

"Yea, but you know. I'm still single and need to mingle. He was on my nipple like the baby he is." She chuckled. "Now, tell me what's up with this mystery thing."

I started our journey forward again with Joni stepping in stride. "Oh, that's just how I keep things neutral. I don't make anything too deep, you know, keep a little mystery. They love to chase. You do that, and they will always keep coming back."

"Hmm, I see. So what's your mystery? I mean you're a mystery as a whole because you're new to Lovey's Bay."

We approached the entrance, and just before I pulled the door open, I paused, swinging my bob, and looked to her with a smirk. "They never know my real name. So, to you and everyone here tonight, my name is Hazel."

I caught Joni's mouth drop before I winked and led the way through the door.

DEACON

Tonight, Rhythm and Brews embraced their blues theme. The sound of guitar strings and soulful voices blared over the speakers, mingling with the chatter of the packed bar. A sea of Black and Brown people filled the seats and the bar, all seemingly enjoying themselves. As for me, amid all the enthusiasm around me, I could only think: *What the hell am I doing?*

Tevin, our crewmate Farris, and I have been holding up the bar for the last thirty minutes. Two whiskey hards and I was still unsure about this whole speed dating thing again. *Am I ready? Do I even know how to date anymore? What do men and women even talk about with each other these days?* Those were the thoughts racing through my mind, and with the mild brain fog my drinks had created, I was far from finding an answer.

"So, ol' man Deac decided to come out with us." The slap of Tevin's hand on my left shoulder had me balling up my fists and narrowing my eyes at him. Tevin stood there, a full glass of beer in hand, grinning widely. "All jokes aside, I'm glad you decided to come out, man! Now, listen, the dating game is a bit different from what it was back in your day. Let me give you some tips."

"Man, if you don't sit your young, five-dollar ass down before I make change," I said, flinching away from Tevin's hand on my shoulder. Farris's laughter rang out in the background. "I might've been out the game for a while, but I can still pull your momma and your sister, young."

Farris wailed louder, stomping his feet. "Deac is back!"

Tevin laughed dryly, nodding his head. "Okay, I'm gonna let that shit slide because you've been in your blue ass feelings for a while. You're jonin' on folks, so that means ol' Deac is coming back, but that's gonna be the last time you say something about my momma and my sister."

The hostess started tapping her mic as I stood up, squeezing Tevin's tense shoulders. I laughed, "Yeah, yeah. There ain't no coming back. I just took a break from getting in yo' ass!"

"Pause, nigga," Tevin said, shoving my hand off his shoulder. Farris and I continued laughing at Tevin's expense as the hostess finally spoke over the mic.

"Okay, welcome to all those who are here for Rhythm and Brew's Romance is Blind event! If you aren't here for it, damn! You're missing out, but tickets are on sale for the next one, but going fast. Get yours before you leave tonight. If you are here for the speed dating event, ladies, line up over there and fellas over here. Make sure to have your ticket ready to present."

I patted my jeans pocket to secure the location of my ticket as the guys and I headed in the instructed direction. It seemed the men and women were entering the smaller dining hall through separate entrances. Silently, I cursed myself, feeling my hands grow clammy as I rubbed them together. To add to my nerves, my mind raced with potential questions and responses. Why hadn't I thought about this *earlier?*

The truth is, I had come up short on viable answers. Even though I joked about my readiness with Tevin, my ego was scratched up by the rust of my game. Before this moment, I had been with Vanessa for years. I didn't have to brush up on my game. I already had the girl. Had. My chest caved at the realization, but I let out a heavy breath, brushing that lingering thought away.

I aimlessly scanned the crowd of women on the opposite side of the room, my pupils dilating as they landed on a familiar face. It was the woman I almost ran into the other week while coming home from work, and then I saw her again at the grocery store. What were the odds that I would run into her a third time? Like each of the other times I've seen her, she was drop-dead gorgeous, but this time I could linger on her much longer to take it in.

I watched her bright smile expand igniting deep dimples in her cheeks. I would've missed the adorable accent to her face if she hadn't absentmindedly flicked her brown and blonde shoulder length hair from her face. I liked her hair color, it complemented her mocha skin…and that dress. She wore a leather jacket over an earth-toned, fitting dress, but even that couldn't cover the fit physique I took note of during our first encounter. I remembered she was toned and had a nice bubbled ass…and that she flicked me off.

My stomach lurched at the thought of our first inter-action. What a way to start, but something inside me told me that seeing her for a third time wasn't just sheer luck. I hope I get a chance to talk to her. Do I even remember her voice well enough to identify her? I clenched my eyes closed, trying to recall the sound of her voice, but I was unsuccessful. When I opened my eyes, she was gone, and the crowd behind me was pushing me forward.

———

"So what happened with your last relationship?"

After stumbling over my answer to this question for the fifth time, I was mentally crashing and burning. I probably was physically, too, and the fact that I was speaking to a divider gave me the grace I thought I deserved, even though their dry "Ohs" felt like death.

What was I thinking about?

The question raced through my mind after each "Switch!" announcement, causing me to retreat deeper into my shell. It was that one simple question that left me stumped and flailing internally like a fish out of water. Every other question, like "What's your name?" or "What things do you like?" felt like a breeze. However, when it came to the question, "So what happened with your last relationship?" I was stuck like Chuck, ready to give up on this whole speed dating thing. Why did we have to dive so deep in the 15 minutes we were talking? That question was loaded with bullets I was still trying to extract from my heart.

"I knew I wasn't ready for this," I grumbled to myself as I leaned back in my chair, taking my third glass of whiskey to the head.

"I mean, I don't think I can come back."

A voice and a giggle from the other side of the divider caught my breath in my throat, tangled in the burn of the brown liquor. I gasped and coughed, feeling the heat of embarrassment rise within me.

"Umm, are you okay?" the melodic voice asked. I could sense that she was either smiling or quietly laughing at me.

I leaned my elbows on the table and let out a sigh-laugh. "I'm good, thanks. What a way to start my 15 minutes."

"It's okay. A bad start to fifteen minutes is only a problem in *other* situations."

My right eyebrow arched as I smirked at her sense of humor. Feeling my shoulders relax, I chuckled and asked, "What's your name?"

"Hazel."

The sultry cadence in which she spoke her name was Cupid's arrow, landing bullseye in my heart. A knowing inside me told me it was her—the woman from the run and the grocery store. I inhaled deeply, trying to gather myself as I sent up a private prayer, *"God, if it's in your will, let this be third time's a charm. Please?"*

"Yours?" she asked, pulling me out of my prayer.

"Uh..Deacon."

"Like, front row of the church Deacon?"

I chuckled. "It's actually Benjamin, but everyone calls me Deacon. And yeah, like "front row of church" Deacon, but I'm far from perfect. My draws might be made of gasoline."

She broke out into sirenic laughter, and my cheeks grew tight from the smile taking over my face. "Okay, so I think I like the oxymoron of the name Deacon. So… Deacon, what got you here at this speed dating thing?"

"My people," I answered honestly.

"What? No reason like, "Oh, I'm looking for my Queen?"

Her soft voice, deepening to mimic a response she apparently received tonight, had me snickering. Again, honestly, I answered, "Nah. I don't even know if I'm built for this. This is just a casual night, ya know?"

The silence that settled between us amplified the chatter around us, and my heart pounded even louder. Just when I thought I fudged again, she spoke, "I feel you. Light and easy… nothing serious."

I didn't know how much time we'd spent together yet, but it felt like it wasn't enough. That's probably why I blurted out, "What are you doing after this?"

"What? I don't know," she giggled in response.

Grimacing at myself, I tried to correct my example of thirst. "I mean… like… what do you enjoy doing for fun? Do you have anything fun planned after this?"

"I'm not from around here, so I don't know much about the area. But you know, I enjoy things that get my heart racing and boost my dopamine." She paused, and I reflected on her words, unsure of where the conversation was headed. I didn't want to say anything foolish if I was mistaken. After a moment, she continued, "Like karaoke, competitive sports, roller coasters. That type of thrill."

My smile returned to my face as her response resonated. "Same. I just want to enjoy whatever I do for fun." It fell quiet on her end again, and I quickly broke the silence. "We have this small carnival on the beach. No rollercoasters, but the Ferris Wheel is huge. It's definitely an adrenaline rush when you reach the top and get to look over the water and the city."

"I've seen that. I've never had the opportunity to go, though."

I shot my shot. "Maybe, I can take you. It's open late on the weekends."

"Alright…it's time to SWITCH!" the hostess announced, imperfectly timing the announcement. The scuffling of chairs moving took over the room.

"Maybe," I heard her reply amid the rising chatter.

"Hey, leave your number with the hostess…please. If you want," I blurted out in full simp mode. Hearing my desperation echo in my memory, I shook my head, knowing that I probably ruined any chances. One simple word from her changed my trajectory.

"Okay."

FALLON

You know how in a scene from a Spike Lee Joint, the character becomes the focal point against a steadily moving background? Spike does this in a way that directs your attention to the character, allowing you to fully experience their true emotions, which you wouldn't grasp without the steady focal camera. Well, if my last few dates hadn't been behind a divider, I feel like their perspective of me would mirror that experience and my lackluster expression would've been duly noted. Until now.

Everything was happening around me as usual while I sat in front of a make-believe camera that was focused on me. What emotions would be picked up now from the lazy half-smile settled on my slightly parted lips and the dazed pupils? Intrigue. An intrigue that wasn't supposed to be there.

Tonight was supposed to be just a fun night of multiple dates—light and easy, nothing serious. So why was I seriously still thinking about that fifteen-minute date with Deacon? In the front row of the church: Deacon. Deacon, a man who could very well sound like a hunk but actually looked like an ogre with a hump? Somehow, I felt like that analogy wasn't true, but even that felt like too much, pondering what he looked like. Thinking of him this much was just too heavy.

"We'd like to thank you all for joining us at our Romance Is Blind Speed Dating Event. Any love connections made? We hope so! The bar is open until two, so go out and mix and mingle. Don't forget to keep your name tags, so your matches can find you!"

I felt my heart skip a beat at the announcement and shifted my gaze to my 'Hazel' name tag. The opportunity to put a face to the man who had captured my thoughts was just moments away. I've never been one to shy away from a good time or meeting a new man. That has been my motto since leaving Damask: meet and enjoy as many men as I choose, doing whatever I want as a single woman. But this potential meeting came with too many feelings I couldn't explain, flooding my mind and my chest. *You're supposed to be feeling things that ignite my vagina walls not creating flutters within my heart,* I scolded myself.

"So how'd it go for you, girl?" Joni's voice behind me pulled me out of my inner scolding.

I scooted back in my chair, making room for me to stand up. "It was cool… a fun way to date."

"Yeah, it was, but why did I end up on a date with Tevin? Remember, the guy I was telling you about?" She folded her arms, trying to feign annoyance, but I could see her pursed lips fighting a smile. "I just can't get away from him."

I chuckled. Calling her bluff, I said, "It doesn't look like you want to. Why though? If he's chasing you, let him chase…and catch you."

Joni smile broke through as she shook her pointer finger at me. "You know. You might be on to something. He chases and pounces well." Joni squealed and I full on laughed at her as we made our way out of the dispersing room. "I think I'm going to go out there and cause a little commotion with Tevin. You coming?"

"No. I think I'm going to call it a night," I said, declining. I heard Joni's disappointment manifest as a scoff, and I turned to her, coming up with an excuse. "I have some things to take care of at my apartment first thing in the morning. I've been here for over a month, and I'm still living out of boxes."

It was true; I was still living out of boxes after a month and a half in Lovey's Bay. I needed to unpack and make my apartment cozy, but that really wasn't at the top of my list. What *was* at the top of my list was getting out of here, getting some fresh air, and clearing my thoughts of this mystery man. I was mentally swatting away the feelings swirling inside me. I had no time for that.

Our walk through the dimly lit hallway was brief, immediately met by the blaring sounds of now upbeat hip hop and the varied voices of patrons enjoying themselves. Joni and I hugged our goodbyes and made a beeline for the exit, slowing just a bit as I reached the hostess stand. I considered Deacon's request for me to leave my number and was close to doing so until Hazel chimed in. Light and easy, nothing serious, my ego reminded me. I nodded, reinforcing that thought, and continued walking, pushing through the door where I was greeted by the cool spring night air. I took five long, confident strides down the sidewalk, feeling pleased with myself for sticking to my guns, when I heard a voice.

"Hazel?"

I recognized the baritone. It was the same one whose deep vibrations sent reverberating waves through parts of me that I wanted to stay cold, and now hearing his voice again triggered tremors simply from the sound of my name… my middle name… my shield from anything that wasn't light and easy. I wasn't one to be rude and ignore someone calling after me, but I considered it—even though, technically, he didn't know if he was calling the right person. My curiosity urged me to slowly swivel on the balls of my feet to… Sidewalk Bully?

His face lit up as he walked towards me. "Your name is Hazel, right?"

I forced a short breath, wanting to feel disgusted that the owner of the voice was the Sidewalk Bully, but as he approached, my eyebrow piqued as I scanned the handsome man, standing over six feet tall, with almond skin and perfect teeth, getting closer to me. The fleeting impression from our previous interaction didn't do justice to the close-up I was experiencing now.

Fluttering my eyes, I finally answered him. "Yeah. Hazel."

"Deacon," he said, extending his hand for me to shake.

I kept my hand in my moto jacket for a reluctant pause before placing it in his. It felt like leather—neither rough nor soft, but a texture that told me he was a working man, with hands that still felt good to the touch. He gave my hand a firm squeeze before running his thumb across the top of it. I looked down at his hand, feeling a tingle in my center, then back up at him.

"I promise I'm not a creep," he said, releasing me and raising his hand as he stepped back. "I thought you might have forgotten to leave your info, so I took a chance to see if you were the one with the beautiful voice."

"So, you came running out after a stranger," I remarked teasingly, adding a smirk to enhance my joke.

If his cheeks could turn beet red, they would have at that moment. He cringed behind his infectious smile and ran his hand through his short curls. He chuckled, "Definitely creepy vibes."

I couldn't help but burst into laughter before continuing my teasing, "So you're a creep and a sidewalk bully, with the name of the saints who sit in the front of the church."

"A-ha!" Deacon's laugh bounced through the air as he threw his head back. He ran his hand over his face before returning his gaze to me. "You're the woman who flipped me off. Wow, what a first impression I made, huh?"

"Mmhmm," I hummed, crossing my arms. I attempted to press my lips together to convey more disdain, but it resulted in a grin instead of a scowl.

Deacon sandwiched my small hand between his two massive ones and stole a breath from me with his puppy dog eyes. "I apologize wholeheartedly for that day. I wasn't paying attention. I tried to apologize, but—"

"Apology accepted," I cut in, my voice soft, partly because I was embarrassed by my actions and then partly because his apology felt sincere. That thing in my chest was happening again and I slipped my hand from his, stuffing it back into my pocket. *Quit it,* I scolded myself.

"So, how am I supposed to make up for that if you skipped out without leaving me your number?" His smile quirked to the left, revealing a dimple that came out of hiding. Ugh, he was becoming more and more irresistible.

"Mm, be creative." I shrugged my shoulders and turned on my heels back in the direction I had been headed, ready to give him a walkaway to remember.

"One night." Those two words made me stop. I glanced over my shoulder at Deacon, who stood there with hope etched on his face and that damn smile. "Give me one night of just a good time. Tonight. If you enjoy yourself, we can exchange numbers to keep the good times rolling. If you don't, I'll never bother you again. I'll even cross to the other side of the street if I see you, so I won't have to deal with you flicking me off again."

Deacon pretended to be struck in the heart, clutching his chest and stumbling back, and I cackled. His laughter mingled with mine as he closed the distance between us. Once in front of me, he gazed down at me and tilted his head, silently asking for my answer. This wouldn't be the craziest thing I've done—randomly going out with someone I just met. Captain Langston was the last, and it was a good time. I felt hesitant with Deacon, not because I thought something was off about him, but because what he was doing to me wasn't right. The way he made my heart flutter and caused me to blush like a girl with a crush was not right. Yet, the thrill of a spontaneous night was knocking at my door, and I wanted to answer it.

"Deal." I extended my hand for him to shake, and he did, holding on for one second, then two, and then a third, nodding his head with a gleam in his eyes.

"Cool. Let's go."

Before I could say a word, Deacon clasped his fingers between mine and led me down the sidewalk. We were passing Rhythm and Brews when I finally managed to chuckle out, "Wait. Where are you taking me?"

He looked back at me with a grin, continued a few more steps, and stopped in front of a pristinely clean red Challenger. The blacked-out rims sparkled under the street light.

"I see you," I subtly complimented as he opened the door for me.

"Fifteen minutes down to the coast. You down?" he asked, as if he could sense me re-thinking this. I was here now and although I could turn back and change my mind, I didn't want to. I nodded and accepted his help into the midnight leather interior.

———

I crave a thrill, a rush, something to make my heart race. That's why I love being a firefighter. That's why my current lifestyle appeals to me. A new fire emergency. A new man. A new experience. The freshness of it all sends goosebumps pricking my skin, makes my heart pound a mile a minute, and causes my face to ache from beaming.

"Wooo!" I remember whooping and laughing hysterically as Deacon zoomed down the long, two-lane highway. I couldn't contain my excitement. He had reached

100 MPH, calling himself ensuring we arrived at our destination in 15 minutes, as he had promised.

"It's actually about a twenty…twenty-five minute drive," I remember him admitting before he pressed his foot on the gas, the engine purring underneath us.

There was a chill in the night, but we sped down the road with the windows down, my hair whipping across my face. I tucked my hair behind my ear to catch everything zooming past us. The sky was a deep blue-black, the darkest color it reaches at midnight. The highway was dimly lit, with a single streetlight on either side about every half mile. It wasn't until Deacon started to slow down that I could make out the coast, lined with pampas grass and boulders. The bay looked still and peaceful under the moon's reflection on the water. It was simply beautiful.

We turned into a gravel parking lot in front of a small, one-story brick building. Several cars filled the lot, which made me wonder how they accommodated the number of people in what seemed to be a shotgun-style layout. As we approached the entrance, I noticed patrons sitting at tables and dancing on the covered patio.

"Welcome to Baby Dee's," a busty woman greeted us as we walked in. There was no missing her cleavage; it was lifted and perky in her baby tee that read Baby Dee's BBQ Joint. You couldn't help but notice her bright smile and the crown jewel on her tooth either as it glimmered as she asked, "Patio or inside? We've got space in both."

Deacon looked down at me as I surveyed the room. The wood-planked walls were painted red, reflecting the red-light special vibe created by the stage lights illuminating the space and the stage at the back. A few empty tables were scattered throughout, with one positioned near the stage.

"Inside. Can we get the table by the stage?" I pointed to the table on the left.

"Absolutely, honey. Follow me," the woman said, patting one of her Afro puffs before grabbing two menus and motioning for us to follow her through the crowded room.

I walked toward the seat facing the stage. Deacon beat me there by a couple of long strides, pulling the seat out for me. I looked up at him, a smirk threatening to settle on my face. *I'm impressed.* Not that Deacon gave off the impression that he lacked common gentlemanly manners, but nowadays, people can appear to have them and still not possess any. *But why does that matter? Light and easy.* I reminded myself as I rolled my eyes to the back of my head, frustrated with my lack of chill.

"I'm Niecey, and I'll be your waitress," the woman introduced, pulling out a notepad. "Can I get y'all started with some libations or somethin'?"

"Ladies first," Deacon said, tilting his head to me.

I smiled graciously and looked up to Niecey. "You think they can make me a Dark and Stormy?"

She placed her pen between her teeth, deep in

thought, and then her eyes widened. "Ginger beer… lime… and what kind of rum do you want?"

"Actually, no rum. Can I get that SirDavis?"

"You got it, babe," she said, jotting down my order. She turned to Deacon. "And you, honey?" She glanced at me and waved her hand. "No disrespect."

Deacon and I exchanged looks and chuckled before I answered, "None taken. He's not my man."

Her full lips formed an 'O' as her perfectly shaped brows lifted. One brow stayed raised as she smirked and glanced at Deacon for his order. He blushed slightly as he requested a SirDavis and Coke. After she walked away, Deacon leaned forward, his elbows resting on the table and his biceps straining against the cotton fabric of his short-sleeved shirt.

"This SirDavis better be good."

I snickered. "No one told you to be a copycat."

He nodded. "True. I wanted to try that Dark and Stormy. Now, that would've been a copycat move. Ginger beer, lime, and whiskey? Sounds bold."

I leaned in, resting my elbows on the table and bringing my hands together. We were eye to eye, and I was getting lost in his dark brown orbs. "That's how I like 'em—dark, brooding, and bold."

Deacon let out a short huff of laughter as he rolled his tongue over his top teeth. The way his eyelids narrowed indicated that he had noticed my subtle flirtation.

"Is that so?" he rebutted. He shifted his gaze from my lips back to my eyes.

Unknowingly, I mimicked him, shifting my gaze to his lips and then back to his eyes, wanting to cease the thin air between our lips. Suddenly, I leaned back in my chair and exhaled, "Yep."

I shifted my awareness away from him and aimlessly scanned the room. He felt like trouble. Good trouble. That's something you don't pass up, but there was also something else mixed in with it all. I felt my skin getting sticky and shrugged off my jacket, draping it over the back of my seat. Just in time, Niecey returned with our drinks. Before the water condensation could mark the table, I lifted my glass to my lips, took a big gulp, and then hissed as the whiskey burned down my chest.

"Big Mama," Deacon mumbled, glancing at me over the rim of his cup while sipping from his glass.

There was something about the way he called me Big Mama that sent a wave of heat rushing through me. Or maybe it was the first wave of whiskey hitting my system. Whatever the reason, I chuckled and swooned in the warmth. I glanced at the clock on the wall opposite us. "Whatever. It's almost midnight. The night isn't young. Stop babysitting yours."

I lifted my glass, challenging him. His teeth glimmered through his wide grin as he tilted his head toward me. Lifting his glass, he clinked it against mine, and we both downed our drinks in one gulp. Another dimple appeared on his other cheek, both deep now. God, could he get any finer? My eyes dropped to the V-neck of his shirt, where the curve of his pectorals peeked out, and I inhaled slowly, imagining him as a nice board to ride.

"Looks like you two need another round. Whatcha think?" Niecey's voice pulled me from my thoughts. She stood there, perched on her hip, grinning while running her tongue over her tooth gem.

I turned my eye toward Deacon, and he met my gaze with an equally devilish grin. My eyes widened slightly, struck by the sense that he was having thoughts similar to mine at the same moment, before I bit down on my lip to hold back a grin.

"We'll take two shots. SirDavis?" He directed the question to me, and my face contorted yet again between thrill and contempt.

"Sure," I answered, not removing my gaze from his. *Bold.*

"Alright, I'll be right back. Y'all stop making googly eyes to look at the menu. The kitchen is closing in thirty minutes."

Niecey turned and sashayed away before Deacon and I could process her quick dig. When we finally did, I covered my mouth with my hand as Deacon and I burst into laughter.

One shot, two shots, and a rack of beef ribs split between the two of us, and we were in a whirlwind of gluttony and swimming in liquid sin. At least I was. I couldn't tell too much with Deacon as he was holding his liquor well, besides glossy eyes and flirtatious looks. I thought I was holding mine well for anyone watching, but inside, I felt like I was floating while my mind filled with filthy thoughts as I watched and listened to Deacon talk.

Just like I explained to Joni my third rule of engagement, I kept a lot about myself a mystery, sharing only that I was from Damask and had been in Lovey's Bay for just over a month. As for Deacon, he was an open book, and I learned a lot, but I can't lie; much of it slipped my mind as I floated on the Tipsy River. The only thing I could remember was that we lived in the same apartment building, and his father was a preacher at a small countryside church.

"You know," I began, turning to look at Deacon. At some point before the band started playing, he slid his chair so that he was sitting next to me with a clear view of the stage. "You know, this is kinda crazy, riding off with you. You could be a serial killer or something."

I cackled at myself, and he chuckled as he scrunched his face. "Nah, never that. I'ma PK kid. I don't have that in my blood."

"That's right, you have nothing but the Blood of Jesus running through you," I cracked.

That made Deacon bellow, clutching his stomach. As he settled, he leaned in, fixing his gaze on mine. He whispered, "Don't be fooled. Do you know what they say about preacher kids?"

I squinted and smirked. "No…?"

The tickle of his breath against my ear sent a chill down my spine as he whispered, "We aren't the most innocent. Don't worry. The Blood flows in other places, too."

Leaning back, I tilted my head enough to look him in the eye, as if it would reveal whether he was a mirage and if he had really just said that. I concluded he was real, and I felt a rush of desire, with my nipples hardening beneath my dress.

"Alright, then, Mr. Deacon," I purred. Seductively, I

smirked and traced my tongue along my bottom lip as I adjusted myself and centered in my chair.

"Too much?" he asked, lingering near my ear as the band started their second set.

I turned my head toward him, our lips nearly touching. The attraction between us could have generated real heatwaves. I studied his pupils, battling the impulse to lick his bottom lip before settling on answering, "I said I liked them bold, remember?"

The bass guitar's chords strummed the opening notes of a classic, "Tell Me Something Good" by Rufus, coming in perfectly timed to halt what would've been an inevitable crashing of our lips. I scooted my chair back, rolling my hips in the seat. "Oh, this is my song!"

"Whatcha know about this, Big Mama?"

There he goes again with that sweet talk. Big Mama was now considered sweet talk because it sugared my panties every time it rolled off his tongue. Had anyone else said it, I'm certain I would've rolled my eyes and ended whatever conversation short, but it was the way his baritone dipped low and the swell of his Southern accent over the syllables that had me squirming in my seat. This was probably the fifth time he called me Big Mama, and I was sure I needed to discard my undergarments now.

I licked my bottom lip, savoring the remnants of the liquor I had consumed as I stood up, pulling him up with me. "Let me show you, Deacon Zaddy."

His laughter boomed, and I snickered, swaying my hips to the beat as I walked backward onto the dance floor. We found a spot in the center of the floor, getting lost in the red light. There was something about the color that ignited passion… lust. The Deacon I met at Rhythm and Brew, stumbling over his words, was no longer there. A bold, confident Deacon had taken his place, and I liked it. He wrapped his arms around my waist while I wrapped mine around his neck, falling into the groove of my sway.

Right. Left. Right. Left. Dip. Dip.

My pearly whites beamed, impressed at how well he kept up with me and the way he moved his middle. He was fluid with his movements like he had hidden skills I wouldn't mind exploring. He added his own roll a time or two, brushing his middle against mine. The already climbing heat between us went up a notch with each collision of our hips, and by the time the band went into the chorus for a second time, our bodies were creating a 5-alarm fire.

"Tell me something good…" I sang along with the band. My back was now against his hard chest while my ass pressed against his manhood. His hands were now resting on my lower abs, keeping me glued to him. I liked the feeling of being smashed into him. He felt like security and I sank even further into him as his fresh, spiced scent wrapped around me. I sang once more, "Tell me that you like it, yeah…"

"Oh, I like it," he murmured, low and deep against my ear. Lulled by the vibration of his voice, I closed my eyes and let my head fall against his chest as I giggled at his response.

Hips rolling and swaying, our bodies were in sync while our hands engaged elsewhere. My right hand roamed up the side of his stubbled face and then caressed his ear, while his right hand rested on my abdomen while the other ventured up the side of my leg. I was tingling all over, my nerves hyperstimulated by the combination of this man and the libations. We lingered in this moment for another verse before I turned around to join in the sing-along of the last line of the verse:

"What I got will knock your pride aside…"

With each word I sang, I swayed my hips as I stepped back. When the breakdown hit, a chorus of "Owws" and "Ayes" erupted, raising the energy in the room to an all-time high. I performed a sultry twerk to the funky beat, swinging my head from side to side as my hair flew around. When my head came to the center, I found Deacon watching. He eyed me as he bit his lip, his dimples deepening.

"Come here, Big Mama," Deacon demanded in the sexiest growl, grabbing my hand and pulling me into him. I giggled as he took his left hand to the small of my back while holding my hand with his right. We did a sexy two-step until the end of the song, where I then led us off the dance floor, heading to the front door.

"I need some air," I announced, fanning myself.

"Go ahead and get you some. Let me pay our tab, and I'll be right out."

The early morning chill felt refreshing against my skin. However, after a moment, the crispness in the air reminded me that I had left my jacket inside. I turned to go retrieve it but paused when I saw Deacon stepping out of the door with my coat in hand. That gorgeous smile seemed to have never left his face since the beginning of our time at Baby Dee's, and if I'm honest, mine never wavered either. The sound of Deacon's shoes crunching over the rocks, the muffled music from inside the building, and the soft crash of the waves were the only sounds between us as he approached.

"You might need this," he said as he opened my jacket for me to put on.

"Thanks." I turned around and let him drape it over my shoulders.

The silence fell between us again as he slipped his fingers between mine. I looked down at our swinging hands before gently closing my fingers around his, brushing away my initial hesitance. Everything I had done throughout the night was mostly calculated. I was over it. My head was in euphoric clouds, and I was tired of monitoring my moves, especially as I noticed us drawing closer to his car. Knowing that the date was nearing its end, part of me wasn't quite ready, but I went with it.

After Deacon tucked me into the car, he pulled out of the parking lot and turned left—the opposite direction from where we had come. Again, I went along with it, never feeling unsafe or worried about where we were going. I rested my head against the headrest as I listened to the chill hip-hop song playing softly. It wasn't long after I closed my eyes that I felt the car come to a stop. When I opened my eyes, I saw we were parked at a cliff overlooking the Bay.

Deacon removed his hand from the gear and lowered his head to look at me. "Can I be honest, Hazel? I wasn't quite ready to end the night. I've really been enjoying my time with you."

The oxymoron of him speaking about honesty while I was still lying about my name amused me, but deep down, I was also enjoying the moment and didn't want it to end. Instead of admitting that, I snorted and simply responded with four words: "I'm enjoying it, too."

I could tell Deacon was trying to figure me out. While I sat with a plastered smile, parts of me still refused to give more than what I was giving.

Light and easy. Nothing serious.

The motto that kept playing in my head reminded me that I was just here for the fun of it all, however it chose to show up. I looked through the windshield, gazing out over the water. "So, what's this place?"

"Lovey's Cliff. Come look."

Deacon stepped out of the car and came around to

my side, helping me out. Gripping my jacket by the collar, I followed him to the front of the car, where he assisted me in sliding onto the hood. This provided me with a great view of the empty beach and gentle waves. I inhaled and exhaled through my nose, feeling my head spin from the lingering tipsiness. Deacon leaned against the wooden rail, gazing out as we both seemed to immerse ourselves in the tranquility of the moment.

This moment was the most peaceful I've felt in a while, and it felt so weighty. Weighty, like a weighted blanket the first moment you place it on your body. The blanket feels uncomfortable until you relax and allow it to cradle you. That's what the moment was giving me—a complete peace and a sense of security.

"Lovey's Cliff is just a chill spot to kick it," Deacon started to explain, still looking out to the water. "Some folks call it Lover's Cliff because of the romantic vibe here. Couples actually use the area as a backdrop to engagement pictures."

"So much *love*. Are you trying to make me fall for you, Deacon?" I asked teasingly, secretly hoping he wouldn't ruin the moment by answering yes.

Deacon turned slowly, his smile still in place, and took two leisurely steps toward me. I stiffened, gripping my propped-up left leg while the other relaxed, awaiting his response. He leaned in, placing a hand on either side of me.

Please don't ruin it. Please don't ruin it.

"Now, that wouldn't be light and easy, would it?"

I smirked and relaxed, satisfied with his response. Wetting my bottom lip, I grabbed the V of his shirt and pulled him to me. "Nope, it wouldn't. I like light and easy."

I don't know who initiated the kiss, but our lips were locked, and I couldn't be happier. I had been craving the feel of his lips since our near collision earlier, and during every other moment, we had taunted and subtly played with the idea. They felt just as good as I had imagined. Soft enough to pull a moan from me, allowing the opportunity for his tongue to interlock with mine. I gasped at the press of his tongue against mine, dancing through my mouth and teasing my tongue.

I scooted to the end of the hood, legs naturally parting as his body settled between them. We were nearly flesh against each other when he began to trail kisses down my jawline, tipping my jacket off of my shoulders along the way. I threw my head back, enjoying his tongue swirling against my neck and his open palm roaming up my right side. His hand stopped just at the cup of my breast, as if he wasn't sure to touch me there. Without words, I gave him permission as I put my hand over his and moved it over my breast. Needing no more direction, he squeezed my right breast as he pressed his lips against mine again. When he noticed the ball he was playing with was my nipple ring, he kissed me harder, it seemingly turning him on. His play turned me up a notch, too, and then threw me over the edge when he pulled the breast out of the scoop neck of my dress and began flicking his tongue over my hardened peaks while tweaking the ring.

"Mmm," I moaned through the clenching of my teeth on my bottom lip. "Just like that."

My egging on kept him curious, finding new ways to bring a moan out of me. He swirled his tongue. Sucked on my nipple. Tugged gently at my ring with his teeth. It all had me singing my praises through the air and grappling to undo his pants. Moving his lips from my breast to my mouth again, he assisted me by pulling his pants and boxers briefs over his ass, letting them drop while he pulled me into him again as he devoured my mouth.

I didn't have to see his dick to know it was heavy. I felt it plop against my thigh with some density. A moan settled in my throat as I thought about how I wanted to feel that steel inside me. Still in a liplock with Deacon, I felt behind me to my jacket pocket, pulling out a condom. I broke our kiss long enough to rip the gold package open with my teeth and then locked my lips to his again as I sheathed him.

"Are you sure you want this dick?" Deacon grumbled against my lips as I sheathed him and then fell back onto his lips. His heaviness was now knocking at my sodden panty-covered entrance.

"You said the blood runs to other places, right?" I panted through a kiss and then gasped at a surprise insertion of two fingers in between my panties. He sunk those fingers into my ocean and stroked methodically while I feigned away the want to bust all over his fingers.

"Mmhmm," he groaned as he suckled my neck while causing my head to spin as he pushed his fingers deep inside me. My mouth dropped, and my voice cracked in bliss as he curved his fingers up, beckoning my cum. My walls contracted around his fingers, ready to break the levy…and then he stopped.

"Why—" I gasped, losing all thought as he moved my panties to the side and sank into me, his girth stretching me with each descent until he couldn't anymore. That's when he methodically began to stroke slowly. In and out. In and out. In and out, until my juices squished to his rhythm and our hips were colliding.

Guttural. That was the best way to describe my moans as he dug into me. My moans pushed from the pit of my stomach each time he drilled into me. He was so thick that it was nothing for him to make me cream a gushy mess with each stroke. My pussy was pulsating at the delight of his fullness taking over her, pounding into her, hitting the mother-fucking bottom.

"Oh, my gawwwwd…I'm gonna cummm…" I whimpered.

"Whew, you're gonna be a problem," he grunted, digging the pads of his fingers into my ass as he pounded harder.

"This dick is gonna be a problem," I whimpered as I

dropped my head back, my climax coming out as a whistling moan. "I'm coming…I'm coming…I'm coming…!"

He blew out another breath as he pounded through my orgasm, each pound causing me to now wail to echo through the air. He wasn't letting up, and I didn't want him to. The tingling through my body, as my adrenaline and climax crashed and burned, was addictive. I wanted to keep feeling it. My nectar kept oozing and squishing between our thighs as he pounded onward.

Deacon pulled all the way out and then plunged back into me, sending shockwaves through my body that ricocheted into more waves of pleasure as he continued his dig into my guts relentlessly.

"Damn, Deacon," I whimpered, grabbing hold of his back as he cupped the sides of my ass and continued the drill of his long dick into my core again. I was suspended off of the hood now, throwing my pussy with each thrust, getting ready to lose it all over again. My legs were quaking, and my clit was rock hard, stimulated by the friction.

"Shit feels too good, Big Mama… God damn…give me one more…"

That was it. I came again hard. The pads of his fingers clamped onto my ass as he bounced me on his dick like a basketball all while I lost all my wits until he pressed into me one last time, grunting out his climax. "Fuck…shit…!"

The way we collapsed onto the hood of his car, I knew it must have gotten dented, but neither of us moved. Still connected, Deacon rested his forehead on my chest, my dress soaking up his sweat. With sleep coaxing my eyelids down, I ran my nails along the back of his head as thoughts of letting him claim my pussy as his ran through my mind. He was trouble. Good trouble.

"**Y**ou're moving mighty slow there, Benjamin."

I looked over my shoulder at Pop, who was standing a few yards away with the weed whacker in his hand, ready to edge the freshly soiled rose bush. I chuckled and joked, "Look here, old man. We have all day."

"You have all day. I'm not going to be out here all day because you want to lollygag."

"I'm not lollygaging, Dad. I just had a long night."

More like an explosive night—an exhilarating night. No other words could sum up the unexpected evening I experienced. I hadn't slept with anyone since Vanessa and I ended. It's probably why when I busted I had more stars in my eyes than the sky had. I could also say another reason was because Hazel…Hazel had me…

"…Going in circles." Pops slapped my back twice.

"Boy, quit walking in circles and get that soil around the flower beds. You're really slowing me up today."

"My bad, Pop." I chuckled at myself and shook my head, moving to the flower beds lining the sidewalk. It was lowkey embarrassing to have my Pop clock me on how out of it I was. If he knew that it was because a woman's vagina sucked all the sense out of me, he would be lecturing me about my morals.

It was my Saturday off and the first weekend of spring. Every first weekend of the season, I visit my parents' home in a small town outside Lovey's Bay to help them around the house. Primarily, I assist Pop, who, at this time of year, takes the weekend to prepare their flowers and yard for the blooming season. Spending this quality time with them is my way of making an effort to connect, as my work schedule is always unpredictable. They are also getting older, both in their early sixties, which makes it even more important for me to check in on them and lend a hand when I can.

This Saturday, however, I had to admit that I was wasting more time than being helpful. I still saw double, my feet moved in slow motion, my head felt slightly tense, and liquor still lingered on my breath even after brushing my teeth. And my eyes? Well, my lids were still adorned with the many faces I was introduced to by Hazel last night: happy faces, sexy faces, and climatic faces.

"Get your mind right," I mumbled to myself as I

knelt down with the bag of soil in hand, trying to gather my thoughts.

Yet, my mind still wandered toward the comforts of Hazel. Who would have thought the woman I passed on the street would be the one to catch my attention at a speed dating event without ever having seen her? Then, she would be the first woman I'd sleep with after my breakup, and it would be amazing.

It wasn't my intention to get between Hazel's legs when I flagged her down outside Rhythm and Brew. All I hoped for was to convince her to give me her number and maybe spend a little more time with her. I don't know what it was about the 15-minute conversation we had that made me so desperate to connect. No, I do know what it was. We just flowed together. She overlooked my lack of game and simply vibed with me. It felt natural; it felt easy—the connection, that is.

Hazel didn't make it easy for me to get her number; she practically had me running down the sidewalk, promising a good time in return. I wouldn't have done it any other way, though. When I finally could put a face to that beautiful voice, it was all over for me. I would've climbed the Lovey's Bay Ferris Wheel like Godzilla just to have a few more moments with her.

Those wishful moments turned into an undeniable vibe. The drinks helped, but the attraction…the attraction was real. The more time I had to look into her sparkling eyes, the more I fell into the sunken place. The more we talked, the more I wanted to know more. The closer we got to each other, I wanted to be closer, damn near living in her skin—and, man, did I get the opportunity to live in her skin. Deep in her skin. Sucked in, even, because her walls collapsed around my dick like there were magnets attached to it. Even before we had sex, the night was the best time I had in a long time.

I completed my gardening tasks, even with my mind still racing through the events of the previous night. Pop had left me in the yard long before I was finished, which was fair. He meant it when he said he wasn't going to do yard work all day. After putting away the bagged soil and tools in the shed, I entered my parents' red brick rancher. I found my mother in the kitchen, mixing the ingredients for homemade lemonade.

"Come sit. I know you're thirsty, baby," my mother beckoned.

Obediently, I sat at the wooden table, watching her pour a glass of lemonade. My dry mouth struggled to produce saliva as I mentally salivated over the sight. Before the glass could touch the table, I snatched it and finished it off with three big gulps.

"Boy, you still trying to eat and drink me out of a house and home," my mother joked, grabbing my cup and pouring another glassful.

"Thanks, Mama," I said, surfacing for air after taking a sip. "When you stop making this delicious lemonade and stop cooking the best meals, I'll stop gobbling up everything in the house. You don't like feeding me anymore, Mama?"

"Oh hush, boy." She giggled as she took a seat in a chair beside me. "You know I love feeding you, but you know what I'd love even more?"

I cocked an eyebrow. "What?"

"For you to give me some grandbabies so that I can plump them up with my home-cooked meals." She smirked, and I rolled my eyes to my head, exhaling hard.

"You're going to have to wait for that a little longer, Ma."

"Mm-hmm. We got pretty close with Vanessa. I just knew I was going to have a daughter-in-law and a grandchild."

"Maa…" I groaned, slumping back into the chair and folding my arms. I'd been in my happy space with my thoughts from last night, and here Mom goes, reminding me of my failure again.

"What?" she feigned oblivion. "I'm just saying, I don't understand what happened with you two."

"I messed up. I dropped the ball. All she wanted was a wedding date, and I couldn't give her that," I recounted the honest truths, from my personal admission to Vanessa's exact words. It all stung, but perhaps if I acknowledged it, it would finally start freeing me from my lingering sense of defeat.

"Mmm." I shifted my eyes off my folded arms at the sound of my mother's hum. When our eyes met, she spoke calmly, "One thing about a woman: when she's tired of waiting for a man to stop shuffling his feet and move, she's going to start moving herself."

"Tuh. Yeah, I see that." I lowered my gaze as her words settled between us, thinking about how Vanessa had literally moved out of our apartment and back to Regency. A sense of somberness swelled in my heart again as I admitted, "I don't know why I was dragging my feet. I thought I was ready."

"Thinking and knowing are two different things. If you were "thinking" you were ready, then you weren't."

I rubbed the side of my face. "I don't get it, ma. If the idea of marriage is in my mind, isn't it a definite thought?"

"Anyone can think about marriage, but did you actually feel it here?" She reached over and placed her hand on my heart. The warmth of my mother's gentle touch enveloped the spot, prompting me to place my hand over hers to keep her from pulling away. She patted the area as she continued, "Do you feel that? That's what it means to know. If you didn't feel that, she wasn't the one. Now, I really loved Vanessa; I think she's a wonderful woman, but I'm glad she moved on. There's no point in you two wasting each other's time if you aren't on the same page about marriage."

I tightened my lips as, once again, her words struck a sore spot. Reality sometimes hits like a gut punch when you least expect it, and this was one of those moments.

Maybe Vanessa wasn't the right one, and that truth stung. There was no doubt that I loved Vanessa. I wholeheartedly did, but Mom was right. I dragged my feet, and while my heart swelled with the warmth of my mother's love, it didn't do the same completely with Vanessa. Though I was devastated by the end of our engagement and her departure, my heart didn't leap out of my chest as if it would stop beating if she left me. Realizing this, and how much time I had wasted, drove the sword called failure a little deeper into my heart.

"When I think about it," I started, intertwining my hand into my mother's and placing our hands on the table. "I feel like I wasted a lot of time. Mine and Vanessa's. Just as much as you want some grandbabies, I want my wife and kids. I want to have a family like I grew up in with you and Dad. I'm in my mid-thirties and still looking for my wife. It almost feels like a bad joke God is playing on me."

"Mm-mm," my mother hummed, shaking her head from side to side. "You chose the path. God gives us free will to do as we please, no matter what, and most times, although we may hit a dead end on our own path, it comes with a lesson. Maybe this was a lesson of learning the difference between thinking and knowing so that you *know* when you come across the woman who's supposed to be your wife. Your daddy knew six months into our dating and married me six months later. Now, does that mean you'll know in the same timeline? No. But when you meet the right woman, you won't drag your feet. Pray about it, baby. Remember your roots. Ask God to be loud and clear about the woman that's for you. And when you do, don't be a dummy and not listen. Ya hear?"

"I hear you, Ma."

Just as she finished speaking, my phone dinged, prompting me to check it to make sure it wasn't the station contacting me. They were the only ones ringing my line nowadays, anyway. It was Denzel, but not necessarily to call me in to work.

Denzel: We're meeting at Rhythm and Brews tonight at seven. Our new crewmate is coming. Are you going to make it?

Me: Yeah. I'm gonna be a little late, though. I'm at my folks' house.

I moved my eyes to the time at the top of my phone. It was only three in the afternoon, but seven felt like a blink away. I needed at least a nap before I could handle another night out. Feeling like I needed to get that nap in pronto, I squeezed my mom's hand before letting it go and sliding the chair back to stand up.

"I gotta get back to Lovey's Bay. I have a work thing in a little bit."

"Okay, baby." She stood up after me, following through the kitchen to the front door. When we reached the door, I wrapped her in my arms. Mom only reached my chest in height, so her head rested there for a moment, a moment I needed. "You be safe going down the road and slow down in that car. I heard you coming down the road before I could see you."

I chuckled at her fuss before I kissed her forehead. "Maa, I'll be fine. I wasn't even driving that fast."

"Mm-hmm." She pursed her lips at me before a smile completed the curve of her lips. "I love you, baby."

"I love you too."

As I headed out of the house, I looked back as I approached my car. I could see my dad in the garage. Before getting in, I shouted, "Aight, Pop! I'm out!"

He looked up and waved as I climbed into the car and revved my engine. As I pulled off, I saw my mother standing at the front door in my rearview mirror. Her words, particularly the part about praying, were still running through my head.

Coming from a family where my father was a retired preacher and my mom his First Lady, prayer was normal in our routine. Somehow, in the middle of my grief, I lost sight of the quiet moments with God. Now was no better time to have a conversation with God as I stepped on the gas and peeled off— with my mother no longer in my rearview.

"Aight, My Guy. It's been a minute, but you know my heart. You know it so well that you know I crave to have my own family like the one I grew up in. I want a wife…some kids. Apparently, I took a road that You didn't guide. I'm taking my hands off the wheel—not literally." I chuckled at myself and gripped the wheel with my right hand a bit tighter as I exited the country road to the highway. "I'm stepping back and asking You to guide me. Guide me to my wife. I really want her. I really want us. Thank you in advance. Oh…make sure she's bad though, my G. That's all I ask, like, Janet Jackson in the 90s bad."

FALLON

If the invitation to come out to Rhythm and Brews wasn't from my new Chief, I wouldn't have been back in the establishment for a second night in a row. Firstly, it was too early to be back in the building after just being there last night, but secondly, I was barely out of my hangover from the night before. Hungover from the drinks. Hung over from the dick. Hung.

Very intoxicated, I was but far from being too intoxicated to remember the mass that filled and stretched me last night. Deacon. That's the name of the equally attractive owner of the pleasure toy for the night. Outside of having probably the largest dick I've experienced, Deacon was a treat to be around. He was fun, and the banter was easy with him. Light and easy. That's the best way to describe the time with him. With us. Just how I liked it, and he didn't make it awkward afterward. No trying to cuddle me, no trying to kiss all over me. We just had a fun time and ended the night with him dropping me off back at the apartments, which is why I gave him my number. He understood the assignment, and perhaps we could have another fun night at some point.

Tonight, I was rolling my collar down and swapping my dress for denim jeans, a fitted T-shirt, the same moto jacket from the night before, and combat boots on my feet. I was meeting my crewmates for the first time, and I was sure it would mostly be cocky men trying to test my ability to perform the duties of a firefighter when the opportunity arose. I didn't need to arrive with my full femininity on display. I needed them to know I wasn't to be fucked with. I could stand my ground. As for drinks, maybe a beer or two. The thought of liquor made my stomach churn, though.

I arrived at Rhythm and Brew around a quarter past seven. Chief Payton mentioned they usually meet at seven, and well, I didn't want to be the first one there for the impromptu meet-up. The bar had only half the number of people compared to the at least a hundred patrons from last night's speed dating event, along with what I assumed was their regular Friday night crowd. The music was more mellow too; it still had an upbeat vibe but was quite toned down. It suited the crowd, mostly consisting of people scattered at various tables and bars to watch the NBA and college games being aired on the TVs throughout the building.

Standing at the hostess stand, I scanned the room and spotted a group of guys, a few wearing what appeared to be company T-shirts. I locked eyes with someone who seemed to be wondering the same thing: whether we were looking at the person we both were looking for. When a smile spread across his brown face and he started walking toward me, I somehow knew it was Chief.

"Fallon?" His greeting sounded like a question as he stretched out his hand for me to shake.

I took his hand and shook it firmly. "That's me. You must be Chief Payton?"

"Call me Denzel," he insisted. "The formals come off when we are outside of the station."

I nodded and smiled, taking in his appearance. He was a handsome man with a strong jawline, a great smile, and a crisp hairline. His dark brown eyes lit up with sincerity. His clean-shaven face resembled that of many other firefighters. There wasn't a speck of hair on his face, not even a mustache, which honestly didn't look good on everyone. A thick mustache sometimes had a bit of a pornstar vibe. I wasn't supposed to think that, nor was I meant to consider that he was a nice-looking man, but those thoughts came and went quickly. I wasn't interested in any kind of relationship with a colleague, especially not with my superior. The last thing I wanted was for my skills to be overlooked or undermined because someone believed I had slept my way up.

Denzel led me to a rectangular table, which was simply three smaller tables pushed together. I was right; the party consisted mostly of men, with the exception of one other woman. Standing beside me in front of the staring crowd, he introduced me, "Hey everyone, this is Fallon Lennox. She will be joining FC143 this week." A collective greeting rang out among them as Denzel moved around the table making introductions. "This is Tevin, Farris, and Joss. Our captain should be here any moment."

The formal greetings began with Tevin, who appeared to be the youngest of the group. Although he and Denzel had clean faces, Tevin's features definitely showed a youthful look—though maybe by just a few years. He wasn't as muscular but had a nice build for his tall frame. As for Farris, he stood a few inches taller than me, with his muscles clearly defined under his company T-shirt. Unlike the others, he sported a well-groomed mustache and goatee, which suited him well. Farris offered me intense eyes and a charming smile that hinted at his interest in a relationship beyond just professional. If I were into workplace flings, he would absolutely be the one. After exchanging a few pleasantries, the guys stood up to head to the bar, while I got settled next to the one person with whom I hadn't spoken much to yet.

" About time Chief brought another female on the

team." Joss extended her right hand over to me, enclosing mine with a dap. "Josslyn, but everyone calls me Joss."

"Okay, Joss. The only female in the crew," I sing-song the rap lyric by Lil' Kim from the classic "All About The Benjamins."

Joss caught on, a familial smile covering her soft yet chiseled face. She chuckled and finished the lyrics with her own twist, "I definitely kick shit like these niggas do."

"Ha! My kind of girl!" I cackled, throwing my head back, but paused mid-cackle. "Wait, are those your pronouns?"

Joss ran her hand over her curly top. "I don't really get into all of that. I'm old school. I was born a female, and I like females. The guys call me bro, and the ladies call me babe. That's all the clarification I need."

I nodded my understanding and chuckled in amusement. Joss definitely gave off the impression that she gets the women. She had a nice build of muscles, with broad shoulders and nice biceps peeking through her fire company T-shirt. Her curly top and tapered sides added to her masculine side and revealed her gorgeous face, completed with almond eyes and a perfect set of teeth surrounded by pink lips.

I leaned in. "So, really? I'm only the second female in the company?"

"Yeah, but not intentionally. Chief's not biased. It's

just not a lot of women coming out to be firefighters." I nodded again and fell silent before Joss continued, "The guys are gonna try to get in your head, but don't trip though. It's all love at the end of the day."

I twisted my mouth to the side and raised an eyebrow. "Noted. They'll find that I'm a tough cookie to break."

"Aye! That's what I'm talking about!" Joss exclaimed, putting her hand out, clasping mine for another dap. "I gotcha back though. We gotta stick together. Plus, Cap be shutting the yappers down. He's a clown with jokes for days."

"Interesting," I said, wondering who the mystery Captain was. I was surprised that he wasn't here yet, but from the sounds of it, he seemed to be cool.

Joss looked past me to the commotion going on behind me. She nodded in the direction. "There's Cap over there."

I turned my head and my jaw slacked immediately. My heart beat tripled and my stomach sank like a boulder in the sea. The sea it sank to, it was my pulsing vagina, because walking toward me with the the same look of bewilderment under his smile was—

"Fallon, this is Captain Benjamin Deacon," Denzel introduced.

What in the Grey's Anatomy?

I needed no introduction. I'd been introduced in a tremendous way just the night before...to my superior.

After just telling myself I would not mix pleasure with work, I am faced with the fact that I have…and wanted to again. The oxymoron. The irony. The epic fail.

"Fallon, eh?" His question came out casual, but his lids narrowed to deeper slits as it dawned on him and me that he was now privy to my real name. Clearing his throat, he extended his hand. "Nice to meet you and welcome to the crew."

Keeping a poker face, I placed my hand in his as if I hadn't already felt his hands in forbidden places. "Nice to meet you too, Captain."

"Deacon. Everyone calls me Deacon, or you can call me by my *real name*, Benjamin."

The jab. It made my eyes balloon slightly at the unexpected moment. I had never been faced with my real identity being exposed, and I didn't know how to respond to this situation. After all, the goal was never to get serious enough to have to reveal that I wasn't Hazel but Fallon. Light and easy was the name of the game. So much for that now.

With a quick drag of fresh air, I pulled my hand away and composed my face with the same confidence I had when I first met him. Even after learning that he is my superior, he's still Deacon. A helluva bang, but still, just something light and fun I enjoyed. No sweat. Pulling my hand from his, I casually stuffed it into my pocket and said, "Well, nice to meet you, Benjamin. I look forward to being an asset to the team."

"Fallon came highly recommended," Denzel chimed in with accolades. He reached over and squeezed my shoulder. "I'm looking forward to adding another strong and dedicated team member to our company."

"That's good to hear," Deacon added. His eyes were still steady on me with clear intent to figure me out. "Where are you coming from?"

Unconsciously, I ticked my head to the side, subtly quizzing his intentions with the question, but I played along anyway. "Damask."

His eyebrows lifted, and lightness took over his energy. "Coming from the big city to the low-key Bay Area. Change of pace? Light and easy?"

I bit on the inside of my lip and fluttered my lashes inconspicuously, catching his innuendo. The simple mention of "light and easy" took me back to sitting on the hood of his car, moments before he had me waxing his hood with my cream. The thought sent goosebumps prickling my neck. The pinch of my teeth on the inside of my lip and the taste of copper pulled me from my daydream. I cleared my throat and swallowed the small amount of blood.

"Yes, a change of pace was necessary. The fast pace of Damask can be a lot sometimes." I ripped my eyes from Deacon and met Denzel's oblivious ones. "Thank you, Chief. I look forward to showing that I was a great decision and addition to the team. If you don't mind, I'm going to visit the ladies' room."

Denzel nodded. "Oh, sure. Before you leave, how about we grab you a drink so we can cheers to you joining the team."

"Sure, but just a beer—something light." I hurried out before turning to find the restroom signs. I walked away with my head held high, even though my insides felt like they were on fire.

It didn't help the situation that Deacon looked just as irresistible as he had the night before, proving that the drinks weren't making him more attractive than he truly was. Then there were the memories from the previous night flooding back as I struggled to keep my eyes fixed on his instead of wandering down his body. My gaze wanted to gravitate toward the parts that still made my vagina react to him: his voice and the way he looked at me. Although his eyes showed confusion and curiosity about who I really was, I could still sense he was thinking about the night before, too.

That has to end here. I reminded myself as I washed my hands after relieving myself. I looked at my reflection, seeing the slight pout settling on my lips. "Damn, I really wanted to take that for a ride again."

After drying my hands under the automatic dryer, I hooked my arm on the door handle and pulled it open, only to pause at the sight of Deacon leaning against the opposite wall. He held two beers in his hands and offered one to me.

"It's a local cider," he informed me. Taking slow

steps toward him, I took the uncapped glass bottle from his hand. Just as I was about to put it to my lips, he asked, "So…who's Hazel?"

My stomach hollowed as I pushed out a breath.

"It's me. My middle name. I never give out my real name to…to…" This was the first time I couldn't form the words. Fling. One night. Hell, I never had to explain myself or what I was doing, and honestly, I didn't plan on it. I sighed, "This wasn't supposed to happen…us crossing into knowing each other on a personal level. It was supposed just to be—"

"Light and easy," Deacon finished for me. He took a swig of his beer before nodding his understanding. "I get it. I didn't expect you to use my number for anything more than that. I just didn't expect to be given a fake name."

His chuckle prompted my own to escape my lips, brightening the mood. "It's not exactly a fake name; it's my middle name. See, you already know too much."

"I would've found out anyway when I looked over your paperwork." Deacon shrugged his shoulders casually, and we laughed a bit more easily this time.

Finally taking a sip of the fruity cider, I looked up at him with raised eyebrows. With a hint of disappointment in my voice, I said, "So, I guess that's the end of that. One and done."

Two Hours Later

"We…can't…do…this…anymore…after this time," I panted between rushed kisses and pants.

Deacon walked me into my dark apartment as if he'd been here before, kicking the door closed behind us. My little legs wrapped around his waist as he monster-walked through, swinging us from side to side. "Where?"

"I don't care," I breathed, damn near agitated by the question. All I knew was I wanted him. Inside me. Now.

How did we get here? Three beers, plenty of laughs and jokes with the crew, accompanied by lingering glances at one another. Deacon offered to walk me to my car, and I accepted. We ended up in the same parking lot next to the Bayside Apartments.

How? How was it that this person, who was only supposed to be a good time, turned out to be my Captain and lived in the same apartment building as me? It felt like the Universe just didn't want this to be the last time I saw Deacon. So be it.

All it took was a hug. A brush of the lips, and then we were trying to swallow each other whole, and I was climbing his body like he was my favorite tree. Shit, the branch that made itself known immediately after I wrapped my legs around his waist, it could be my favorite tree. It really could.

Deacon dropped down onto my couch with me sitting on top of him. We hadn't released each other's lips once and stayed locked and sealed as we fumbled with articles of clothing, only pulling away to pull each other's shirts off. Skillfully, he snapped my bra off, releasing my girls. My nipples were taut and hard from the crisp of the air and they allured him to fondle them to harder peaks. He played with my nipple ring like a kid with a new toy. Tonight, I was his wind-up doll. As he tweaked my nipples, I came alive more and more.

Feeling my dominance, I challenged, "Being that this is your last time, I hope you do more than play with my nipples."

"Last time, eh?" He egged on, flipping me over so that I was lying on the couch.

"Mm-hmm."

Deacon covered my mouth with his, kissing me hard and deep as he unbuttoned my jeans. The zipper released itself, and I assisted in the removal of my jeans by lifting my ass as he pulled them down and off. I wasted no time, undoing his jeans and putting my hands inside, feeling his long erection in his boxer briefs. I creamed at how hard and veiny he felt.

"Don't play with it," he groaned as I stroked it through his boxer briefs.

I nipped his lip. "You're the one still in your boxers. Give it to me already."

"Bossy much?" He mumbled onto my lips, chuckling.

"Yes," I admitted, pulling at his briefs, tugging them down as he slid down my panties.

"I like it," he admitted with a smirk. He sat up on his knees, his rod swinging with each move as he dug into his wallet and pulled out a condom. "But tonight, I think I'm gonna have to fuck that bossy shit out of you."

I giggled as I sucked on my bottom lip, watching him sheath himself. My mouth watered at the sight of the condom stretched for dear life over his masterpiece. Master. Piece. He leaned down, eyes still on me, lining up to my center. When I felt him plunge into me, my nerves jumped and unraveled. Stretched and filled by him, I oozed intoxicated moans as he wound his hips and dug his way until he hit the bottom. In and out. Long and short. A hypnotizing combination of movements, creating havoc over my brain and body.

Sigh. What a cruel, wonderful joke the Universe played on me with this one. A nice shiny toy. Given and taken away.

"Welcome to Robin's Bend State Park to anyone who hasn't done training or fought last year's wildfire with us here. When the bus stops, file off of the bus, and I'll give you your room assignments. There will be a cabin number on the paper that will match an actual cabin. You have about two hours to get unpacked and comfortable before coming together as a unit and starting dinner."

Deacon stood between the two rows of seats as we bumped down the dirt road. Catching his eyes, I rolled mine toward the window I was leaning against, choosing to watch the green foliage on the trees pass by. For the last two weeks, it had been easy to forget the two intimate nights I had with him, given that we had been on different work shifts. I meant it when I said there wouldn't be another night with him. Except, I didn't realize we would be spending a weekend together for training. Technically, we aren't spending another night together, but hell if this didn't put us too close for comfort in my decisions. I didn't need the distraction when it came to being a part of this crew.

Over the last two weeks on the job, I realized Joss was right. The crew wouldn't stay off my back, as my feminine presence became the focal point with their jokes and assumptions about my abilities. They were terrible comedians, hitting me with the typical, "Can you lift that?" or "Are you sure you want to mess up your nails?" Thank God they're not paid for their jokes. I've heard them all, and they only annoyed me instead of making me curl up and cry like they expect. Little do they know, I've overcome the most oppressive relationships: my ex-fiancé and my mother. Their jokes seem minuscule.

The bus's engine roared, and the brakes screeched as we came to a stop in front of a literal campground. Tall, foliage-covered trees surrounded us, and several cabins were lined up in two rows ahead of us. A smirk crept to the corner of my mouth as I thought about spending a weekend kicking some egotistical ass in competitive training scenarios. I cast my eyes toward the obnoxious laughter coming from two of my targets, Tevin and a guy named Nate.

"You ready, roomie?" Joss nudged me in the side, interrupting my daydream of taking down the guys in competitive spirit. My smirk faded a bit as she added, "You know they'll probably put us together."

"Yeah, I guess."

"Hey, it beats bunkin' with these ninjas." She leaned into me. "Did you know grown-ass men still act like high school boys and smell like them, too?"

I snickered. "Oh, I know. My crew and Damask weren't any different—except we had twice as many women in the company. Even with us around, they still guffawed like high school class clowns in homeroom."

"Damn, I keep forgetting you aren't wet behind the ears. So, you know what training weekends are like, eh?'

"Kinda. Damask Fire is a little bigger, so we didn't do weekend-long training. Our trainings were always scattered throughout the week, but nonetheless, I know how strenuous it can be. I'm good for it, though. They'll learn I'm not this soft new girl soon enough."

The chatter that once filled the bus began to grow distant as the crew began filing out of the bus. Joss stood up, throwing her bookbag over her shoulders. "Hey, don't take it personally, though. Everyone gets "hazed."

She made air quotes with her fingers, and I pursed my lips and rolled my eyes at what she thought would be comforting to me. It wasn't. It just reminded me of what I left behind in Damascus: being reduced to just being a woman. Don't get me wrong—there's nothing wrong with being a woman. I LOVE being a woman; it's the notion of what a woman should be that bothers me.

"Just look cute and let him do all the work. Darling, you're going to be a very kept woman..."

The memory of my mother's words that day when she witnessed me defying one of Travis's "orders" lingered in my mind. It was during one of my mother's visits, and we were having dinner at our home—well, Travis's home, which I was then privy to after becoming his fiancée. The house was a mansion, spacious and open, but it felt stifling. Suffocating, really, because he was slowly sucking the life out of me. Yet, for the love of Travis and his pursuit of City Attorney of Damask, I maintained the image and the lifestyle.

Why do we do that? Why do you fall into this false belief that you must be a Stepford Wife to an influential man? I subconsciously embraced this idea from watching my mother do the same: give up her life in Damask and marry a British man. Thomas Munford was his name. He was a great man to my mother and a father figure to both Parris and me, even though he wasn't our biological father. She wanted for nothing. We wanted for nothing. So why not follow in my mother's footsteps? Well, because my then-fiancé, Travis Marshall, was no Thomas Munford. He had an ego as big as his substantial bank account, along with a control issue that only emerged after I became engaged to him, and when I expressed my desire to keep the one thing that was important to me: my career.

I had been with the Damask Fire Department for five

years before meeting him, and I worked hard to get there. After taking a two-week leave to focus on our rapid engagement and even quicker wedding planning, I was ready to return to work, to my peace. Travis had other plans and suggested that I resign.

"No! I'm not leaving my job. I bust my ass to get the respect I'm getting in this field!"

I remembered pushing away from the dining room table, nearly knocking over the chair I had occupied. Travis and my mother jumped with different yet equal shock. My heart raced as if I were a kid whose favorite toy had been taken away. At that time, my career was my favorite thing, and Travis was trying to take it away from me.

"Respect? If you have to work that hard for respect, then what are you doing? You know what respect is? Respecting the man who's giving you all those nice clothes and jewelry you're wearing right now. This house. Do you know how many women are lined up wanting to take your place? Ha! Respect."

Travis' words stung so much that I remembered clutching my chest as tears burned the corners of my eyes. They took an inch off me, making me feel small. And for him to say it in front of my mother and then stormed out of the room, I felt defeated, especially since my mother didn't console me but instead told me to "just look cute and let him do the work." I felt unsupported on so many levels.

"Lennox, you good?" I glanced over the top of the seat, my face clenched and still lost in my memories, when I saw Deacon standing at the front of the now-empty bus. His thick eyebrows furrowed together, clearly surprised by my demeanor.

I squeezed my eyes shut, forcing my thoughts to the back of my mind, but the tension remained, throbbing at my temples. I let out a heavy sigh and collected my things, walking down the aisle and brushing past him. "I'm good."

———

I didn't realize how much I needed the invigorating sensation of the early April air against my sweating skin. With my pores open, I ran through the trails of Robin's Bend Park, climbing ladders and maneuvering heavy hoses, feeling the high I craved in everything I did, completely in my element. What made this moment even more gratifying was that I was dusting every person who tried to reduce me to their twisted perception of a female firefighter. They weren't going down without a fight or a joke, though. All day, Tevin tossed a joke my way, and Nate would alley-oop with a remark that felt personal. I took it personally, despite Joss continually reminding me not to take it seriously. It was personal for me and fueled my desire to complete this last obstacle for our Saturday training at the top.

"Alright, this is our last obstacle before we take it in for the day. This should be a fun one, the Smokin' Maze."

We stood in front of Deacon and a maze of tall bushes. He pulled a small fob from his pants pocket and pointed toward the maze, causing white smoke to begin billowing from hidden machines, quickly filling the pathway.

"Inside the maze are the Citizens of Lovey's Bay. Not real humans, but plastic representations of them. You and your partner must navigate the maze, find all the trapped citizens, rescue them, and make your way out. You have thirty minutes to finish your run. Here are the pairs..."

I crossed my arms, already knowing the direction this was headed. I was pretty sure I would be paired with Joss since she had been my partner all day. I was starting to think Deacon was involved in this exclusion until I heard my name called and found out I was paired with someone other than Joss. It could've been anyone but the person he paired me with.

"Fallon and Nate."

An exaggerated scoff billowed from the pits of my stomach, silencing the group. I cut my eyes at Deacon, who challenged me to speak up with a raised eyebrow.

"Aye, the feeling's mutual," Nate spoke up. "I'll give you a head start if that helps."

"It looks like she's been dusting you all day, Nate," Farris said, stepping up to him. His actions surprised me a little, even though Farris has been subtly showing his admiration for me. I noticed Deacon whip his head to Farris with a look of surprise as well. "Who really needs the head start?"

"And where exactly have you landed in all of this? Last place?" Nate shot back.

"Aye! We're not doing this!" Deacon barked as he snapped a finger. Both guys quieted down, bringing their attention back to him. "I don't know what's going on here, but we are a family, and this challenge is a *team sport*. Friendly competition! We got that?"

Deacon scanned between Nate and Farris, holding his glare on Farris for a longer pause before turning toward me. Although I was shocked by Farris's defense of me, I felt more confident in his support within the crew than I did with Deacon. His generic ass statement didn't address the bullshit that was obvious to others besides me. Not wanting to feed into it verbally but wanting to show through my actions, I simply said, "I'm good, Cap. The problem doesn't lie with me."

"Okay, now that this is settled, let's get started. We have about two hours before sunset. Tevin and Joss, you're first up."

As if nothing had happened, we all dispersed, with Tevin and Joss heading toward the entrance of the maze. Joss looked over her shoulder to me as she jogged away, giving me the "OK" signal. I shrugged, feeling annoyed and eager to wrap this up. Farris strolled over to me.

"You're killing his ass out there. That's why Nate's panties are in a bunch," Farris assured as he stopped in front of me. He searched my eyes as he asked, "You good?"

"I'm swell," I answered sarcastically and chuckled. "I'm used to being the strongest woman on the team and threatening weak men. I'm not worried about Nate."

Farris whistled. "I like that energy. You bad, Fallon."

His subtle compliment coaxed a chuckle from my tight lips, softening my entire demeanor. This seemed to be contagious, prompting a surprisingly charming smirk to appear on his lips. I looked at him a moment longer, admiring the handsomeness that radiated beneath the beads of sweat forming on his forehead and trickling down the sides of his face. A shadow fell over, blocking the sunlight that had once shone brightly, shifting my gaze to the body that cast it. Deacon stood peering over Farris' shoulder with narrowed, under-entertained orbs.

"Everything good over here?" he grumbled.

Farris turned to Deacon and placed a hand on his shoulder. "Everything's copacetic. Just checking on Lennox."

Deacon glanced from Farris to me and slowly nodded.

"Cool," was all that he answered before turning around and walking away. I furrowed my brows, confused by the glare and his impromptu interruption. It further added to my annoyance.

I watched each pair go through the maze for an hour and a half. They donned protective gear to shield themselves from inhaling the smoke, yet they still came out at the end of each run, out of breath and fighting to take the gear off. When it was Nate and my turn, I snatched on my gear and set myself to sprint off when giving the signal, poised and ready to show how it should be done.

"Giddy up, cowgirl." Nate's taunt made me crane my head toward him with a menacing sneer. He cackled just as Deacon called for our start.

Cowgirl? I'll show you a fuckin' cowgirl. A badass cowgirl.

I bolted, elbowing Nate as I ran past him. I let out a heat-infused grunt as I kicked my legs into high gear, nearly kicking myself in the ass with the soles of my sneakers as I weaved through the smoke-filled maze. The smoke was thick, as if we were in a real-life fire emergency, making it hard to see where I was going and where to turn, but I pushed through, finding my way and still keeping a lead over Nate. At one point, I couldn't hear the thump of his feet behind me, which sparked confidence that I could slow down and ease my breathing a bit. I was heaving, my chest rising nearly to my chin as I tried to take in as much air as possible while slowing to a jog in front of a dead end, leaving me with only two choices: left or right. My hands hit my knees as I allowed myself a moment to rest and make a decision, but that lasted only a couple of seconds as I heard Nate's footsteps powering up from behind. I looked over my shoulder to see that he had found one of the fake humans.

Determined not to let him win, I zoomed off to the right, frantically searching from side to side for the last body. Tucked away under a bush, I spotted a nude-colored plastic form a short distance away and dashed toward it, snatching it up and tucking it under my arm. I glanced back and saw Nate just steps behind me, then turned to see the opening at the end of the tunnel with the rest of the crew staring and cheering us on. I took off again with Nate by my side.

"May the best man win."

His words made me see red. Made my blood boil. Made me want to prove a point. I pumped my arms and legs harder, gaining a lead, but then Nate powered up and was back at my side until he tripped. I halted, looking back to see his citizen and him sprawled on the ground. I considered going back to help. That thought came and went as I took off to the finish. Clearing the bushes and catching a beam from the setting sun, I dropped my person and raised my fist to the sky, roaring.

"Yes! I fucking did it!" I hollered, doing my victory dance. The crowd around was cheering, but a harsh tone silenced them.

"You did it, but your crew mate just died!" I spun around to Deacon, who was glaring down at me as he closed in. "If this was a real emergency, you would have allowed your fellow crewmate to have died in the fire because "you fuckin' did it." Not only your crewmate but the person he was rescuing."

My breathing steadied just as my thoughts did in response to the truth of his words. As much as I wanted Nate to burn in hell, in a real situation, I wouldn't let my crewmate or a victim die in an emergency without at least trying to rescue them. I removed my protective gear with my head still low and avoided Deacon's gaze. He stayed put as he dismissed everyone, resting a hand on my shoulder to keep me from moving. I lifted my eyes to him, no longer able to hold back my frustration.

Deacon's scold came out low and steady. "Whatever that was, stays right here. We are a team and family, and we aren't carrying that into real-life situations."

I was seething inside from embarrassment, targeted by jokes and incredulous remarks from weak men, and then scolded by my Captain, the only person out here who had seen me naked. Now, I stood figuratively naked, exposed to my ego being verbally ripped apart. I hadn't realized how tight my mouth was bunched until I finally released the tension to speak.

"One thing you'll learn about me is that I am selfless. I will fight through the most horrendous emergencies for the sake of protecting and serving. I can't say that I fully believe my "family" here would do the same for me. If it was me that had tripped back there, do you think Nate would've come back for me? Would he have been scolded in the manner that I have? No. He got away with berating me all day with not even a peep from anyone but Farris. Not even you. But I hear you, Capo."

I shrugged off his hand from my shoulder and stormed away.

Ever since the last time Fallon and I were together, I'd been curious about her. Even though she declared that it would be the last time we'd be together in that way, I couldn't stop thinking about her. I observed her, not in a stalkerish way, but just to learn more about her. It wasn't difficult because we shared some similar habits, like morning runs. I discovered that when she wasn't scheduled to work, she would go for her run between seven and eight in the morning; most of the time, it was seven, especially now with the days getting longer.

That's why I got up at the crack of dawn this morning, hoping to catch her on her way for a run. After what happened yesterday, I felt I needed to talk to her, and at this hour, during her run, it would seem less suspicious. I don't know why I was worried about that. A captain and a crew can go running, right? My guilt over being with her in ways I yearned to experience again made me paranoid. While I've managed to keep my composure throughout the weekend, it was hella hard, especially watching her go into beast mode during every training session or obstacle we tackled. She was strong and determined, and it was sexy as hell, especially with how great she looked in uniform. She made the fire department t-shirt and shorts look dangerously appealing with her natural curves.

I stepped out of my private cabin at quarter to seven, thinking I'd have time to stretch and act like I wasn't waiting for her, however, when I scanned the quiet campground, among the chirping of birds, I heard soles hitting the dirt path and a voice. A distance away, I saw Fallon already on the trail and talking to herself.

"Interesting," I said to myself. *Perhaps she's reciting affirmations.* She looked like the type who would have a list of affirmations, and I chalked it up to that as I started into a light run to catch up with her without scaring her.

As the distance grew smaller, I couldn't keep my eyes off the view of her from behind. She wore a matching navy sports bra and form-fitting running shorts, stopping right under the curve of her ass. Fallon was petite, but she packed amazing curves, clearly created and toned by her workout routine. A small waistline complimented her curves, making her hips sit out beautifully. And her ass, although contained in the spandex, its bounce couldn't be contained by it.

"Hey," I tried to say softly enough not to sound creepy, but not so loud that I startled her. My effort failed; I still startled her. She reached up to her ear, revealing that she had earbuds in.

"Zaria, hold on," she huffed, slowing down to a stop. Her orbs still held the annoyance from yesterday. "Yeah?"

"My bad," I said, raising my hands. "I didn't know you were on a call."

"Yeah, I am." She folded her arms over her chest and moved her eyes as if she were listening to the Zaria person in her ear. She rolled her eyes and mumbled, "Bye, Zaria."

"Mind if I take a run with you?" I asked after she tapped her earbud. She shrugged and began to run at full speed.

"Fair," I said under my breath, picking up my pace to catch up with her.

Fallon had every reason to feel the way she did, although I also had a valid point. The silence between us was thick, drowning out the sound of our feet on the gravel and dirt path. If it had been anyone else—Tevin, Farris, anyone—starting a conversation that included my apology along with a discussion about what was right and wrong would have been easy. This was difficult because, though I was her Captain, I also wanted to shed that title and be the man who had an aching interest in this woman. Remembering that we agreed to forget the moments we shared before knowing our work roles, I pushed the feelings aside and put on my Captain's hat.

I caught Fallon's attention by grabbing her arm and pulling her off the trail. She gaped as she realized what I was doing and stumbled, nearly falling into me. I seized her other arm, steadying both her and myself as we stood between the surrounding trees.

"What…are you doing?" She stammered, dropping her arms from my grasp.

I crossed my arms and looked at her square in her pretty brown eyes. I almost lost track of thought, peering into them, but regained myself. I cleared my throat and confidently said, "We need to discuss yesterday."

She folded her arms again and looked away. "What else is there to say, Captain? I was told I was wrong, and I accepted that."

I stepped into her view, wanting to meet her eyes as I corrected her, "You were partially wrong, not completely. I owe you an apology. I didn't take into account that Tevin's jokes and Nate's remarks were offensive to you."

Fallon's facial features softened a smidge, but her eyes were still slits.

"I didn't care about the jokes. I can handle jokes. I came from a fire company full of men. I know how to handle you all. But I never had to deal with the kind of hate Nate was giving off. No. I have, and I *refuse* to have another man try to make me little. I worked too hard to get to where I am and to be who I am now. *No one* will take that away from me."

Her words were laced with something from her past. Hurt. Trauma. An experience she wasn't willing to go into. She didn't have to because I was hot inside thinking about what someone could've done to make her feel small or less than. I wanted to fix this, make her not feel those things, but what could I do to heal her past?

I pulled Fallon into my chest, wrapped my arms around her shoulders, and held her. My actions were just as surprising to me as they were to her. I felt her body stiffen underneath me and then relax as she placed her hands on my back.

"What are you doing?" she mumbled into my chest, yet not moving from my embrace.

Overstepping a boundary, we placed between us. Acting impulsively. That was what my mind conjured, but instead of admitting that, I admitted something else.

"My Dad used to say at the end of his sermon, "Sometimes all people need is a hug." I figured you needed a hug." She snickered, letting that be the only sound between us as she melted even more into my arms. "Nate's being put on leave, but you'll never have to deal with him again. He's outta here."

She pulled back, looking up at me with wide eyes. "What? Fired? I don't know if that's necessary on my behalf."

"Not fired, but after his leave, he's going to another firehouse. Chief's already working on the paperwork."

Shock overtook Fallon's face. The corner of my mouth twitched, wanting to form a smile, but before it could fully emerge, Fallon found comfort in my arms again. Her head rested on my slowly rising chest as the soothing sensation of her arms gliding up my back made my body tingle with a feeling I hadn't experienced in a long time.

I didn't think too hard about it. Instead, I let the feeling fill me up as I whispered, "Hey."

Fallon looked up at me, and before she could say anything, I pressed my lips to hers, the touch light to test the water. Her head jerked the slightest as she moved her eyes up to mine before she closed them and returned the kiss. Her lips provided a firmer touch, and I unwrapped an arm and placed her chin between my fingers. Tilting her head, I kissed her intently and then deepened the kiss. Our tongues danced a slow grind, a perfect rhythm for me. I didn't want to rush the moment but savor the feel of her soft lips against mine. I wanted to savor the serenity that came with her being in my arms. I wanted to feel the prickling sensation that took over my body just a little longer.

"Deacon…what are we doing?" she whispered against my lips.

I gave her a peck.

"Kissing."

She pecked back.

"Should we be kissing, Captain?"

I planted my lips onto hers firmly as if it could wipe away the formality. "Right now, I'm Deacon, and it's just a light and easy kiss." *Smooch.* "Can I kiss you?"

It was too late for the question, but I asked it anyway. There was no answer needed. Fallon stood on her tiptoes and hooked her arms around my neck, inviting me into the warmth of her mouth again.

"It's nothing but G.O.A.T.S on the team. Put some respect on 'em!" Tevin shouted over the noise at our table. Rhythm and Brew was a madhouse, given that it was the start of the NBA playoffs. I'm sure the conversation we were having was also happening at every other table filled with basketball fans.

"There's too many superstars on the team," I chimed in. "Every year, they're fighting for the spotlight and losing the playoffs."

"True."

"Deac, got a point."

The co-sign from Denzel and Farris ruffled Tevin's feathers. "Tsk, man, y'all sound like some haters to me."

"Haters?! How are we hating on a losing team?" I retorted, laughing loudly. I leaned over and knocked on the side of his head with my fist. "Hello? Is anything up there?"

Tevin swatted, his face balling up more as the table erupted in laughter. "Aight, D. Just because you got a big muscle head doesn't mean you treat everyone else's head the same way."

My eyes ballooned, and I went for the jugular. "Oh, so you're admitting that there's nothing in between those elephant ears?"

The table erupted again. Tevin tried to fight his laughter, twisting his mouth to the left and right until he broke. "I see jokin' ass Deacon is back. I'm gonna let you live because, for a minute, you were mentally checked out."

"Now, Tevin has a point," Denzel added. "We're glad you're back, Deac! We were beginning to worry. You had Tevin taking over your spot, and he's no comedian."

Laughter broke again at the expense of Tevin. Dryly, he said, "Aight, you got jokes too, eh? Y'all get off my neck. We talkin' about Deacon now." He tilted his head to me, smirking. "You did what I told you to do, didn't you? Got you some new new."

The table went mute, and all attention was on me. I twisted my mouth and snorted, trying to play it cool while thoughts of Fallon ran through my mind. "Nah. I'm just in a good spot now. Letting the past be the past."

My answer was a half-truth. I had been releasing the

past and moving on. After a while, I realized that holding on to all the whys that came with trying to figure out what went wrong with Vanessa and me wasn't helping; it was keeping me in my sorrows. I couldn't make room for what I prayed for if I continued to wallow in my pity. It was clear that time wasn't waiting on anyone, and I wasn't going to waste any more time on the manifestation of my wife. Fallon's presence in my world kind of helped, too.

I couldn't lie. When I was introduced to her as Fallon instead of Hazel, I felt some kind of way. She lied about her name, and I didn't know what else she was capable of behind all her beauty. However, as she was part of the fire crew now, I had no choice but to see if she was a scammer or not. My reservations didn't last long after I met her in the hallway that night, and she fessed up. My dick was longer than my holdout, and I proved that too later that night.

Fallon had an unusual pull on me that made it hard for me not to want to be near or feel her, even after she laid the law about not letting sex between us happen again. I respected it because, honestly, I didn't know how I would navigate through work with her, knowing I had access to that magic box between her legs. Her pussy was the perfect kind of warm, the perfect kind of snug, and she looked beautiful in the moment.

It wasn't just the sex that drew me to her, though.

The more time we spent at work, the more I got to see her in her element and learn that she was genuinely an amazing woman. She stood firm in her power, her confidence being a huge turn-on, but even behind her tough exterior, I could tell she had a soft spot buried underneath it. I saw it when we took that morning jog at Robin's Bend, which is why I couldn't resist the distance and kissed her. I'm glad I did because that brought the wall back down with her. She let me back in.

We hadn't introduced sex back into the equation, though. A few texts throughout the day, longing stares when in the room together, flirtatious words behind the normalcy of working together. I think we both didn't know how to navigate back into that without knowing our roles in the workplace, but the tension was there. I wanted her again and again and again. Maybe it was the newness of learning someone new, or that she was just a drug I wanted to be high off. Whatever it was, I wanted it. I wanted more of her.

"Yeaaah, it's a female," Farris commented. I turned my attention to him as he continued. "Look at his face. Smirkin' in his daydreams and ish. I got a feelin' I'm fittna be just like you." He rubbed his hands together as a sheepish grin spread across his lips. "I'm going to help Fallon with some things at her apartment."

My eyes widened and my body tensed in my seat as the focus shifted away from me to him. Grateful for the change in questioning, I felt like I was about to burst, clenching my jaw tightly to contain the surge of panic. When did they start talking? Why did she ask him for help? The ringing in my ears faded as he expanded on his thoughts.

"Yeah, man, she told me to come through and help her with this TV stand, so I'm going through there tomorrow. I'm gonna ask her out. See what she's about."

"Oh, shit!" Tevin cackled. "So you're going to be the first one to the 'L' from her?"

Denzel and Tevin cracked up. I huffed a dry laugh as I opened my text thread with her, scanning for any mention of a TV Stand needing to be put up. I found nothing, and that made my stomach knot up. We conversed about everything, but her needing help with anything in her apartment wasn't one of them. I felt some kind of way about it, even though Tevin was right, Farris would get an 'L' for the attempt to take her out. I cringed at the idea that he would even have the opportunity.

I was over listening to Farris fawn over Fallon. The sound of the legs of my chair loudly scraping the wooden floor halted the conversation at the table. "Hey, I just remembered I have some things I need to do before I start my shift tomorrow. I'll catch y'all this week."

The crew looked at me confused but didn't protest. Quick head nods and goodbyes came from them before I swiftly walked away, as they continued their conversation about Fallon…basketball—something that I had no interest in at this moment. My mind was on a fast track ahead of my body. While I went to the bar to close my tab and then promptly left the venue, my mind beat me to Bayside Apartments. What my mind didn't do was come up with an excuse for me knocking on Fallon's door.

I stepped back from the door, blowing out a sobering breath. *What the fuck am I going to say when she opens the door? Shit, is she even going to be here?* All the important questions that should've been pondered before I left Rhythm and Brews crowded my mind with no resolve when Fallon swung her door open.

Dressed in a cropped T-shirt and cotton shorts, her bob fixed with the top in a hair tie, and a clear, shocked face, Fallon asked, "What are you doing here, Deacon?"

Staking what's mine, ran through my mind, but what came from my jarred mouth was, "I heard you had something that needed to be assembled."

Yeah, tell her the other truth. I cringed at myself for giving up the information I wasn't supposed to be privy to. Her mouth dropped, and instead of waiting for her to say anything, I mumbled, "Excuse me," and slid past her and entered her apartment. My pupils zeroed in on the boxed TV stand lying on the floor of her living room, and I headed in the direction of it, scanning how her living room was starting to look "lived in."

When I first visited, the state of her apartment was similar to mine, still in boxes. The boxes that were once stacked in the corner by the balcony were no longer there. What replaced it was a side table and a ceramic lamp atop it. A bamboo plant was tucked in the corner behind it. The lamp was turned on along with the flat screen sitting on the floor, clueing me in that I interrupted her watch of a crime show with Queen Latifah.

"Soo… what made you think I needed help—wait. Were you guys pillow talking?!"

I looked up from the box I had started ripping open, eyebrows crinkled. "Pillow talking?"

"Yeah. You and Farris and whoever else was involved." Fallon threw her hands in the air as she walked deeper into the living room. I continued taking the pieces of light-colored wood out of the box, discarding the instructions. Seemingly talking to herself, she fussed, "Why didn't I think that this man wouldn't say anything?"

"It's Farris. He's been drooling over you since you walked in the door," I answered for her. "Where's your tools? Screwdriver? Drill?"

"What do you mean…Farris…drooling over me? Wait—what…and he was going to bring all the tools. I don't have any."

"So you did ask him to help you assemble this, knowing I'm only two flights up," I accused through clenched teeth. I stood up from my crouch position in front of the wood frames and attachments.

Fallon shook her head quickly and threw her hands up. "Pause. I did not ask him. It came up in a *friendly* conversation that I needed to put this stand together, and he *offered*. I wasn't going to ask any of you to help. I'm capable of doing it myself."

I could see her confusion about the whole situation while she stood firm in her capability to be Superwoman. I didn't doubt her ability to be her. Her tenacity and will to be a badass did something to me every time. Even right now.

I started taking long strides to the door, but then pivoted and made my way back over until I was standing directly in front of her. She lifted her eyes to me, her lids going between stretched and slits as her mental and her body confused her on how she should feel. My chest heaved as I grabbed her by the back of the neck and crashed my lips into hers, slipping my tongue into her mouth. A moan slipped from her mouth as I witnessed her melt to my touch, and I buried my tongue into her mouth with hopes of stamping her tonsils with my name. I pulled my lips from hers, fighting the urge to throw her over my shoulders, clear off the dining table behind us, and eat her like she was my mother's steak and potatoes meal.

Grunting back my desire, I said, "If you need something. Call me. Light bulb went out? Call me. Need a picture hung? Call me. I don't care what it is. I love that you are Superwoman, but you ain't gotta wear your cape all the time with me around, and you for damn sure don't need to ask another man. I'll be back. I'm going upstairs to get my toolbox."

"I didn't ask…ok…" Fallon's failed protest trailed from her mouth as I stalked back to the door. I didn't care whether she protested or not, as long as she knew I was the man for any job she needed completed.

Watching Deacon work was better than watching the TV sitting on the floor beside him. I had lost track of what was playing on the TV; it all blended into mumbo-jumbo as I concentrated on the entertainment before me.

Deacon had stripped down to his undershirt and toed off his shoes when he returned with his toolbox, getting comfortable without asking me whether it was okay. I wasn't going to argue about it. I enjoyed the sight before me. I sat on the arm of my sofa with my legs crossed and the tip of my index finger grazing my lip as I watched the muscles in his back bulge and contract with each movement.

I squirmed in my seat, my hips wiggling and reacting to my sweet spot pulsing. It had been doing that with every thought since he validated the Superwoman in me and affirmed his desire to be the reason I put away my cape sometimes. I had never felt secure like this with anyone, not even Travis. My ex tried to force security by being overly controlling. Deacon stood on business and said what he wanted. Not forcefully, just sure. This notion was attractive to me. It made me feel seen while confirming the security of letting my guard down. Let my guard down. That was another thing that wasn't supposed to be happening within me: getting comfortable with a man enough that I was lowering my gate from around my heart. Yet here I am, in the middle of a battle with my mind, body, and urges to pounce on him.

I shook my head, trying to push away the fuzzy and intense feelings clouding my judgment, but at this point, sound judgment was out the door. That had left the moment our lips touched on our last day at Robin's Bend. I had demolished my rules about not fraternizing in this way with a colleague—Benjamin Deacon. Farris never had a chance with me. While he was a very hand-some man, my attraction was heavy with Deacon, and keeping that in check was far more grueling than I had anticipated from working so closely with him.

And then, after he got rid of Nate and made me feel seen, I realized the line of professionalism was nearly non-existent. He literally transferred the man for disre-specting me. The gesture was extreme, yet so damn chivalrous and sexy. It was enough to make that boundary I had in place to go "poof" and shatter all my walls.

Sigh, what have I gotten myself into?

"Now let's see how well I did," Deacon mumbled. He got down on one knee, lifted the TV, and placed it on the stand.

I slid off the arm of the sofa and tiptoed over to the side of him. Deacon stepped back as I inspected, turning my nose up playfully. I moved my eyes to side-eye him and caught him with his mouth twisted as if he knew I was on some bullshit. I snickered before saying, "Thank you, Deacon, although you really didn't have to do this."

"Hell, if I didn't. What do I look like letting Farris do something for—"

"For whom?" I challenged, my eyebrows lifting with the octave of my last syllable. I looked up at him with piercing eyes, waiting for his response while my brain and heart fought for control.

Deacon closed the space between us, peering down at me unwaveringly. "Someone I like."

"Abort! Abort! Abort!" My alter ego, Hazel, screamed in my mind, but the pounding of my heart was much louder. My heartstrings strummed a romantic tune. I could picture my little alter ego stepping on a string of my heart, trying to prevent it from continuing to strum.

"You're supposed to like me, Captain."

A nervous laugh slipped through my lips as Deacon wrapped his arms around my waist. I didn't flinch when he nipped at my bottom lip. Instead, I melted into his chest as his touch caused my jaw to slack.

"And you're supposed to like me, Fallon," he murmured, offering his lips to me. I accepted them, pressing into his and softly pecking. He whispered onto my lips, "Now we're two people like each other."

I do, my heart wanted me to admit, but my brain produced the deflecting words, "You're putting words in my mouth now."

Giggles fell from me as he planted kisses on my left cheek, my right, and then onto my lips, each peck growing more intense.

"Am I?" he questioned, pulling away to smirk at me. Words formed but never made it past my parted mouth as Deacon swiped his tongue between the slit of my lips. I forgot all the words as my knees buckled and swooned at the electricity surging through my body from this one touch.

I cursed myself for how he controlled my body with the simple act of kissing me. That's all I've let him do: kiss me, and each time, my body betrayed me. My body craved more. His body craved more. I could feel how it reacted to me just as mine responded to his. Yet, I was still trying to hold on to the thread of morality and not sleep with my superior.

...But my superior has amazing dick...

I hadn't had any form of a dick since the last time Deacon and I christened my couch, and that wasn't even me. I was supposed to be in a new city, with my new job, taking a joy ride on a new adventure—man—when I chose to. Somehow, my body wanted one joystick I had been depriving myself of for over a month. Again, what has gotten into me? Holding out for some dick I put myself on timeout from?

"When are we going to stop playing this game?" Deacon groaned into my mouth, squeezing at my love handles. "I love kissing you, but I want to kiss other places."

"Hmm," I moaned at his words. Wrapping my arms around his neck, I pulled closer for a tongue-heavy kiss, hoping to buy myself some time because my mind was no longer fighting with my heart but with my pussy. She was percolating at the thought of his mouth on her, and I wanted nothing but to let him do just that. Yet, I was still wrestling with the facts. Deacon was my captain.

My mind won this time. I drifted my hands from his neck to his chest, gently pushing him back and breaking our kiss. "I'm sure you do, but your time of bombarding has ended. Good night, Deacon."

"Bombarding? What?" The words rolled over a chuckle as he held his hands out to his side.

I moved my eyes to him, scanning over his heaving chest and unmistakable bulge in his jeans, completely ready to reconsider my decision. I stuck to my guns, though, needing to figure out how I even got to this point in the first place. Sighing reluctantly, I switched my way to my door and opened it.

"Yes, bombarding me after your pillow talk with the guys. So, thank you, Deacon, for putting my TV stand together, but yes, it's time to say good night before we cross into territories we won't know how to navigate."

Deacon chuckled as he swiped his shirt from the floor and slipped into his shoes before ambling over to me, pausing only when we stood chest to chest. I wet my lips as the last of my breath escaped me. Curving his index finger, he gently lifted my chin until our lips met for another sweet, agonizing kiss. Pulling away, my orbs moved from his lips to his eyes and then back to his lips as I breathed in his air, craving his touch once more.

With certainty in his rasp, he assured, "I know how to navigate those territories very well. You know that."

Big dick energy. A shaky breath oozed from me as my nipples hardened. *God, what is happening to me? I am putty with this man.*

Nearly whining, I replied, "You know what I mean. You…me…work."

"Fair enough…" The words fell from his mouth as he brushed his lips against mine before planting a smooch against them. Accepting his fate, he sighed heavily before giving me a few more pecks, trailing one kiss after another before he released my chin and stepped to the opposite side of the threshold.

As if he wasn't ready to let me go, he wrapped his

arms around my waist again, pulling me into his warm body. I wasn't ready for him to go or for him to let me. Still, I couldn't bring myself to completely fall back into giving him all of me, especially now that the thought of being found out by our crewmates was accompanied by tingling feelings that invaded me whenever he was near.

We reluctantly drifted apart, our hands being the last to disengage. I watched Deacon walk off, further and further, until I heard someone clearing their throat. I turned my head in the direction.

"Mm. Deacon, huh?" Joni queried, snaking her head and folding her arms. Her lips were pursed as if she had just heard the juiciest gossip in town. Technically, she had stumbled across some gossip that would be pure gold to some. I opened my mouth to say something, but Joni spoke before I could. "Don't worry, I'm not gonna say anything, girl, but you're gonna spill the tea to me later."

"I'm sure you all are familiar, but today I am here to review CPR techniques for your annual recertification. We will go over the proper way to perform chest compressions and mouth-to-mouth. Unfortunately, our test mannequins have been recalled due to toxic materials, so we will be practicing on each other."

The local paramedic's announcement sent confused mumbles and then silence across the fire garage. That's until Tevin spoke.

"What about toxic breath? Can we recall this session because some of these mugs breath hotter than a pigs ass with diarrhea."

The whole room erupted in laughter, prompting a chuckle from the paramedic. I laughed at Tevin's silly ass and then called for order. "Alright crew, settle down.

Tevin, zip your trap. Last I heard, you're the only one with the yuck mouth."

My joke did nothing for the settlement of the room as they burst into laughter once more. Fallon was even giggling behind the hand that covered her mouth.

Denzel stepped up to the plate. "Okay, okay. Now that we've got the giggles out, let's pair up and get this cert done."

I stood back and watched as everyone began moving and pairing off. My eyes darted to Farris as he headed straight for Fallon. *This nigga*, I thought, as if he knew Fallon was off-limits. He didn't, and technically, she wasn't. She wasn't officially mine, but she was definitely off-limits to Farris. With my left eye twitching, I took a deep breath before regaining my composure and casually yet deliberately made long strides toward Fallon, meeting Farris just as he approached her. Fallon's eyes widened slightly as she flicked her gaze between Farris and me.

"Farris, I think the new volunteer might need your help," I said, more so as an order. I waved my hand over my shoulder in the direction of nothing in particular.

"Fallon's new," Farris protested. His eyebrows crinkled as if this grown man wanted to pout.

I turned halfway to him, my right brow raised. "That's why I, the Captain, will help her. Now, to the volunteer."

Pulling in a deep breath, Farris exhaled and moved

on and out of sight. I turned to Fallon, wearing a grin, only to meet her narrowed eyes and pursed lips.

"You're giving very much obvious," she said under her breath, moving towards a more open space.

"How? I'm performing my Captain duties, making sure our new female crew member feels comfortable."

"Mm-hmm," she hummed, not buying what I was selling. "Get on the ground."

"There goes, Big Mama. So bossy!"

"Stop it!" she hissed as she whipped her head toward me. Her face contorted, stifling a grin and glaring at the same time.

Chuckling, I raised my hands in surrender before lying on my back on the cold cement. Fallon followed suit, kneeling to my right as the paramedic began to explain and demonstrate how to perform chest compressions. Fallon peered past me, intently watching the demonstration. I watched her with equal focus, noticing how she gnawed at her bottom lip with her teeth. The way her plump pink lip resisted her grazing teeth was tantalizing, and I found myself thinking of ways to steal a kiss before the day ended.

"Alright, now that you all are reacquainted with the technique, it's your turn to perform."

At the announcement, Fallon rolled her eyes down to me, twisting her mouth up. She leaned in with her hands on her knees, close enough for only me to hear her threaten, "Don't lose your life." My jaw dropped, furrowing my brows with confusion about her threat. "Don't act like you don't know what I'm talking about. Act like a good victim, and let me pass my certs."

I tilted my head to the side, pretending to be disappointed. "You're threatening my life when you're supposed to be saving it?"

She scoffed and rolled her eyes as she placed her hands on my chest. "Deacon, chill. You know what I mean. Don't try any slick shit."

"I don't know what you're talking about," I denied, adjusting my head to the center and lying stiff as a board.

Fallon started the chest compressions, repeating the sequence after a small pause in between, giving the instructor time to come over and check her form. After getting the head nod of approval from the instructor, she leaned back on her heels, placing her hands on her knees again. I moved my eyes down her body, stopping at the spread of her hips as it rested on her heels. I found her irresistible, even in her department T-shirt and shorts. Sensing my gaze, she moved her eyes down to me, tucking her hair behind her ear.

"What?" She asked, her eyes squinting.

"I can't look at you?" I murmured, wetting my lips.

"Not like that," she said through clenched teeth, her lips framed by a fake smile. "Quit flirting."

"Stop looking so beautiful, then."

The instructor's voice interrupted my flirting,

allowing Fallon to blow out a breath she seemed to have been holding in.

"Okay, now we will perform the full sequence together, chest compressions and then mouth to mouth."

Fallon and I met eyes again as I wet my lips exaggeratively and put on a cheesy grin. She snorted, "Your ass is so damn silly."

"Save me, Big Mama," I begged playfully, shaking out my shoulders before lying stiffly again and closing my eyes. I heard her call out the Lord's name in vain before leaning into me and beginning the chest compressions.

Press. Press. Press.

Thirty seconds went by as she pushed the meat of her palm into my chest. Completing, she leaned in to give me two rescue breaths.

First breath.

Second breath.

On the second breath, I skillfully swiped my tongue into her mouth. I heard her suck in a breath through her nose before I popped open my eyes. I met her big doe eyes and I danced with her tongue again as my heart filled with glee at her surprise.

Beep! Beep! Beep!

Long blaring beeps filled the garage, followed by the monotone of the computerized system speaking:

"Fire Emergency reported at 505 Boardwalk Way.

Priority 1. Fire Emergency reported at 505 Boardwalk Way. Priority 1…"

In a matter of seconds, the garage's calm turned into turmoil as feet clattered across the floor. Each of us quickly sought our protective gear and clothing. Any jokes or unseriousness that had once filled our crew vanished in the blaring alarm of a life-threatening five-alarm emergency. Heart pounding, I rushed through the firehouse, listening to the ongoing announcement and trying to recall the location from memory.

"What the fuck is fire doing poppin' off on the beach?" Tevin asked rhetorically as he fell in step with my jog toward the front of the engine.

The question made a lightbulb go off in my head as the location dawned on me.

"That's the small residential area, isn't it?"

"Shit, I think so."

"It is. I just looked at the system's map," Denzel chimed in, his long strides catching up with us. "It's the home right on the beach. The one they should've deemed unsafe years ago. It's too close to the shore, for one. Let's get a move on it!"

The adrenaline rush during a fire emergency is unlike any other. The mind becomes crystal clear and laser-focused on the task at hand. A feeling of superhuman strength takes over as we move, as if we have the weight of feathers on our bodies instead of 50 to 70 pounds of protective gear. And then, there's the excitement.

Beneath all the calm and the rush lies the thrill of being relied upon to make things better.

The April showers had descended upon Lovey Bay all month, and today was no exception. Spurts of heavy rain dominated most of the morning before tapering off to the misty rain we were experiencing now, a little after midday. Observing the weather conditions, I was already weighing the pros and cons of managing whatever we were about to face. All of this would be sensory overload for a normal person, but for me, it energized me as I navigated the engine through the streets of Lovey Bay.

"Make a left up here."

I followed Denzel's directions, making a left turn and leaving the city streets of Lovey's Bay. I passed through the green light onto the street next to the boardwalk. The route we were taking led to the two-lane highway that Fallon had driven down the night we met, dawning on me that I hadn't seen her since we received the alert.

"Everybody back there ready to go? Know what their duties are?" I queried, glancing at Denzel briefly. I cleared my throat, hoping my inquiry sounded like a Captain checking for order and not a man checking on his woman's well-being.

"Should be," Denzel answered before pressing on the radio attached to his gear. "Everybody knows their roles when we get there, crew? Tevin and Farris, you man the water supply and hose. Fallon, you're on search and rescue..."

"Got it."

Hearing the one voice I had been waiting for hollowed my stomach and allowed me to focus. I tuned out the rest of Denzel's rundown of duties, pressed down a bit harder on the accelerator, and let the sound of the siren spur my urgency to reach our destination. In no time, I was slowing down, staring at a raging fire with thick, charcoal smoke billowing above it. I came to a stop to assess the situation. Among the many challenges of controlling the blaze, waves crashed against the unstable stilts supporting the house. With each crash, I could see the stilts threatening to give way.

Creeping down the steep pathway towards the house, I peered over to Denzel. "You see what I see?"

"Yep. We don't have much time to make sure this house is evacuated before it goes sailing into Lovey's Bay."

Static. "LBPD is at the scene, and the family is saying they're missing a child. We need rescue asap."

The announcement blared loudly through Denzel's radio as I shifted the truck into park. After a quick scan of the scene, I spotted a man with a woman and a boy who looked about eleven, clinging to him. Soaked from the rain, sweat, or perhaps both, they all gazed at the flames, while the woman cried hysterically.

"Do we have a description of who we are looking for?" I asked as Denzel and I walked over to the family. I looked between the man and woman, remaining calm, but my heart thudded deep when the mother spoke.

"It's my daughter! My baby girl! I thought she was holding on to her brother's hand…." The woman's head was buried into the crook of the man's arms before she could complete her sentence.

"I'm going in," I heard Fallon say over my shoulder.

I glanced at her, momentarily captivated. Her eyes were dilated and full of determination, and I could see the furrow of her brows beneath her helmet and mask. She rubbed her gloved hands together as she shifted her stance, clearly waiting for one of us to give the word.

Over Fallon's head, I watched the raging flames dance as Tevin and Farris began to tackle the fire. The whirring of the ladder deploying and the breaking of windows to ventilate the smoke-filled house mingled with the crackle and roar of the fire. My chest sank as I thought about Fallon entering those conditions.

"C'mon guys, we don't have much time," she reinforced, waiting for the okay, but hardly. Her petite body was already halfway in a sprint position when Denzel finally gave her the okay, the answer I was not expecting.

Moving Denzel off to the side, away from the family, I murmured, "Denzel, are you sure? We hardly have a clear view of what she's going into."

Denzel's expression wore confusion. "Do we ever? We never know what we are getting into, but we do it.

It's her job, Deac. It doesn't change with her being a woman."

I shook my head. "No, that's not what I'm saying. Look. I'm going in with her. Yes, she's capable, but it's her first major incident."

Denzel nudged his head in the direction of the home. "Go on then, stop standing around!"

I took off in a light jog before I took on a skip and went into full speed run, seeing Fallon disappear in the cloud of smoke, heading to the ladder.

Did I doubt that she could handle the job of finding this little girl? No. From the way she navigated our makeshift obstacle at Robin's Bend, I knew she was the best for the job among our crew. It's just… it's Fallon. She had a hold on my heart, squeezing it and making it hard for me to see her as just one of the crew doing the job they signed up for. As I followed her up the ladder, still a ways behind, I watched her rush onto the raised deck and then disappear into the burning home. At that moment, I saw her as the woman I adored, risking her life, and she wouldn't go down on my watch. I wasn't going to lose her before I could ever say she was mine.

I knew I was taking a risk. The moment I stepped out of the truck and saw the waves crashing against the stilts, which looked like battered No. 2 pencils that had been plucked to death against a desk, I understood the danger. At any moment, after a wave crashed, those stilts might crack, just like that pencil, and the house could drift off into the bay—or sink like the Titanic.

Hearing that a little girl was trapped in the smoky, fiery inferno triggered feelings. If I had to name those feelings, it would be desperation, empathy, and a need to protect. So, I didn't wait for anyone. I didn't wait for Denzel to finish his declaration before I went. I didn't wait for the ladder to finish propelling completely. I didn't wait for Deacon when he called after me.

The cascading smoke almost pushed me from the entrance of the home. It was thick and full of charred embers, making it unsafe for the trapped child to ingest. I entered the home from the back into what was vaguely made out to be a family space and a kitchen off towards the front of the home. Everything was engulfed in hot orange flames, making it hard to identify the best way to move through.

"Mommy!" I heard a small voice in the distance call out. It wasn't really distant, but it was in another part of the home—maybe even outside.

"Mommy, help me!"

I felt my heart in my throat the second time I heard her plea, and for a moment, I was transported from the house back to Damask—Travis's house, right after the heated argument we had about my leaving the fire department.

That was the day he struck me. It was the first time he had ever done that, and the first time I had ever feared him. I remembered holding the side of my face where his knuckles had connected from his backhanded slap. My cheekbone vibrated from the impact, and through my watering eyes, I saw…no one over his shoulder.

I knew my mother had heard the commotion. She was still somewhere in the house when we began to argue, and I knew she could hear the clatter of the accent table I bumped into as I tried to pull away from Travis's grasp. I knew she heard the crack of his hand against my soft face. It sounded like lightning striking. I remembered because my body jolted as if I had been a tree hit by lightning. Yet, I didn't hear a footstep. I didn't hear a peep from her, even though inside, I was pleading for my mother to help me.

Protect me.

Save me.

A piercing shriek jolted me from my memories, and I dashed through the maze of smoke, letting her cries lead me. I found myself at a door in the kitchen area that opened to the front of what I now recognized as a wraparound balcony. Outside that door stood a small girl, no more than six years old, at the balcony railing, which was swaying.

"Shit."

My chest was heaving now, and my eyes were fixed on the little girl as I realized the true danger of this situation. Without hesitation, I swung the door open and bolted onto the balcony, but I stilled as I realized just how unstable it was. It was swaying like loose hips on a dance floor, and with too much pressure, our dance in the fire would end in the water.

Big brown eyes stretched at the sight of me. Pouting, she asked, "Where's my mommy?"

"She's downstairs…" I replied, as my memories and present converged. Tears filled my lash line and streamed down my cheek before I understood what was happening. I shook my head quickly, trying to banish my memories while carefully moving toward the girl. "I'm going to get you back to your mommy, okay?"

The little girl nodded her head, her mahogany cheeks stained with tears. She clung to the railing, gagging occasionally from the smoke. I had to get her out of there immediately, not knowing how much smoke she had already inhaled. Reaching her, I knelt down and asked if I could pick her up. With another nod from her, I scooped her up, and she clung to me, burying her head in my gear. As soon as she felt comfort in my arms, I heard the crack of one of the stilts.

"Fallon!" I looked up to see Deacon standing at the door, his arms out, trying to determine balance. At that moment, I felt a security blanket cover me as my eyes met his intense stare. "We gotta get off of this balcony *now*."

Reaffirming his statement, the balcony tilted and swayed again. I bumped into the railing, hearing a large creak and then crack. Behind me, I saw the rushing water. I looked back towards Deacon, whose backdrop was the raging flames. I mentally prepared myself for the only way out of this: by water.

Staying cool and collected, I rubbed the back of the little girl in my arms. "Hey, what's your name, pretty girl?"

She coughed and answered, "Amina."

Another crash of waves smacked the beams, and another crack was heard. "Okay, Amina. I need you to be Superwoman with me, alright?" She nodded. "We're going to fly, okay? And we're going to land in the water. But before we land, I need you to hold your breath really big, okay? And don't stop until we pop up from the water. Okay, big girl?"

"O-o-okay," she sniffled. She was trembling in my arms now.

"Don't be scared. I won't let anything happen to you," I assured her with the words I wished my mother had spoken to me. On queue, just as I suspected, another roaring crashing wave made its debilitating contact, and the weak beams creaked loudly before snapping.

"Fallon!"

The harshness and fear of Deacon's voice was the last thing I heard before gravity was lost. I hadn't realized how far up we were until I looked up and saw Deacon, a distance away, jumping in behind us. How ironic it was for my heart to soar as I realized he was coming for me.

"Activate your superpower, Amina. Hold your breath…now!"

I felt her tiny body heave as she took a huge breath, and then water rushed around and over our heads. With all my strength, I kicked my feet, pushing against the water and the weight of my gear, feeling us start to rise back to the surface. Then I felt us being pulled as we broke through the surface. Unable to see anything, I could hear Amina gasping, and then my arms felt light. Gasping and reaching, I searched for her frantically.

"Amina…Amina!" I forced out, but my voice was muffled by the protective mask I still had on.

"Fallon…Fallon! We got her. I got you!"

My vision unblurred, finding Deacon in front of me. He was free of his helmet and protective mask, face drenched with water.

He really came for me. Me. Why me?

The questions clouded my mind and heart; my pulse was rapid and uneven. It felt like a heavy boulder sinking into my chest, and I started to search for my next breath as it seemed to slip away with each passing moment.

Deacon's eyes showed terror before he held onto my stiffened body with one arm and began ripping off my headgear and mask. As soon as it was off, I inhaled deep and exhaled deeper. I inhaled deeper and exhaled deep. The unevenness of my breath continued as tears burned my eyes and then came flooding down my cheeks. Behind my tears, I was back in the memory of being in Travis' home with Amina's sweet voice calling out for her mom to help her. In my mind, it was me calling for my mother…to help me.

I don't know how quickly or when Deacon got us to shore, but he did, all while I was mentally and physically breaking.

"Yo, is she good? Medics are on the way."

"Stay back! Give her a minute!" Deacon barked sharply. I didn't know who was asking, but I recognized Deacon's voice distinctly. I also knew his arms, feeling comfort as he enveloped me, shielding my privacy while I broke down within his embrace.

DEACON

If my melanated face could show it, it would have revealed the moment the blood drained from my face. I felt like a newly transformed zombie, pale and void of emotion when the balcony dislodged and Fallon and the little girl fell into the water. Had this house been positioned away from the shoreline as it should have been, I would've still been worried about the impact of them hitting the sandy bottom, but it was water. Raging unyielding water, made even more violent by the windy and rainy conditions we'd been experiencing. What was once shallow shorelines now felt like being in the middle of the ocean due to the natural shift of the shoreline over time. There was no telling how deep the water was at this point—there was no sign of a sandy bottom when the waves rolled back. Just water. Just water.

"Fallon!"

My voice didn't even sound like mine when her name slipped from my lips. There was so much emotion behind it. This wasn't the first time I'd witnessed a heroism unfold before my eyes. This is what we do as firefighters. We are heroes. We rescue those in danger. But…this was Fallon. She was the woman who had my head all in the clouds, craving every moment that my lips might touch hers. She was the one who lived behind my eyelids each time I closed them. Who would save her? When our eyes met the instant the floor gave way beneath her, I was almost certain I saw that same question reflected in her gaze.

Me. I'm going to be the one to save her, my mind answered as my legs and body took over, running toward the broken, weak edge and jumping in behind her, peeling off my turnout gear as I descended. As the layers fell away, so did the weight, and my acceleration toward the rushing water increased. It wasn't fast enough because I saw Fallon and the girl sink into the depths before I smacked into the water. Her eyes were on me, void of any emotion, as if she wasn't there. That caused the notion of fight or flight to kick in within me. I fought. I fought the air, kicking and winding my arms well before I hit the water, ready to search and rescue my future beneath the unknown depths of the liquid darkness.

My future. The thought of Fallon being in my future

has been like a whistling whisper for some time now, first drifting through my mind the night I heard her voice over that partition at the speed dating event, and then becoming more pronounced over the past month and a half. The words echoed in my ears and settled in the depths of my chest, unable to wrench themselves free. I didn't want it to. I couldn't. Fallon's unbelievable beauty, her badassery, her tenacity… it all drew me to her—making me want her.

As I crashed into the water, my body mirrored that sensation. The gurgling of the water flooded my ears, and I grappled with the underwater debris of weeds and rocks while I searched for the two. I feared that the weight of Fallon's suit would drag her and the little girl down, jeopardizing their chances of surfacing safely. When I found her, no amount of strength or obstacle could prevent me from pulling them to safety. With a death grip on her gear, I somehow managed to pull her and the child she held tightly to the surface. Denzel, Tevin, and Farris were there, with Denzel working to pry the little girl from Fallon's arms. Fallon still appeared as if she were in another universe, her eyes bulging, pupils dilated, and her breathing shallow.

And then she blinked. Her eyes met mine, and it was like a flick of a switch how fast her dazed state turned into something else. Her shallow breaths became long and heavy drags and then heaved like she was gasping for air. My gut tightened while my heart pounded my chest as I wrestled with her headgear to give her fresh air. Her breaths slowed once it was removed, but her tears flooded her face just as quickly as her breaths once were. She broke. Tough Fallon broke, and it left me gutted yet protective of her.

"Yo, is she good? Medics are on the way," I heard Tevin asking, his voice filled with the same worry that coursed through me. I could hear his footsteps growing closer as I sat on the shoreline with Fallon cradled between my legs, limp and sobbing.

"Stay back! Give her a minute!" I barked, taking my left hand and waving him away. I could hear him stop in his tracks and the voices of medics that Tevin indicated were on the way.

"Fallon…Fallon…shhh…I need you to take some deep breaths for me, mama. Deep breaths." I kept consoling her and guiding her, even though, for a moment, it felt like it was doing no good. Her sobs and heaves were heavy, as if she was releasing something heavy. This was more than just this rescue. It was something else I wasn't privy to, but I didn't force the need to know. The only thing I needed was for her to be okay. I needed her to know she was safe. I wanted her to understand that I was going to sit here and talk her down from the attack on her mind no matter how long it took.

———————

"Fallon did one helluva job."

From my peripheral vision, I noticed Denzel stop and stand next to me. We were back at the fire station, and I observed from a distance as Fallon underwent some debriefing assessments—physical, mental, and emotional evaluations. This was the standard protocol many of us have followed after a major fire incident like this one.

"Yeah, she did," was all I offered him as my eyes strained to find anything that might suggest the opposite of what she showed now.

Unlike before, Fallon was at ease, breathing normally, and even wore a faint smile that lit her face just enough to mask the puffiness of her eyes from her break-down. As if she sensed my presence, she glanced my way but quickly dropped her gaze to her hands while the paramedic checked her pressure again.

"I'm gonna let her go home for the night, but I want someone to drive her. She looks well, but I saw how she cracked earlier. I want to make sure she gets home safely."

"You know she isn't going to go for that," I mumbled, inhaling deeply as I watched her hop down from the table she had been sitting on.

"I know, but it's an order. I'll tell her—"

"Nah, I'll tell her. I'll take her home too," I offered, not thinking much more about my response until a few silent beats went between Denzel and me. I looked over at him, finding him wearing a look of inquisition. "You good with that, Chief?"

"Yeah. That's cool," he agreed, his eyebrows furrowing, further indicating his suspicions. Denzel is one of my closest friends, but even so, I still hadn't clued him in on what was happening between Fallon and me. What was I supposed to tell him? Nothing I could think of to explain the situation sounded ethically professional. As much as I wanted to share with him, there was no way to do so without potentially compromising either of our jobs.

"Alright, well, I'll get her home and come back."

"No, go ahead and take the rest of the shift off. It was just as grueling for you as it was for Fallon. I'll call in a couple of crew members from the next shift to come in early."

I didn't protest Denzel. I dapped him up and then headed over to Fallon, who was leaving the common space toward the locker room. When I caught up to her, I gently touched her forearm to get her attention and pulled her further into the empty hallway.

"Hey, so Chief wants to make sure you take it easy for the rest of the evening, so I'll get you home."

Her weary, brown eyes narrowed as she refused. "I'm good. I can finish up the shift."

She started to walk away and into the locker room, but I grabbed her swinging hand and pulled her into an empty sleeping room next to the locker room. All the while, she questioned what I was doing. Once behind the locked door, I pinned her with worried eyes. I could see her eyes widen as she folded her arms.

"Do you remember how you were when I pulled you out of the water?" I asked, taking slow strides toward her. I looked down at the crown of her now wavy, damp hair as she avoided making eye contact with me. Attempting to encourage her to look at me, I gently placed a finger under her chin and lifted. She turned her eyes away. Giving up on my efforts, I sighed. "What happened back there?"

"Cap, I-I...I won't let it happen again," she stammered, removing her chin from my touch and making her way towards the door.

I caught her by the hips and pinned her to the nearest wall, moving my head each way that she moved until she finally gave in and looked at me. "I'm not worried about your ability to handle an event like this. I'm Deacon right now, not Captain Deacon, and who I saw back there wasn't the Fallon I know."

"But what if it is?" she said, her voice cracking. As the setting sun rays shone through the window and warmed her face, I could see her eyes beginning to water.

"Okay, and if it is, I want to know that side of you too," I admitted, cupping her face and gently stroking her cheek with my thumb. That simple gesture caused a heavy tear to slip from her eyes. The chords attached to my heart twisted as I watched it trail down. I longed to kiss away her sorrows but remained composed and committed to listening. She blew a hard breath and shook her head as she began to talk.

"I…I just…something about that moment took me back to a time I felt helpless…" Her voice trailed off. Sucking in her bottom lip, she exhaled and closed her eyes. "My ex…he hit me once. I never saw it coming. Never thought he'd ever put a hand on me, but he did, and when he did, my mother was in town—downstairs. I knew she could hear the commotion, and she did nothing. Said nothing. I think, hearing that little girl call for her mom to help her put me back there." She paused and then rushed out, "I know, this is no place for that. I'm grown—"

"You're also human, too," I interjected, wiping at the tears wetting my thumb. The thought of a fool putting his hands on Fallon had my jaw clenched, and me speaking through my teeth. "And trust me, if a joker tries to even put a finger on you again, they'll be eating through a straw with their feet."

My candid remark aroused a short laugh from Fallon. "That'll never happen again. I'm too good…too strong…"

Fallon broke again, squeezing her eyes shut as her waterworks painted her face again. It was killing me inside to see Fallon this way, to see her in tears and I found myself acting on my earlier notion to kiss away her tears. I planted my lips on each salty tear as it trickled.

Her eyelids. Her right cheek. Her left cheek. Her top lip. Her bottom lip.

"Deacon," she whimpered, moving to place her hands atop mine, cupping her face.

"No," I protested, already knowing she would tell me to stop. "Let me kiss the pain away."

I took her bottom lip between my lips, tugging softly and pulling a whimper and another sob from her. I pulled back just as she opened her glassy eyes to me. Fallon blinked away the fresh tears before asking, "Why? Why do you want to..."

"Why not?" I asked, answering her lost question. Locking into her gaze, I answered earnestly, "Fallon, you're everything. I'd do anything to see you happy...to see your beautiful smile again. Let me. Let me kiss away the pain."

Fallon pinched her eyes closed as she exhaled, seemingly to let go of her fight. With tears still trickling down her cheeks, I proceeded to kiss away her pain, wetting my lips with each tear on each cheek, lining kisses along each side of her jaw, and then pressed my lips to hers again, ever so soft. This time, she kissed me back and wrapped her arms around my neck. My hands glided down the side of the fresh company T-shirt she wore and then under the cuff of her butt, hoisting her up. She wrapped her legs around my waist as our pecks turned into longing, languid lashes as I backed her into the wall.

I was very familiar with Fallon's mouth, as it was the only thing she permitted me to feel, but this time it felt different. My heart expanded just as much as the space between my legs. Fallon always felt relaxed in my arms, but this evening, she seemed open to more. She didn't stop me when I trailed my lips to the crevice of her neck, suckling gently yet firmly. Instead, she let her head fall against the wall and let out a soft moan. She didn't protest when I walked us to the bed in the corner, laying her across it. She relaxed and lifted her arms, helping me as I pulled the T-shirt up and over, tossing it to the ground.

I scanned her body, layered only with a sports bra and her shorts, and her feet still with the slides she had been wearing. I skated my eyes back to hers. They were glassy still, but no more tears. I could still see the pain living in her eyes. I continued my mission to kiss away her pain. Moving down the bed, I ran my hands down her silken legs and removed each slide. Sitting on my knees, I lifted each foot, massaged it and then covered each toe with my mouth, sealing each with a kiss. Circling my tongue around her big toe, I pressed my thumb firmly in the center of the bottom of her foot. The spot was like a button that made her legs relax open further. Her breath caught before she released a soft, shaky moan as she felt me kissing up her thighs as I moved to guide her shorts down. She lifted, assisting again as I gathered her panties with the shorts and removed them.

I climbed back up again, holding myself up with my hands, eye-to-eye and nose-to-nose with her. I scanned her eyes, still glossy but now holding less pain. She searched my pupils as I did hers before I leaned down and claimed her lips again.

"You okay?" I whispered.

Fallon nodded as she held onto my neck, pulling me in for another smooch. I gave it to her, only settling there for a moment. I still had work to do in order to kiss away the last of the pain. I kissed down her soft stomach, and then positioned myself between her thighs and pecked.

Right thigh. Left thigh. Her mound.

Her hips twitched as she sucked in a shaky breath. Locking my arms underneath her legs, I nuzzled my nose in between the folds of her sex until the tip touched her clit. I could smell the sweetness of her arousal and my mouth began to salivate. I swiped, immediately being obsessed with the cream she already had pooling at her center. I went in for more, alternating between long licks and French kisses to her center, completely in a zone to make her replace the pain with pleasure.

"Deacon," she whisper-moaned, reaching down to palm my head.

"Hmm?" I hummed, answering and purposely adding another sensation to her pleasure. I hummed low and long, the vibration eliciting a whimper from her and the quake of her legs. Clasping my hands on her abdomen to keep her there, I tongue kissed her pussy once more before latching onto her clit, alternating sucks and taps to her swollen pearl.

Suck. Flick. Suck. Circle. Suck. Suck. Flicker. Flicker. Suck. Suck. Suck…

Fallon mashed my head into her pussy—also now known as my happy place—as her hips began to buck, her body contracting forward. Still latched to her bud, I listened to her whimper, "I'm…I'm…coming… Deacon…"

"Mmhmm," I acknowledged, as her release drenched my lips. I licked each drop of her slick and creamy release. It was a beautiful mess. I cleaned her thoroughly, lapping through each wave of smaller orgasms she produced until her whimpers turned into slow exhales, my indication that she was no longer in pain.

FALLON

A hand across my bare stomach stirred me from the light slumber I was still in. Like clockwork, my body was nudging itself awake naturally just before my alarm would sound. I slowly blinked my eyes open, catching the slither of sunrise peaking through my sun-blocking curtains, confirming that daybreak was approaching, along with the obnoxious alarm. Lifting slightly to reach for my phone to silence my impending alarm and check the time, I was pulled back by that same callous hand and into a hard chest—and morning wood. I looked down at the mahogany-colored hand, following it as it cupped my right breast, thumbing my nipple.

I wet my bottom lip as I exhaled, "Good Morning."

"Good morning, gorgeous."

I turned completely over to meet the eyes of the

owner of the raspy baritone. Deacon's sleepy eyes locked on mine through half-open lids. Even with them not fully open, I could feel the…I didn't know what to call the emotion in his eyes. It was like a combination of wonder, lust—and adoration. One season ago, I would've quickly dismissed Deacon from my bed because he was looking at me with such intimacy. However, in the middle of this scorching summer, I wanted nothing but to be in his skin and locked into his adoring gaze.

This morning, I welcomed him as he curved his arm under my waist. Scooting me into his naked body, he nuzzled into the crook of my neck, pecking and tasting my skin. In the same motion, he cupped my breast so that my pebbled nipple protruded as he massaged and tugged at my ring, igniting tingles in my center and a soft moan. Adding to my pleasure, he moved the warmth of his mouth to my happy point. His teeth clanked against my ring, and he tugged at my ring and then flicked his tongue.

I didn't question what I was doing anymore when it came to Deacon. I'd lost all care of the rules I once had about dating, cuddling—everything. He was even sleeping at my home or vice versa for consecutive days sometimes, especially when our days off coincided. Deacon gave me a spark in my soul that crumbled every brick wall that guarded my heart and mind from feeling. *I was feeling.* Feeling things that were similar to what I once felt for Travis, but different. Deeper.

Knowing our time was limited before we both had to get ready for work, I wasted no time climbing over his wide hips and sitting upon his throne. I oozed a gratifying moan as his erection stretched and filled me. There was very little pain now that sex was a normal, almost daily activity between us. There was nothing but exhilarating fullness as he stuffed my walls. He was so thick, the sinking of his shaft stimulated my clit all the way down. It was so exhilarating that I trembled mini orgasms every time. When I recovered from my body quake, I placed my hands on his stomach for balance. I rocked and rolled my hips with the position of my arms pushing my breasts together. Deacon groaned and licked at his lips, salivating at the sight.

He let out a breath, shaking his head and grunting, "Goddamn, Big Mama… work that shit. You're so fuckin' beautiful."

Big Mama. Beautiful. The pinch and tug at my nipple rings. The deeper dig inside me as I rocked my hips. It was all a sensory overload, and I was fighting for composure. I don't know if it was a blessing or curse when my phone chimed and my brother's name was announced.

I paused my gyration and leaned to retrieve my phone.

"You don't want to do that," Deacon threatened, doubling down with a thrust up. With my breast dangling in his face, he trapped a nipple in his mouth and gently tugged.

I gasped and whimpered through another thrust, "Deacon…fuck…I gotta get this call."

With a mouthful, Deacon groaned disappointingly as I snatched my singing phone and answered the call.

"H-Hello?" I stammered as Deacon pushed up into me one last time before stilling his movements.

Parris came over the line with inquisition in his voice. "Why do you sound like that?"

"I'm just waking up, Parris," I whined as Deacon sat up and started feasting on my twins. The stimulation of his tongue and his dick inside of me had my walls contracting, making this position not the best one to be in while on the phone with my overprotective brother. With reluctance, I lifted up and rolled onto my side of the bed as I huffed, "What's up?"

"Are you sure you're good?"

Still taunting me, Deacon rolled onto his side and nibbled on my thigh.

"Stop!" I whispered-yelled and giggled.

"Wait, ugh, Tweety," Parris groaned. "You have a boy over there??"

"Parris, I am thirty years old. I have a man here, not a boy." I rolled onto my side, grabbed the first shirt I found on the floor—Deacon's Fire Company shirt—and tossed it on as I hurried away from the bed and his grip.

"Ughh," Parris groaned exaggeratively.

Snatching the curtains open and letting in the sun, I fussed, "Parris, you called me in the wee hours of the morning. You should've texted if you were going to be grossed out because I am entertaining."

I heard Deacon scoff. Looking over my shoulder, I winked at him and mouthed, "I'm just joking," before I padded to the bathroom.

"Who is this guy?" Parris grumbled.

I moved the phone away from my ear, lifting the corner of my lip as if he could see my disdain. I pressed the Speaker button and set my phone on the counter, maneuvering around Deacon's toothbrush to grab mine. "I'm sure you didn't call me to find out who's digging all in my guts."

"For Christ's sake, Fallon," Parris retched on the other end. I quietly giggled, geeking at the reaction I hoped to provoke from him. I could picture him now, veins bulging at the sides of his head as he tried to shake the image from his mind.

"What?" I feigned oblivious.

Sighing roughly, he shifted the topic. "I didn't mean to call so early, but it's the only time I have today to tell you. Mum is coming to the States in a couple of weeks. She'll be staying with Tinsley and me in Stonecrest during her visit." Parris paused, seemingly trying to gauge my reaction. I had nothing to say until he made his point. I knew there was more to come. When he realized I wasn't going to speak, he went on, "You should come—no, you're required to come. It's a family gathering, slash engagement party thing. You know, since we cut down our guest list."

Parris and Tinsley's wedding is a major event. It's not as if it wouldn't be with her being the superstar she is, but strange things have been happening around Tinsley that have led to increased security, making everyone tight-knit and tight-lipped about everything from the destination to the guest list. Wetting my toothbrush and applying the minty paste, I asked, "Can't I just wait until the wedding to see Mom?"

"Tweety, come on," he groaned. "Do it for me. At least, if things go left, it can go left in a barnyard where you two can squabble out of sight. I told you before, I can't be worried about you and Mom and the safety of my wife."

"Aww, look at you," I cooed with my mouth full of suds. I spat before continuing, "Being all soft and husbandly."

"Cut it. I will never be equated to soft," Parris curtly shut me down and moved on. "So, can I count on you to be there?"

I spat again and disgruntledly grumbled. "Okay. I'll be there. You're lucky you're my favorite brother."

"I'm your only brother, Tweety."

We shared a laugh before I turned on the faucet to rinse my mouth. Parris went back to his probing.

"So, who is this guy and when can I beat him up?"

Through the mirror, I watched Deacon enter the bathroom. I smized and chewed on the inside of my lip, admiring him discretely. He was partially dressed in only his dark navy basketball shorts from last night. His pectorals were bulging, as was his still very prominent morning wood. Intentionally, Deacon brushed up against my backside as he leaned in to retrieve his toothbrush, igniting a phantom feeling of him inside of me.

"So?" Parris pressed.

I rolled my eyes at his insistence and heard Deacon chuckle from behind.

"Mind your business, Parris."

Parris scoffed, "You're my business."

"Bye, Parris!"

Without waiting for his response, I pressed the end button. I caught a glimpse of Deacon's puffed-up cheeks before he exhaled the breath he had been holding in a fit of laughter.

"Don't mind Parris."

"Oh, I'm not," Deacon assured, settling down. "He doesn't know I'm a dog that bites back yet."

My jaw dropped partly to spit out the rinsing water and partly at his remark. "Oh my God. I'm not gonna have you and my brother fighting to prove your machismo."

Deacon switched places with me, positioning himself in front of the sink as I moved over to the shower. He shrugged and gave a playful smirk as he said, "I hope that's not how our introduction goes. From the sounds of it, we'd get along. We both don't take any shit when it comes to you."

I hadn't thought about Deacon meeting Parris until now. Instead of paralyzing my nervous system, a warm tingling sensation washed over me along with the thought that Parris would like him. I looked over my shoulder, my smile quirked to the side as I worked to keep my blushing at bay. "Probably so. He would like anyone who isn't my ex, though."

Deacon clutched his chest and stumbled backward in true Fred Sanford fashion. I shook my head at his dramatics and peeled off the T-shirt as he elaborated on his performance, "Ouch! So I'm just anybody?"

Though it was said humorously, this was a question we'd never discussed. And even though Deacon was the only man I'd slept with since meeting him, I wasn't sure how to answer. In public, among our fire family, we were friends. Coworkers. We kept our interactions platonic and subtle, with the exception of a few flirty hand caresses and fleeting brushes of our skin. To everyone around us, we shared that familial bond like the rest of the firehouse.

Now, the fucking we do behind closed doors would be blasphemy to the idea of being "brother and sister," and I was thankful that the brotherly love was just a figure of speech. Sex with Deacon was leg-shaking— literally. I don't know what kind of award he was trying to achieve, but he was in first place in everything he did in bed. The way he ate my pussy? First place and unnerving. His stroke game? Unheard of excellency that had my body convulsing with back-to-back orgasms. Being with Deacon had me questioning all of my sexual experiences, including the longest experience of them all, with Travis.

Have you ever had sex with someone and questioned whether you were ever being sexed properly prior? That's what I asked myself one time after I experienced shooting stars in the back of my lids from an explosive orgasm. Sex with Travis wasn't awful, but it wasn't this. It wasn't attentive like Deacon, noticing every way my body ticked, contracted, or released whenever he kissed, sucked, or curved his dick. He paid attention and noted what made me unravel, and he made me feel good while doing so. No, he made me feel worshipped. His kisses were adorning. His touches were like he was handling a precious jewel. Deacon treated me with care, far more care than I expected for something between us that had no title.

"You're not," I finally answered before my mind could register what I was admitting. When my mind caught up, I pressed my lips tight to conceal any more words and stepped into the shower.

DEACON

It was an unusually quiet Friday morning at the firehouse, especially entering into the Fourth of July weekend. With the holiday falling on a weekend, it was usual for us to expect at least one call about a drunken patron doing something reckless overnight. However, the slow pace of the morning was welcome, giving Denzel and me a long-overdue workout session at the firehouse gym. Tevin joined us when he saw us heading that way.

Contrary to the span of time that had gone by since I had a good weightlifting session, I felt invigorated. Other extracurricular activities—sexual activities— had been keeping my cardiovascular and muscular health in good shape. As I pushed my heaviest weight in a set of assisted chest presses, my eyes clouded over to earlier that morning with Fallon's positioned to ride me to glory.

She was beautiful all the time, but it was her morning glow that got me wanting her to sit on me every morning we woke up together. Bare-faced, yet a natural sheen covered her skin, and her naturally plumped lips were always extra pouty when she arose in the morning. Sleepy amber eyes hooded would look down at me, and I couldn't front. I tried to fuck the shit out of her so I could watch her satin wrap unravel while she unraveled.

My ego played a role in my efforts, but what truly motivated me was making her feel good. As much as I loved seeing Fallon be a boss lady in her own right, I also loved witnessing her in her softer moments. I cherished the times when she let go and allowed me to please her. I found that, most of the time, everything I did for her was my attempt to help her embrace what the ladies refer to as the "soft girl era." If anyone deserved it, it was her. She may have had a tough exterior, but I've learned she has the kindest heart and simply wanted to feel safe in exposing it. This revelation alone opened my heart in ways I had closed off after my failed engagement with Vanessa. I didn't think I was capable of being open again without scaring off another woman. So far, Fallon was here and not running away.

"Pause! You can't be smirking at me like that while I'm spotting you."

Blinking away my thoughts, my vision unblurred to Tevin grimacing down on me. I scoffed, "Lil' Tevin, no one wants your scrawny ass."

I pushed up through the last count, and Tevin grabbed the weight, slightly struggling to put it back on the bar before retorting, "Man, I'm not scrawny…and I get women. I may be smaller than your musclehead, but they say the dick is bigger."

Tevin grabbed his dick before cackling and walking off. He went mute when I arose from the bench and quipped, "Okay, little man. Ask your mama how big my dick is. She'll tell you it's a lot of muscle in *that* head."

"Now, why you gotta bring my mama in this shit?"

Tevin took quick steps toward me as Denzel and I fell out at his expense.

"I'm just playing with you, my dude," I said earnestly, reaching out once he was at arm's length to squeeze the back of his neck.

"Yeah aight," Tevin huffed, moving his head from my grasp. He gave me a sly grin and said, "I'm not playing, though. Your head really looks like a big ass muscle. You need to get that checked out."

Denzel rounded us, taking the lead out of the gym and into the kitchen. Settling down from the hysteria, he turned to us. "Okay, okay, guys, let's chill. I wanna wrap with ya'll about this weekend anyway. I'm doing a little something at the house and I need you two there."

"Food involved?" was the first question out of Tevin's mouth.

Shaking his head, Denzel chuckled. "Yeah, food is involved. It's kind of a cookout, but…" He stepped closer to us as if there was anyone else in the empty kitchen. "…I'm going to propose to Nina."

"Say word?!" I dapped Denzel and pulled him into a hug. "Congratulations, man."

"Thanks, man. I'm inviting everyone from the company who isn't on shift, but it's important that you two are there. You were there when I met her."

"Tuh, were we," Tevin added. "We watched you fall in love at first sight with the most accident-prone woman in Lovey's Bay."

"Ehh, he has a point there," I egged on.

Denzel chuckled, shrugging. "True, but I wouldn't change it for the world. So, can I count on you guys to be there?"

"For sure, my guy."

"Yep, as long as the food is hot and ready, I'm there."

I turned to Tevin, looking him up and down. "There's gonna be plenty of food for your little ass to muscle up on."

———

By mid-morning, the firehouse was bustling with activity, the crew moving around energetically. After my post-workout shower, I put on my blues—a navy-collared firehouse shirt and fireproof pants— and headed to my office to go through some emails. I was pulled away from my task by a light tap on my door. I had a sense of who was on the other side.

"Come in."

Just as I thought, Fallon slipped through the small opening, closing the door behind her. She sauntered over, wearing the same outfit as I was, but damn, I'm sure it looked better on her than on me. Her shirt and pants fit much more snugly, accentuating those curves I loved to peruse. I responded to her smirk with one of my own.

"Good morning, Captain," she purred as she rounded my desk.

I stood up as she closed the distance between us. I couldn't resist seizing the moment to press my lips against hers before murmuring, "Good morning, Lennox."

"You forgot this." She reached into her pocket and pulled out my watch.

"Oh shit, I didn't even know," I mused, lifting my wrists and eyeing them.

"I know. Here."

She pulled my left wrist down and fastened the smartwatch to it. The simple gesture drew a deep breath from me, filling me with a sense of peace in her presence. When she finished, I intertwined my fingers with hers, prompting her to look up at me with those damn dreamy eyes. For a moment, I was lost in them before I blinked out of it, remembering where we were.

I cleared my throat. "How was your morning jog?"

"Good," she said, letting go of my hand and sitting on the edge of my desk. "I talked to Zaria, and she'll be flying in this afternoon, so…no staying over this weekend."

I plopped back into my chair, leaning against the reclining back. "Fair. Will I get to meet this Zaria since she's cutting into my time with you?"

"Oh, my God, Deacon," she gawked, kicking her legs. "It's not like you don't see me every day, but yes, you'll meet her. She'll be with me at Chief's shindig."

"Cool. So Chief told you about it already?"

She nodded. "Yep, we'll all be there. With that being said, be on your best behavior. You like teetering on the line of showing and telling them about us."

Fallon's voice lowered as she spoke as if we weren't behind closed doors. I grabbed hold of her leg as it swung up, using it as leverage to pull me and the chair between her legs. She yelped as I admitted, "I do. You like it too."

I ran my hands up the top of her thighs, squeezing at the top as I coerced them to open wider. She didn't stop me, but she hissed, "Deacon. Not now!"

"Why not?" I asked, not really seeking an answer. The warmth radiating from her center as I pressed my face against it had me bricking up. "We got sidetracked earlier, and I won't have you to myself for the rest of the weekend."

"Everyone's out there," she whispered, then gasped as I kissed the inside of her thighs through her pants.

"Okay. That's never stopped anything before," I reminded her, recalling the times we sneaked away to dark corners of the firehouse for a quickie. We were in my office, not quite dark, but still suitable for us to finish what we started this morning.

I didn't wait for her to protest. She didn't offer one either as I unbuckled her belt and slid her pants down her hips. Wiggling her legs, she assisted me in the removal, revealing her shapely smooth legs. She sat atop my desk in her shirt and a skimpy little pair of thongs. Picture fucking perfect.

I lifted my narrowed eyes up to hers. "Who are you wearing these little things for?"

She giggled. "Who else, Captain? Are you going to waste time asking questions, or are you going to finish what we started?"

I moistened my lips as I locked eyes with her and shifted the fabric covering her mound to the side. "Say less, Big Mama."

She giggled again and then it fell into a stolen breath as I tested her waters with my fingers, entering two, slow and deep. She was an ocean already, my fingers being coated with her effortlessly. The glisten of my fingers as I removed them tempted me to taste her. Closing in the space, I covered her lips with my mouth, closing them around her clit. Short breaths fell from her lips as I pulled her pearl out of hiding and then flicked my tongue up and down as I stroked her with my fingers. Being jealous of my fingers, I replaced them with my tongue, groaning as she coated my tongue.

"God damn," I mumbled as I went in for more, pulling her essence onto my tongue and then lubricating her clit for another slippery round of tongue pulses.

Her moans were symphonic to my slurps and groans. Her taste was addictive and I could've stayed there, satisfied with listening to her melt as she palmed my head, but I was on a mission to make sure we were both good for the weekend of abstinence. She had the same thoughts, apparently, closing her legs slightly and pushing me from between them. I rolled back in my chair and watched her hop down from the desk.

"I love the way you eat me out, but I need to feel you, Big Daddy."

Big Daddy. Daddy Deacon. Whatever she called me made my blood rush from my brain and to my dick and fueled my desire to give her a performance that would have her screaming out one of those names. Unbuckling my belt, I leaned up and smacked her ass. "Bend over then, baby."

With a soft grunt at the contact of my hand, she obliged, bending at her hips. I watched her ass spread, revealing the thin fabric of her thong that disappeared between her dripping folds. I slipped my fingers under the material, and fisted it as I let my pants drop as I stood. At the slight penetration, her walls sucked the head of my dick inside. I sucked in a cool breath, ensuring I didn't bust the moment I fully entered and then pushed my full length inside of her, pulling a whimpered moan from her. The warm, gushy mess surrounding my dick forced a grunt from me. I stroked slowly and deeper with each. I couldn't hold my groans back, her pussy gripping my dick and my groans each time I pulled back. With a slippery thrust, I hit the bottom and took control, changing the tempo to strong, long, and steady strokes. My dick grew harder inside her as I watched her ass ripple as it smacked against my thighs.

"Fuck, Deacon," she moan-whispered as I stretched her thong to give me more depth.

I thrust into her hard. "Uh-huh, what happened to Big Daddy? Daddy Deacon?"

"You gotta earn that," she taunted. With that, I pulled all the way out and then pushed into her, my thighs smacking her ass as her thong snapped. She whimpered and cursed her pleasure. Her taunt turned me on and my ego up. Sinking my fingers in the sides of her ass, I began to pound into her, rocking the desk with each thrust. Her silent whimpers grew louder yet stifled between her teeth and lips, but I wanted it all. I wanted to hear her call out my name.

Pound. Pound. Thrust. Pound. Pound. Thrust.

"Ahh!" Fallon moaned, gripping the side of the desk

with one hand and cupping her breast over her shirt with the other.

"That sounds good, but you know what I want to hear," I said, steadily pounding into her. Fallon was a fighter, unrelenting but I knew how to undo her. I pulled out, but only long enough for me to spread her cheeks wide, insert my tongue in between her walls and pull some of her cream onto my tongue. I licked up her split, making her arch her back, and then circled her other hole, depositing her essence there. Taking my thumb, I pressed into her forbidden spot and then plunged back into her.

"Fuck...." She whimpered, but it wasn't what I was looking for.

I drilled into her relentlessly, working her asshole while holding on the the last of my wits. And then, Fallon began to unravel. Labored, ragged breaths fell from mouth as her walls tighten around my dick. Her legs shook with each push into her. She was near, but I wasn't satisfied yet. I thrust my hips into her and moved my thumb in and out.

One thrust. Two thrust.

"Say it, baby."

Knock! Knock! Knock!

Fallon stiffened and tried to run, but I pulled her hips into me, grunting, "Don't run." And then called out mid-stroke, "I'm on an important call!"

I heard steps walking away as I returned to my pound

Fallon's pussy with my finger still lodged. Within seconds, she was unraveling again, whimpering, and moaning through her orgasm.

"Fuck, Big-fuckin'-Daddy…shit…Deacon—"

"That's —*pound*—what the fuck—*pound*—I'm talking about! Where you want it!"

I was seconds from exploding when I pulled out and in seconds Fallon swiveled and dropped to her knees, opening her mouth wide to accommodate my dick. The picture alone had my dick pulsing and ready to spill, but when she began sucking up and down the half she could fit in her mouth while moaning and playing with herself through another orgasm, I exploded.

"Shit, Big Mama…" I grunted as my abs contracted and I emptied my seeds into her mouth. I came hard, shooting off and coating the back of her throat. She didn't waste a drop, swallowing each round that left my dick.

Big fucking Mama shit.

"Welcome to Sable Pearl. Your table is ready. Please follow me."

We were greeted by a slender woman with deep brown skin, dressed in a sleek, all-black outfit that matched her chic demeanor. Her pearly white teeth sparkled as she smiled at each of us—me, Zaria, Joni, and Joni's friend Nina—before she twirled on the tips of her red bottoms, her lightly bumped long bob moving with her. We followed her through the buzzing restaurant, which wasn't loud but rather humming with conversations confined to the tables of the guests, accompanied by a smooth acid jazz playlist that set the ambiance. Our final destination was a table for four on the patio overlooking the Bay.

"This was a great choice, Joni," I exclaimed as we neared our table.

The patio maintained a nautical vibe with its white-painted wooden structure. The restaurant's chicness was reflected in the table setting, featuring black linens, elegant centerpieces made of seashells, and a unique touch of black pearls that complemented the restaurant's name. Our table offered a stunning view of the sunset over the bay, elevating the ambiance even further.

"Don't thank me. My girl Nina is the one that put me this spot."

Stepping away from the railing, I turned to Nina. "How'd you find out about this spot?"

Nina lit up at my question. She was a petite, gorgeous woman, sporting a cute pixie cut that highlighted a face card I'm sure never declines. Her big almond-shaped eyes widened at me as she replied, "Oh, my boyfriend introduced me to this place. We're always trying new restaurants, and this is one of our favorite finds."

"Yeah, Nina is kinda banned from the kitchen, so they eat out a lot," Joni said as we all took our seats. She nudged Nina playfully.

Nina rolled her eyes, taking light of the joke. "Ugh, when are you all going to get off my case? My kitchen blunders are so last year. I got the man. He knows I don't cook well, so he treats me to fine dining. It's a win to me!"

"That sounds like a win to me," Zaria chimed in, high-fiving Nina.

I settled into the plush chair and crossed my legs

while the two women shared a laugh. It was a good night with good people. Zaria touched down in Lovey's Bay just before happy hour, giving us just enough time to get to my apartment, shower, dress, and then head across the hall to Joni's place for a quick glass of wine to celebrate the hour. This also provided ample time for us to make introductions and exchange pleasantries. Zaria and Nina were somewhat new faces, with Zaria being my best friend and Nina being Joni's bestie. It was an easy blend of friends, making dinner feel like a casual gathering of old friends reconnecting.

Shortly after we were comfortable at our table, our waitress came over and took our orders for drinks and appetizers. Nina spoke up first, raising her menu and pointing.

"Oh, how about a bottle of Ruby Noir. That's the housemade wine, right?"

"Yes, that is one of our housemade wines," our waitress explained. "It's a rich red wine that pairs well with most of our dishes."

Nina glanced over the table. "How do you all feel about that? It was so good the last time I had it."

The table agreed on the wine before I suggested, "How about you bring us one more bottle? Put it on my tab."

The waitress jotted down our drink order and orders of oysters and calamari before quickly leaving our table and ushering in Joni with little-known facts.

"You know that Nina's man is your boss," Joni said, leaning in and tapping the space in front of my placeholder.

"Really?" I tilted my head, my heart racing as I realized there were only two men she could be talking about—the one I was secretly involved with and Denzel. I was hoping it was the latter.

"Joni stays telling all my business," Nina joked. "But yes, I'm dating Chief Payton."

"Denzeeeeeellll," Joni crooned and then cackled. "Gon' head and say his name the way you do when you're talking to me about him."

The table chuckled at Joni's silliness, and I wondered if she needed any more wine for the night. At the same time, I exhaled, grateful that she didn't mention Deacon's name.

"Oh, my God, Joni. Put me on blast, why don't you," Nina said bashfully.

"Shit, don't be shy." Joni waved her hand toward Nina. "I'd be calling his name like that too if I were you. That man is hot."

"So, I take it that all the men in Lovey's Bay are fine," Zaria chimed in, pretending she was taking notes. "Noted."

"Now, that's one thing I can agree with," Joni added, wagging a finger in the air. "Lovey's Bay has a surprising number of good-looking men, both single and married. So keep your head on a swivel."

"That's noted, too," Zaria confirmed, tapping the air with her finger. "Lovey's Bay might be a good move."

I whipped my head toward Zaria. "Since when have you been thinking about moving here? You didn't mention it to me!"

"It's just a thought, Fal. Don't get your panties in a twist. I've been thinking that maybe I need a change too. Damask can feel so phony sometimes. Plus, I miss my BFF."

Zaria leaned over and gave me a side hug, prompting "Awws" from Joni and Nina.

I gave Zaria an air kiss. "It would be nice to have another woman on the crew. I mean, there's Joss, but she's more like one of the guys."

"You're a firefighter too?" Joni jumped in. "Lord, how did I end up surrounded by firefighters? It's all Nina's fault. If she wasn't burning down her apartment, I wouldn't be an honorary member of the crew. Fallon, you know that apartment across from mine that's blocked off? That was Nina's old spot."

My eyes bulged as the image of the boarded-up eyesore came to mind. The doors bore traces of soot that suggested a bad fire. I looked at Nina, whose face had turned beet red. Sparing her any further questions, I said, "I'm glad you're okay, girl."

Nina shot Joni a look as she agreed, "Me, too, but that fire wasn't my fault. It happened because of a random firework." Zaria and I gasped in unison while

Joni nodded her head, confirming her story. "Denzel saved me. That's when I knew he was the one."

"Let her tell it," Joni said, pursing her lips. "That girl really gave that man a run for his money—literally. Nina could've run right alongside Sha'Carri Richardson the way she sprinted away from that man."

Zaria's "oop" transformed into a soft "Oh" as a handsome man with salt-and-pepper hair—mostly salt—swaggered up to our table carrying two bottles of wine, followed closely by our waitress with our glasses. His white chef's coat indicated that he was a chef, and the few buttons undone at the top revealed the outline of a well-built chest, suggesting he might spend some time at the gym.

"I thought I'd do the honors and bring you the house wine myself and express my gratitude for your generous support. I'm Chef Maxwell Vaughan, the Executive Chef here at Sable Pearl."

A collection of "Hellos" and "Nice to Meet You" flowed over our table as Chef Vaughan flashed his model-esque smile and graciously nodded to each of us. The chef, who seemed to be over 6 feet tall, was pleasing to the eye. He had a debonair and mature flair, complete with his full mustache, beard, and neatly combed wavy curls. Chef Vaughan popped the cork from one of the bottles as our waitress set a glass in front of each of us. He poured half a glass of the ruby red wine for everyone, with Zaria being the last to receive hers.

"So, Chef Vaughan," Zaria purred, leaning back in her chair with her glass held aloft. "What's your recommendation from this delicious menu?"

"Please, call me Maxwell," he insisted. I could've sworn his teeth sparkled as his smile brightened. "Well, you all made a great choice with the fresh oysters and hand-breaded calamari. All of our seafood is local, sourced from the Atlantic Ocean just east of us. In my humble opinion, I'd say…"

Maxwell proceeded to offer us dishes to suit different tastes, but his interest was focused on Zaria. The subtle exchange of glances between the two was noticeable among the three of us who served as bystanders to the show, each of us exchanging sly looks with one another. Zaria and Maxwell paused their moment just long enough for us to place our orders. They shared one last look before he excused himself.

"So…did you cum?"

"What?" Zaria's honeyed complexion flushed as she tousled her humidity-enhanced body waves.

"Girl, anyone could see food wasn't the only thing you two were talking about. Look at you, your eyes all low and sex-filled."

Zaria giggled and then settled with an airy sigh. "A girl can have fun on her vacation, can't she?"

"I'm not mad at it, honey," Joni hummed.

"So, how long are you here for?"

"Just for the weekend," Zaria responded to Nina's question, turning her attention to her.

Nina's face lit up. "Oh, you should come to the cookout Denzel and I are having tomorrow. Fallon, you're coming, right?"

"Yeah," I replied, taking a sip from my glass. The bold taste of the drink, finishing with a hint of spice, prompted me to pause and savor the sip. "I was hoping it would be alright for me to bring a plus one."

"Of course!" Nina chirped, clapping her hands together. "The more the merrier. This should be fun!"

This was *not* turning out to be fun. In fact, running into Vanessa after not seeing her for almost a year was awkward. What made it even more awkward was having Fallon there, witnessing it all with a frozen expression that was somewhere between pleasant and uncomfortable. Worst of all, I couldn't say anything without raising suspicion.

The crew was all there—Farris, Joss, Tevin with his friend Joni, and Fallon brought her best friend, Zaria. Outside of the crew, there were several other guests who seemed to be family members of the two. Typical for the height of summer, it was a scorcher, and instead of gathering on Denzel's large back patio, we were scattered. Those who appreciated the warm weather were on the patio, while most of us found comfort in the cool of the house. Everything was copacetic. In the midst of regular camaraderie, Denzel and I tended the grill.

"Fallon's friend is kind of cute," Denzel said while flipping the chicken on the grill. He tilted his head toward me, wiggling his eyebrows with a clear hint that I should talk to her.

"She is." I winced and shrugged. "I don't know if she's my type, though."

"What? She's beautiful and friendly. What's your type if that's not it?"

Fallon. That's how I wanted to respond as I peered through the glass of the back door at her. She was engrossed in conversation with the ladies, her smile lighting up the room alongside the yellow strappy sundress she wore. It suited her perfectly, highlighting her beautifully toned thighs as she crossed her legs. Instead of admitting to the bane of my current existence, I said, "Don't get me wrong. She seems like a great woman, but she lives in Damask. I don't know if I want my first potential love interest to be long-distance."

Denzel closed the lid of the grill, setting the utensil aside before wiping his forehead with the hand towel draped over his shoulder. "I hear you, but I heard she's considering moving here. At least, that's what Nina told me last night."

"Hmm," I murmured, unsure of what else to say. As much as I wanted to tell Denzel that the only person I wanted to keep getting to know was Fallon, I hadn't discovered the right way to express it to him.

I was saved when the backdoor swung open and Tevin offered us two beers. I accepted, and before any further talk about hooking me up with Zaria started, I caught the closing door and went inside. Just as I was trying to get comfortable in the empty chair a couple of feet away from Fallon, Denzel walked in, resuming his efforts.

"Zaria. Have you met Deacon yet?" Denzel motioned to me, awkwardly directing the attention of the room towards me. Sensing the situation, I noticed Fallon squirm in her seat, clearly uncomfortable. If I wasn't mistaken, she nudged Zaria in the side and whispered something to her.

Zaria wore a warm smile as she turned her attention to me. "I don't think I've officially met him." This was true. Although we met months ago over Facetime, we haven't met in person since she arrived here for the weekend. "I've heard about him through Fallon—everyone, really."

Denzel's expression shifted to intrigue. "Ahh, nice. I hear you're thinking about moving to Lovey's Bay. Maybe you and Deacon can connect before you head out. He's probably the best local to give a tour of the city."

Fallon choked on the gulp of beer she had just taken, and Zaria's eyes widened slightly before she resumed her neutral expression. As for me, I was sweating bullets as if I were still outside. A chorus of squeals from another part of the house drew everyone's attention. When Nina brought in the source of her excitement, the sweat trickled down my forehead.

"Guess who made it!" Nina squealed. "Everyone knows Vanessa, right?"

"Oh shit," I heard Tevin chuckle not too far away.

"Not everyone, honey," Denzel said, giving Vanessa a hug. Everyone in the living room, except Fallon, was part of the crew when Vanessa and I were dating. Those who knew her were aware of how fucked up I had been after our engagement ended and her sudden departure. Nina also knew since I had spent a few days at their house after Vanessa kicked me out of the apartment.

Nina shook her head. "Ugh, where are my manners? Fallon and Zaria, this is Vanessa. She's… uh…"

Nina distorted her facial features as she struggled to find her words, glancing between Vanessa and me for assistance. This was the first time Vanessa and I made eye contact. Vanessa remained the beauty I remembered, with big, round curls framing her face. Her round cheeks glowed as she flashed her signature smile, even amid the awkwardness. She gestured with her hands.

"Ahh, let's get rid of the elephant in the room." She extended her hand to Zaria and Fallon. They stood and accepted it cordially as she introduced herself, "I'm Vanessa, and I was Deacon's fiancée."

"Oh, wow. It's great to meet you," Fallon replied.

Vanessa gave her a polite nod before retracting her hand and pivoting toward me. "Deacon."

"Vanessa," I said, rising to my feet. "It's been a while."

"Enough time to grow a baby." My heart sank before she snickered. "It's been nine months since I last saw you, that's all."

I chuckled, realizing her joke as she closed the distance and wrapped her arms around me. Shocked, my body froze for a moment before I embraced her in return. Her hug felt familiar—familial—and my body relaxed as my heart settled into that feeling.

Vanessa leaned back to look up at me. "How about we have a chat and clear this awkwardness out of the way?"

I did a quick scan of the room, noticing all eyes on us, including Fallon's. Her gaze sparkled with something I couldn't quite identify. Uncertainty? Sadness? Shock? I couldn't tell. My eyes twitched as I tried to communicate with her silently, hoping to convey that there was nothing to worry about before I turned my attention back to Vanessa. "Sure."

The weight of everyone's gaze stayed with us until we stepped out the back door. Vanessa led the way down the steps from the patio through the private entrance to the beach. She paused in the middle of the sandy beach, far enough away that the chatter from the house became almost unrecognizable beneath the sound of the crashing waves nearby. She turned to face me, her hair bouncing in the light, warm breeze that swept over us.

"How have you been?" Her voice was low and slow as she spoke.

"Uhh, good...lately," I answered earnestly. "How about you? You left Lovey's Bay and no one heard from you."

"*You* didn't hear from me," she corrected with a half smile. "I've talked to Nina, hence why I'm here now."

I crossed my arms as I nodded. "Fair. Well, I'm glad to see you're doing well."

"Same. I'm glad to see you doing well, too."

Silence fell between us, as if we were both trying to choose our words. I was wrestling with all the questions I had buried in the back of my mind over the last several months. They were now rushing to my frontal lobe, fighting each other to be the first to roll off my tongue.

"It took me a while...to get back to myself," I finally said, spooking myself. "You just left without any answers."

"Benjamin." She crossed her arms and fixed her eyes to me. She only used my first name when preparing for a serious conversation. "You had all the answers because I always told you what our problem, but since you have amnesia, you moved slower than a snail when it came to us getting married. You always had a reason or excuse, with work being the most prominent."

I rolled my eyes, recalling her nonstop complaints

about my work. "Vanessa, you knew what kind of work I did when we first met. You were with me for four years—"

"The job wasn't the problem. The problem was that during the first two years we were together, I kept wondering if I was wasting my time in a dead-end relationship, only to receive an engagement ring and still have the same concerns two years later. And your reason? Work, work, work. I understood the demands of your job, but the way my Grandma Hattie raised me, a man doesn't drag his feet when he wants what he has. Then I had to ask myself, were we just in this because we felt comfortable but not truly happy?"

Her eyes stung me just like her words. If I had acted solely on emotion, I would've sunk back into the feelings that my sentiments at the beginning of our breakup were true: she didn't want me. However, when I truly pondered the question, perhaps it wasn't so much that she didn't want me, but rather that we both craved the comfort we provided each other, despite the complete happiness we had lacked for months before our relationship fell apart.

"I don't doubt that we ever loved each other. I loved you, Benjamin Deacon. But sometimes love just ain't enough if you're not happy. I wasn't happy being a fiancée for two years, and although I understood your role at the Fire Company, I realized I hated being second to your job." She glanced at the shoreline for a moment before looking back at me. "Be honest, Benny, were you really happy? We argued more than we loved during the last few months of our relationship."

I rushed out, "I was…" and then my words trailed off as I decided to be truthful. "I wasn't happy anymore. I loved you too, Vanessa. Don't ever think I didn't. I thought I wanted to get married. I still believe I want to get married, but… I only recently realized that it wasn't to you." My revelation to her turned into a revelation for myself. My throat dried as I recognized that the only person I've spent time with who made me realize I wanted to marry them was—Fallon. I blinked, returning to the moment and the empty yet knowing expression that now crept over Vanessa's face. "I'm sorry, Vanessa."

She shook her head. "No. No need to be sorry. I knew that, which is why I left. We were both unhappy."

"No, listen to me," I plead, taking her hand in mine. "I'm sorry for essentially wasting your time. I wish I could take it back. I wish I had known what I know now so you wouldn't have had to wait for me to figure my shit out."

She grabbed my other hand and squeezed both assuredly. "Thank you. Water under the bridge, that's what it is now. I'm happy now. So happy." Her eyes grew, reinforcing her contentment. She blinked hard as her bubbly smile started to emerge again. "Sounds like you're happy, too."

Sighing, I smiled and admitted, "Yeah, I am."

A figure behind Vanessa caught my attention. It was Fallon, who had caught wind of the moment Vanessa and I were having. The moment she noticed I saw her, she quickly turned, ready to make haste. I dropped Vanessa's hands and waved Fallon over, calling out, "Fallon! Come here." She stopped moving and looked over her shoulder at me, seemingly questioning whether she should. I pleaded with my eyes while mouthing, "Please," before she started to walk over slowly.

FALLON

She's gorgeous.

This sentiment echoed in my mind the more I took her in. When Nina entered the living room with her trailing behind, the first thing I noticed was her hair—it was thick and fluffy, full of bouncy curls. Then, when Nina introduced us and she turned around, her face card was undeniable. A big, beautiful smile framed by red-painted full lips was complemented by large brown eyes that sparkled because of her radiant smile. And her style! She was a pure diva; her curves, with big bosoms and round hips, were accentuated by the dress she wore. She. Is. Gorgeous.

As if having Chief try to hook Deacon up with my best friend wasn't enough, seeing Deacon and his ex reunite didn't help my efforts to keep my body temperature from soaring into the triple digits. I couldn't hear anything they were saying, even though they were only a few feet away from me. I hated that I was holding my breath in hopes that it would minimize the distraction of hearing what was said. When they walked away, I released a sigh, silently scolding myself for my desperate thoughts. It's his ex, and I'm his—I don't know. It's not even a thought I should be having. I was really supposed to be keeping it light and easy, but here I was, falling for my Captain.

"I wonder what that's all about," Joni mused, scooting the chair Deacon left empty beside me and taking a seat there.

"Joni, you're so nosy," I laughed, but inside I was quietly questioning the same thing.

She stared at me. "Aren't you curious about what's being said between you and your boo?"

"He's not my boo," I murmured, scanning the people within earshot.

"Girl." I turned to Zaria, whose lips were pursed in disbelief at me. I rolled my eyes at her betrayal and then looked back at Joni, who was piercing me with the same look.

"Now you know I know that's a lie. Not with the way that man goes in and out of your house. He's the only man I've ever seen regularly at your apartment."

I scoffed. "Are you stalking my door?"

Joni snickered. "I don't need to stalk your door, girl. He leaves for work at the same time I do."

"Oop!" Zaria squealed. She reached over to me and high-fived Joni. "See, Joni is my type of girl. Stay on her neck while I'm not here, okay?"

The two shared a laugh at my expense, and I couldn't help but snicker. Nina pranced over and sat on the edge of the table in front of us. "What are you ladies talking about? I want in!"

"Oh, we're just trying to figure out what Deacon and Vanessa are talking about and get Fallon to start claiming her man," Joni said, making me drop my jaw and prompting a "Mmhmm" from Zaria.

Nina glanced back and forth between Joni and me, puzzled. "Wait, who's your guy?"

"No one."

"Deacon," Zaria and Joni said in unison.

I shot Joni a side-eye and then darted it to Zaria. "Zaria, you're supposed to be my girl, and here you are spreading my business with Jabba Jaws." I heard Joni gasp as I spilled Zaria's tea. "I didn't tell everyone who you were with all night last night."

Zaria sipped from her glass of wine and shrugged. "I don't care. As a matter of fact, I'll tell them myself. Chef Vaughan."

"Whaat?!" Joni pulled her chair closer, eating up all the gossip. "You talking about that salt-and-pepper

Maxwell? I mean, I know his name is Maxwell, but he's as smooth as the singer, too."

"Mm-hmm. Him," Zaria admitted with a grin. She glanced at me. "See how easy it is to tell the truth?"

I opened my mouth to say something, but Nina put her hands between us, centering her gaze on me. "Wait, let's backtrack. You're dating Deacon?"

"We aren't really dating, we're just—"

"Fucking." Zaria and Joni answered for me.

I scoffed. "What are y'all Double Mint Twins now?"

The two laughed while Nina's expression turned into a frown. "Oh my gosh. If I had known, I would've told you she was coming. I'm sorry, Fallon."

"Nina, girl, it's okay," I consoled, rested a hand on Nina's thigh as she started to tear up. "No one knows about…whatever Deacon and I are doing, and I want to keep it that way for the sake of work."

"Yeah, girl," Joni said, sliding over to the table with her. She rubbed her back. "We're just being nosy and teasing. No need for you to cry, girl."

Nina tittered, wiping her eyes. "I'm sorry. I don't know why I'm so emotional today. I just didn't want anyone to feel uncomfortable. It's already tough that this is the first time they're seeing each other since she left him high and dry."

My back stiffened at the new information. Joni nodded slowly and confirmed, "Mm-hmm. Tevin said he was a mess after she left, sulking around and not himself. He was down bad."

I raised my hand, silencing them from giving me any more details. It was already too much as I thought back to the speed dating event where we met. At the beginning, he was so unsure of himself, as if it were his first time in the dating scene. Now, with the information Nina and Joni provided, it made sense, but it deepened the uncertainty about what the conversation between the two could be about. Was he still hung up on her, and was I just a comfortable rebound?

"I'm going to get some fresh air," I said, feeling myself turn flush again.

I stood up and headed out the back door as if stepping into the heat wave would improve anything. Anything would be better than being bombarded by Deacon's past and my swirling thoughts. I shielded my face from the sun, hoping it would stop the sweat beading on my skin, but it was no use. I was perspiring for more reasons than just the heat. What I hadn't considered was that I would be intruding on Deacon and Vanessa's intimate moment. When I reached the beach, I saw them hand in hand.

"Fallon! Come here!" Deacon shouted for me. I was already on my way back when his voice stopped me in my tracks. I glanced over my shoulder at him, unsure if I should approach. He waved me over and silently pleaded. With a bit of hesitation, I made my way to him and Vanessa. Once I was close enough, Deacon took my hand and pulled me to his side.

"Vanessa, this is Fallon, my lady."

I scanned his brown eyes, absorbing the title he had given me. His pupils dilated, and a hint of a smile settled on his lips, encouraging one to spread over mine.

"So you're the woman who's making him smile again," Vanessa replied, her smile widening. She placed a hand on my forearm. "It's good to meet you again. Now, if you two don't mind, I'm going to head back up to the house. I'm hot and hungry!"

After one last glance between Deacon and me, she walked away. Once Vanessa was out of earshot, I asked, "So, you're a lady, huh?"

Deacon took my hands in his and ran his thumb over the back as he repositioned himself directly in front of me. "Yeah, if that's okay with you."

My heart raced as I hurriedly said, "Benjamin, I don't want to be your rebound from Vanessa. I was a rebound in my last relationship, and I was the one who actually had the ring."

"Not you calling me by my first name," Deacon chuckled. I tried to pull away, but Deacon squeezed my hands, keeping me in place. I fought not to look into his eyes, yet he wouldn't move from my view. "Fal, look at me." I fluttered my eyes to his. "You've never been a rebound. Ever. When I met you, I was in a place where I was ready to move on with my life. I wasn't pining over

Vanessa; I knew that was over. In fact, I prayed for you."

I scoffed, disbelieving. "Prayed for me."

"Yes. Prayed for you. I prayed for God to guide me to my…my person. I literally let God take the wheel, and there I was, meeting you."

My heart swelled as Deacon stared down at me, unwavering and unflinching. My eyes filled with tears, threatening to spill over. For the first time in a long while, they were happy tears. I fought to contain them, but my heart raced, urging me to blink rapidly. I lost all control of the small droplets cascading from my eyes.

Deacon reached up, wiping away my tears. "Aww, Big Mama has feelings."

"I don't," I grumbled with a chuckle, letting go of his hand and wiping my face.

Deacon caught my hand mid-wipe and brought it to his mouth, pressing his lips against the remnants of my tears. "It's okay for you to feel because I feel it, too. And let me tell you this: you will never have to worry about me mistreating you. I'm not built that way. I'm a one-woman man, and I only have eyes for you. And my hands? I'll use them only to please you, baby—never to harm you."

Those were the last words he spoke before his lips brushed against mine ever so softly and gently. I moved the hand he held to trace along the back of his neck as I opened up, allowing his tongue to soothe away all doubts and fears from my mouth and heart. With every ounce of my being, I knew Deacon was genuine and sincere. I recognized he wasn't Travis and that he would treat me with respect and love—everything I had been trying to shield myself from when I moved to Lovey's Bay. I didn't want to feel anything. I was too afraid to let someone back in like that. Deacon effortlessly washed those feelings away.

"So?" Deacon asked, pulling back to look at me. "You gonna be my Big Momma?"

I chuckled at his nickname for me. What used to just turn me on now also warmed my heart. "I guess so, Daddy Deacon."

His laughter rattled his throat as he kissed my lips. "I like the sound of that."

We shared another moment in our solitude from the rest of the world before heading back to the house. We made the trek, still holding some space and a sense of platonic connection between us. Without needing to say it, we both understood that our relationship needed to stay just between us when it came to our crewmates. When we reached the entrance back to Denzel and Nina's property, everyone was crowded on the patio. We climbed the steps and saw Denzel and Nina in the middle.

"The nation may celebrate today for a specific time in history, but for me, I'm honoring the day I realized

Nina was my person. Many of you may know that we met by chance during a fire emergency—"

"Yeah! Nina almost burned down her kitchen!" Joni interrupted, making everyone laugh. Nina swatted at her.

Denzel chuckled and continued his speech, never moving his eyes or hands from Nina.

"She was, but I'd like to think of it as the day she burned a place in my heart. However, on the 4th of July, I could've lost her if I hadn't been there to save her. To save my future."

Denzel dropped one of Nina's hands and reached into his shorts pocket, pulling out a felt ring box. Nina stepped back, raising her hands—one to her stomach and the other to her mouth. Denzel continued, "We've been through a lot. Some ups and downs, some running around and finding our way back to each other. But when we found our way back, we stayed. We worked out our issues, and we became one. Today, Nina…my Fire Goddess…I want to ask if we can become one officially. I want you to be Mrs. Nina Payton. So, will you? Will you marry me?"

Nina didn't give him a chance to fully take his knee before she jumped into his arms, screaming repeatedly, "Yes! I'll marry you. And… and… I'm pregnant! I was going to wait to tell you, but…"

Nina began sobbing into Denzel's mouth as he pulled her lips to his, showering her with kisses and his excitement over her announcement. I wiped the back of my hand across my eyes, brushing away the tears I shared with the happy couple. I had only known Nina for a couple of days, but I was genuinely happy for her. I always felt joy when someone found the love they deserved, and now, here I was, believing that maybe I would find mine too. It was as if Deacon sensed I needed reassurance; he discreetly grabbed my hand and inter-twined his fingers with mine.

If anything brought me peace about this quick trip, it was the opulence of The Bellevue Hotel. I followed Deacon as we were surrounded by the impeccably maintained vintage fixtures that, according to my research, were original from its opening in the 1920s. Those pieces were accompanied by modern features that aligned the boutique hotel with the present, but the vintage elements captivated me. The grand, sparkling chandelier, the winding twin staircases, and the polished marble counter behind which the hotel attendant stood.

After Deacon and I made our relationship official, I invited him to join me on the trip to Stonecrest for Parris' engagement party. The question didn't come out smoothly; it was filled with jittery nerves and uncertainty. It wasn't that I didn't want him to meet my brother—it was my mother. Honestly, I haven't even seen or talked to her in months, the last time being right before I left for Lovey's Bay, when she scolded me about leaving Travis. It was a scene straight out of Waiting to Exhale. You know the one where Savannah is talking to her Momma, who infamously says, "He's a good man, Savannah." Yeah, that was my mother, in all her British accent glory, pleading for me to stay with this man because he was a "good look."

"If a good man is going to try to beat my ass for wanting to keep a piece of myself and cheats on me, I don't want it, Mum! And I don't say this respectfully!" I remembered shouting at her before storming out of the luxury restaurant where we were having brunch.

The memory of my exit sent chills through me as I stood beside Deacon while he checked us in. Those waves of nerves settled just by looking at him towering next to me. His height and muscles exuded protection, and his presence in my life eased my worries and made me feel secure. At that moment, I felt especially confident with him alongside me this weekend. I didn't expect him to go overboard and act as my bodyguard or anything. Deacon simply calms my soul with a gentle touch or kiss. I anticipated just that from him—his gentle giant presence.

"You look gorgeous, honey," Deacon said as he entered the hotel bathroom with me. I was putting on the final layer of plum lipstick. He stood behind me, running his hands down the sides of my floral sundress before he knelt and kissed the crook of my neck. I admired his affection through the mirror, noticing how our outfits complemented one another. My floral dress had a white background adorned with purple and blue florals, while Deacon wore a simple white short-sleeve button-up and dark denim.

"Thanks," I cooed softly, wrapping my arms around his as he held me close. "You look good yourself."

"Eh, just a little something." He looked at me through the mirror. "I just checked Maps. It's about a 20- to 25-minute drive from Regency to Stonecrest. You ready?"

I took a shaky breath and exhaled, locking eyes with him. "I suppose it's now or never. I apologize in advance for anything rude my mother might say."

"No apologies needed, Fallon," he reassured.

I distorted my mouth. "Yes, it is. She's not your usual mother-in-law."

I stiffened, and my jaw dropped as my words registered. Deacon's gentle smile transformed into a big, cheesy grin. "Mmm, mother-in-law, huh? Noted."

His grin never left as he pulled me back into his chest again, enveloping me as he snuggled and kissed my neck. I squealed, "Deacon! I slipped up and said the wrong thing."

"No, you didn't. You're speaking it into existence. From your mouth to God and my ears." Deacon squeezed me once more and then pecked my matte lips. "C'mon, let me go meet my mother-in-law."

———

The drive to Stonecrest was picturesque. After departing from the bustling city of Regency and heading west on the highway, the city skyline gave way to tall trees adorned with vibrant green foliage. As we exited the highway and followed the directions to Henderson Farm, those trees were joined by sprawling farmland and grazing horses.

"This is different," I remarked as we drove down the gravel path toward the farm. "I've never known Parris to be the country-living type."

"Love will introduce you to new things. Besides, country living isn't so bad. I grew up in a more rural area —not quite as rural as this—but there's something about the tranquility found in "the sticks.'"

I furrowed my brows. "The sticks?"

"Yes," he insisted with a chuckle. "All there is around here are sticks, trees, and farmland."

Nodding in understanding, I asked, "Would you ever move back? To the country?"

Deacon parked the car next to the line of cars already there and turned off the engine. "Yeah, I've thought about it. Maybe one day. My parents have my name on the deed to their house, so when they're gone, I'll inherit it. It's a thought, but right now, I'm enjoying life by the water."

"That's nice of them."

"No, it's *necessary* for them to keep our land as part of our legacy. I'll take you out there one day so you can see it and meet my family."

My body tingled and warmed at the thought of meeting his parents. Deacon winked at me before getting out and helping me out of the car. We walked hand in hand, following the sounds of music and laughter until we reached an open space beyond the barnyard. Parris and I spotted each other almost immediately, with him pulling Tinsley in my direction.

"Tweety, I'm glad you made it." Parris wrapped his arms around me, enveloping and smothering me.

"Parris, you're going to mess up my makeup!" I squealed, my voice muffled by his barricading arms. He loosened his grip, freeing me from his hold. As I finger-combed my hair back into place, I stepped beside Deacon, whom Parris was already glaring at with narrowed slits for eyes.

"Who do we have here?" Parris asked, his voice rough and stoned.

"Put your claws away, Parris. God!" I huffed, then chuckled. I intertwined my fingers with Deacon's as I introduced, "Parris, this is my man, Deacon—well, Benjamin—"

Deacon stuck his hand out. "Benjamin Deacon, but you can call me Deacon.

Parris grimaced at Deacon, then extended his hand to shake. "Deacon. Your man, huh? You're the one who's always at her place when I call?"

"Parris!" Tinsley and I scolded in unison and then giggled, exchanging glances before moving in for a hug. We greeted each other warmly, as if it wasn't our first official meeting, while the guys exchanged pleasantries. Finally, Deacon was introduced to Tinsley.

Tinsley wrapped her arm around my shoulders and said, "I'm so glad to have you two here. Come, there's plenty of food, and the party is just getting started."

Meeting Tinsley was just as I expected. She was America's sweetheart—kind, sweet, and welcoming. I could see why Parris fell in love with her. Along with her warm spirit, she was undeniably beautiful. Her long hair fell in beach waves over her bare shoulders and cascaded down the very cute off-the-shoulder denim corset-style top and shorts. She perfectly complemented the theme of their Down Home yet elegantly decorated engagement party.

Everything was going well. We mixed and mingled, mainly because I was trying to avoid my mother for as long as possible. However, that came to a halt when we found our seats at the table where she sat, her shoulders up and her nose even higher at the head of the table.

"It's about time you came and spoke to your mother," she drawled, sipping from her cup.

"Oh, I wouldn't miss the opportunity to speak with you, Mum," I replied through a forced smile and gritted teeth. I felt Deacon's arm wrap around my shoulder, his hand offering comforting rubs on my arm. I took a deep, calming breath as her head tilted slightly, peering behind me at him. "Mother, this is Benjamin, my boyfriend."

She scoffed. "Oh, we're back at square one with boyfriends now, eh?"

Eyes wide, I opened my mouth to say something, but Parris interrupted. "Mum, Benjamin works with Fallon. He's a captain at the fire company she's with."

"I… I met her before I found out she was coming to join our crew," Deacon clarified as he extended his hand to my mother. Slow to accept, she offered her limp hand as if she were waiting for him to kiss the ring. I bugged my eyes at her while Parris whispered something in her ear. She turned her hand to the side and gave a delicate handshake.

I could already foresee this going terribly wrong, and it was the last impression I wanted to leave Deacon with at my mother's first meeting. I sighed, "Mother, can we have a moment in private?"

With a smug tone, she replied, "Of course, darling."

Without waiting for her to get up, I shrugged Deacon's arm off my shoulder and stomped toward the far end of the gathering, putting myself by a wooden fence. Mother strutted toward me without a care in the world, her cup in hand. Despite her ugly ways, Aubrey Lennox was beautiful. She showed none of the telltale signs of aging. In her early 60s, she still had all the grace in her walk, glowing butter pecan skin, and minimal fine lines. She wore her natural hair sleek, reaching her bra strap, but today, with the August humidity in Greenbrook, her pressed hair was slightly puffy with more volume. She came to a stop in front of me, her big round eyes peering through low lids while the flow of her dress settled as she did.

"What is it?" I asked, folding my arms across my chest. "What is it that I know you want to say? Say it to me now because I won't let you embarrass me in front of Benjamin."

"Embarrass you?" she scoffed, rolling her eyes away before turning them back to me. "I can't embarrass you. You've chosen the life you live."

I blinked rapidly, taken aback. "Wow, Mum. What exactly is the problem with the life that makes *me* happy?"

She raised her hand before sipping from her cup. "Darling, don't play stupid. You had it all. You had the life. I groomed you—"

"You groomed me to settle with a man who didn't respect me emotionally, mentally, or physically isn't something to be proud of, Mother."

"Oh, my Heavens, Fallon. It was one time…a mistake. That's what Travis said—"

"Are you really serious right now, Mother?!" My voice cracked and went up an octave as I stared at her in horror. "You're actually taking Travis's side over mine right now?"

Defiantly, she turned her gaze away from mine as she crossed her arms. She remained silent for a long moment, with only the distant sounds of the party and the neighing of the horses filling the air.

"Fallon Hazel Lennox. I went through hell and high water to ensure you and Parris had the best. You attended grade school abroad and lived a comfortable life that one could afford. All I ever wanted for you is to keep living the same life I provided for you, free from worry. Yet, when you met the man who could give you that, you threw it all away for your dreams of becoming a *firefighter*."

The disdain that draped her speech about my career weighed heavily on my heart, twisting and contorting it. It sank into the depths of my stomach, making me nauseous at the thought of how she believed her entire monologue made sense. It didn't. It was twisted and caused my stomach to knot at the mere idea of it.

"Did you ever think that I enjoyed what I was doing as a firefighter?" My voice cracked as I asked her what I knew would only be a rhetorical question. "Better yet, that I could succeed in my career choice and be a great wife to a man who respected me? All you think about is me being with a rich man. Well, that rich man blacked my eye, Mother, and you did nothing! You didn't even flinch!"

I was yelling now, and I could see Deacon and Parris approaching us over my mother's shoulders. I looked at her; she seemed unmoved except for the roll of her tongue against the rim of her mouth. Her silence thickened my throat, and I unconsciously balled my fists. It was like nothing I said made a difference, let alone was worth a response from her. I let out a frustrated groan and started to stomp away.

"I just wanted you to be happy, Fallon," she finally said. Her admission changed nothing for me; it only proved she hadn't heard a word I said.

I stopped walking and turned to her, finding her now facing me. Through my swelling tears, I declared, "I'm happy! I'm happy to be valued at my job and by my boyfriend! Yes, I'm back at square one, but dammit, Mother, I'm happy, fulfilled, and respected. I don't give a damn if I never get it from you!"

The drive back to Regency was awkwardly quiet, but the energy radiating from Fallon spoke volumes. I witnessed the altercation between Fallon and her mother but wasn't privy to what was said, only aware of the hurt and the pool of tears that were desperate to be released from her eyes. Fallon was painfully strong, willing the tears to stay at bay, never letting them fall, not even once we were confined in my car after she insisted on spending thirty more minutes for Parris's sake. That was her, from what I've learned over the past five months of knowing her. She was strong and often put herself on the back burner in doing so.

Once back at the hotel, silence enveloped us as we entered the elevator. We rode up five floors, listening to its chime with each stop, and then stepped out, continuing quietly until we reached our room. I placed my key on the sensor, unlocking the door and let Fallon enter first.

"You wanna talk—"

My back hit the wall, stifling the rest of my question.

"I don't want to talk. I just want to fuck. I want you to fuck me," she demanded, removing her hand from my chest and dropping down into a squat, busying her hands with undoing my shorts.

"F-Fallon," was all I could muster while I watched her peel down my jeans and briefs and catch my swinging hard-on in her mouth. Grabbing hold to the side of my ass, she opened wide, engulfing as much of me into the warmth of her mouth. I forced out a gritted "Fuuuuckkk" as she slurped up my shaft and bobbed feverously. I got lost in the trance of her melodic slurping and moaning as my dick went further and deeper into her mouth. When my head hit the back of her throat, and she gargled onto it, my dick pulsed as my men started gathering. I pulled her face from my dick, regretting it the moment the cool air of the room hit it. She pinned me with an intense look.

"I'm going to fuck you, but we're going to talk afterward. Got it?" I panted, trying to regain control of myself.

Fallon stood up and walked away, pulling her dress over her head, and huffed, "Whatever."

Her demeanor left me stuck, not knowing what to say. I'd never seen Fallon like this, her sexual aggression filled with anger, but I was willing to give her what she wanted to make her feel good. I stepped out of my jeans and briefs and followed her to the bed while unbuttoning and stripping my shirt off. Fallon was braless, leaving her to just shimmy out of her lace panties before she climbed on the bed and sat up on her elbows with her legs propped open. I knelt down on my knees at the edge of the bed and pulled her legs until her lips below touched mine.

"Fuck," Fallon panted as my tongue circled her clit before I sucked. Through a strained moan, she demanded, "Harder."

I moved my eyes up to her pained ones and proceeded to suck on her pearl harder, indenting my cheeks with each pull. Hardly supporting herself on her elbows, she shook with each pulse of my tongue and vacuum-strength suck on her clit. She threw her head back and growled a guttural moan. The sound of her desire turned me on despite the anger behind it. I swiped my tongue flat between her folds before entering it into her gushing center.

She moaned again as she threw her pussy onto my tongue, gritting, "Just..like…that!"

Dick throbbing, I cupped the side of her ass as I tried to reach for the middle of her cream filling with my tongue. I groaned hungrily as her juices spilled onto my tongue and down my face. My tongue slipped and glided over her glistening pussy, feeding my gluttony for her.

Before I could satisfy my gluttony and before I could bring her to her climax, I felt Fallon's toes on my shoulders, pushing me off.

My eyes widened, and my mouth fell open as I watched her scoot further onto the bed and get on all fours. "I want you inside of me."

"Fallon—"

"Please," her voice cracked as she begged. She looked over her shoulder at me with those pained eyes again.

Fallon could be a demanding lover, but this was different, and it had me concerned while turned on. Yet, I gave her what she wanted, what she said she needed at this time. I climbed onto the bed, lining myself up with her. Before I entered, I leaned over, kissing her shoulder blade, whispering, "I want to see your beautiful face."

"Not now...ahh!" Fallon declared, falling into a whimpering moan as she pushed into my dick, her walls opening like floodgates allowing me to slide in. The feel of her walls wrapped around my dick seized an unexpected breath out of me.

"Goddamn, Fallon," I moaned as she threw her pussy back, taking the dick for herself. I grabbed hold of her hips and mastered a steady tempo, sliding out and then burying my dick inside her slowly. At the rate she was going, I was going to bust before she did if I didn't gather some control.

"Harder, Deacon," She gritted, meeting my stroke with her own tempo.

I pulled out to my tip and then thrust my hips into her, inciting a whimpered moan from her.

"Yes! Harder," she begged. She laid her head on the bed and deepened her arch as she reached back, pulling her cheeks apart. It was a fucking beautiful sight as I gave her what she wanted. Pound after pound, I watched the white cream from her pussy cover my dick.

"Harder," she whimpered again, and I did, so hard that my thighs were smacking her ass, and my balls were colliding against her pussy.

"Fucck!" I roared out, digging my hands into her hips.

And then I heard it. I heard sniffling, and I became confused. I pulled out and flipped Fallon over. I was met with her tear-stained face. My stomach pitted, and my breath froze as I rubbed on her legs.

"Am I hurting you?"

She wiped her eyes vigorously. "No. I need you... I need to feel... Please..."

Fallon's words fell as crackled breaths as she silently sobbed into her hands. My heart crumbled watching her emotions pour out through her tears. Her words echoed in my mind, and I realized exactly what she needed. I leaned over her as she moved her hands from her eyes and whispered, "Please."

I pushed into her, slowly and with care this time,

stroking in and out of her still-moistened walls. She inhaled and exhaled as her eyes drifted closed again as she wrapped her legs around my waist and her arms around my neck. I lowered so that my lips were lingering over hers as I continued to massage her walls.

"Harder," she whispered.

"No."

Her eyes opened as her eyebrows met. "Deacon, I need—"

I delved inside of her, holding still once I hit the bottom. She sipped in a shaky breath as her walls convulsed around me. I pecked her lips. "You don't need pain. You've been feeling pain for a long time. I'm going going to give you love. I'm going to make you feel loved."

Fallon opened her mouth, but before she could form a word, I covered her mouth with mine, languidly swiping all remnants of her protest away. I felt her body relax under me as she met my tongue with hers, and I began creating love with each slow, gentle stroke inside her. Love sounded like the squish of her juices and her soft moans as I moved my kisses down to her neck and then cupped her breast. I gently suckled and nibbled and teased at her nipple rings, my dick jumping at every roll over her hard nipple against my tongue. I moved to the other breast and gave it the same love, all while stroking more love into her. Her hands trailed my neck and raked through my curls, sending tingles through me and straight to my dick.

I plunged further as I groaned and moved my lips to hers again. I stayed there, hovering over her lips, looking deep into her soft eyes. Behind the sadness, I saw her joy, fighting to come through. The amber of the setting sun showered Fallon's face, illuminating the richness of her brown skin. She was beautiful. She was angelic. She was mine. She was love.

I kissed her deep, tangling my tongue with hers as my stroke grew to a mid-tempo. My body buzzed as my nerves unraveled at the feeling of her. She felt so good and so wet. I didn't know how long I would last like this with her. Fallon wrapped her arms around my neck and her legs tighter around my hips, pulling me closer and flesh to her. Her walls contracted around my dick, pulling twin moans from us.

"I love you," I declared into her mouth, hoping those words would embed themselves in her heart. Her eyes ping-ponged, searching for mine. My forehead creased with the intensity of the emotion overtaking me as I held my gaze steady on her and repeated, "I love you."

Her eyes filled with tears as she found no deceit in me. She brought her lips to mine, kissing me passion-ately, then looked at me again and whispered, "I love you, too."

This time, I devoured, ceasing to let her go. I swiped my tongue deeper with each plunge of my dick into her as she rocked her hips into me, creating an unnerving friction between us. Sparks were setting off—in my dick, in my body, in my vision— as I went from plunging to pounding. My ragged pants and Fallon's whimpers filled the room as we fought to stay connected through body and mouth. I clenched my teeth, trying to stave off my cum long enough for Fallon to climax. Within remarkable moments, Fallon's walls clenched, and her release came crumbling down. Soon after, I met her in the land of bliss.

I fluttered my eyes open to find Deacon staring at me. Propped up on his elbow, he looked at me with the kindest, most loving eyes I've ever received from a man. He reached over, tucking a stray hair behind my ear before leaning in and kissing my forehead.

"Good Morning," I cracked out.

The corner of his lip curved up. "Good Morning. How are you feeling?"

I murmured, "Good," as I snuggled closer to him, feeling the warmth of his chest relax me.

"Good. So, you want to talk about last night?"

Taking a deep breath, I remembered the angry sex I initiated that left me feeling completely joyful and loved. His words echoed in my mind, too: "We will talk later."

Later was now, and I realized I wouldn't be able to dodge the conversation.

"What you witnessed was a typical experience with Audrey Lennox. I'm always talked down to for choosing myself over a rich man who disrespected me. Yesterday, she basically doubled down on taking his side. You know what she said to me? I squandered an opportunity." I scoffed as her words replayed in my mind. "She would prefer I live a lavish life while feeling fearful and unhappy rather than see me fulfill my passion as a firefighter and pursue real love."

Deacon lifted my chin so I was looking at him. Simply meeting his sincere eyes caused my walls to come crumbling down, and tears filled my eyes. I squeezed them shut, willing the tears away.

"Mm-mm. Don't fight your tears," he murmured, pressing his lips against my eyelids. Each gentle kiss caused the floodgates to open wider, overwhelming me with a wave of emotions.

"Why are you like this?" I whispered, feeling him still kissing my tears away.

"Like what?"

I blinked up at him. "So good to me."

"Don't you know you're worthy? I'm this way because you deserve to be treated well. To be loved. To feel safe. Fal, you're safe with me. Cry. Get angry and use my body like you did last night." Deacon blew out a breath and then laughed. I giggled as he shook his head.

"We're in the trenches together, baby. We're walking through fires together."

I inhaled a cleansing breath, still overwhelmed by feelings that were once foreign to me: worth, true happiness, and genuine love. I reached up and pulled Deacon close, claiming his lips as my own. Then, he shifted me onto my back and claimed what was his: my body.

"Alright, babe. We're all checked out. Let's hit the road," Deacon announced, stepping away from the front desk. I felt a bit sad leaving the beautiful hotel behind, wishing we had one more day to stay. I started to roll my luggage, but Deacon tapped my hand, shooing it off the handle. I obliged and let him take it. Just as we were about to enter the revolving doors, he paused mid-stride, threw his head back, and turned around. "I left my keys at the counter."

"We can't go anywhere without those," I teased as I watched him walk back with an extra spring in his step. I imagined he felt as renewed as I did. After releasing my heart's sorrows and being made love to this morning, I felt like a new person. An unstoppable person. A loved person. I felt ready to leave the drama of my mother and my past behind and return to Lovey's Bay, which truly felt like my new home. Just as I turned around, though, my past stared me right in the face.

"Fallon."

The man for whom I made a 500-mile effort to be far, far away from identified me. And as he strolled toward me, the distance I had tried to maintain became non-existent. Dressed sharply, groomed, and wearing a smile that once could charm me was my ex-fiancé, Travis Beaumont. He attempted to wrap his arms around me, but I placed my hands on his chest, re-establishing distance.

"Don't touch me," I scolded, my heart pounding in my chest.

The harshness in my voice didn't faze him as he smirked at me, yet he stilled at my request. "Darling, you're still mad at me? I thought at least we'd be cordial."

His ridiculous suggestion made me feel uneasy. I tried to ignore it and ask the only question that mattered right now: "What are you doing here?"

"So you can ask questions, but not me?" he asked, still wearing that smug grin. I stood there, unmoved, waiting for an answer. He snorted, "Official business. You might be seeing more of me around here."

I tensed at his revelation but jerked my arm away as he reached to touch me, stammering, "Well, it's a good thing I-I don't live here."

"You good, babe?" Deacon's warm body pressed against my back as he intertwined his fingers with mine. The simplicity of the moment eased my stifled breath and calmed my heart.

"Babe?" Travis's thick eyebrow arched as he shifted

his glare from Deacon to me. I felt the menace lurking in his dark eyes, tightening my grip on Deacon's hand.

"That's what I said," Deacon reiterated, his baritone rich and steady.

Deacon's lack of retreat made Travis narrow his eyes at me and grit out, "You move pretty quickly, don't you?"

"You're one to talk, Travis!" I spat, feeling offended and amused as I recalled this mistress. "How's Lindsey?"

"Oh, so you're the punk who likes to put his hands on women," Deacon barked, releasing my hand. He began to move around me toward Travis, but I grabbed his arm.

"Deacon, no. Let's just go. Please." Deacon glanced at me, as if to ask if I was sure. I nodded quickly, intertwining his fingers with mine as I grabbed my suitcase. "C'mon." I looked at Travis. "Don't come looking for me."

I had to tug on Deacon's hand to get him to follow me out of the hotel, and with some hesitation, he did. We had taken a couple of steps away from Travis before he became froggy.

"You should probably listen to her, Preacher Man. Just keep walking."

Deacon stopped suddenly, making me bounce back like a yo-yo. "It's Deacon. Don't let the name fool you, my boy. I turn into a demon over this one."

Deacon's grip on my hand felt like that of a parent

holding tightly onto their child to prevent losing them. He wasn't going to lose me, and I believed every word he spoke. The fury in his eyes as he led me out of the hotel indicated that he would go through the pits of hell for me. Deep down, something told me that Hell was in town for much longer than I wanted.

Lovey's Bay stood in stark contrast to the fast-paced, glamorous Hollywood mecca known as Damask. Instead, this bayside city focused on community, hosting numerous family-friendly events each season, such as today's Labor Day Community & Hurricane Preparedness Event. Harbour Pointe Park's green landscape buzzed with families and children enjoying bouncy houses. Scattered around the edges of the park were vendors selling a variety of goods, including Fire Company No. 143 in our designated corner.

We attracted the kids by offering interior tours of the fire truck for younger children and hosting a Tug-O-War competition between the teens and the firefighters. I wasn't really there to pull a rope with teenagers eager to prove a point. Instead, I helped with all the demonstrations, starting with a sandbag stacking demonstration to illustrate how it prevents flooding.

Right now, I found myself at the table where guests could get emergency kit essentials and checklists to ensure they were prepared for their own needs. The table didn't need much supervision, but Joss came over shortly after I took over. She plopped down on the edge of the table, wiping the beads of sweat from her forehead.

"Yo, those kids are on some Survivor shit over there. Like, it's Tug-O-War. Nobody's winning any money."

"I see," I chuckled, nodding toward the game taking place at that moment.

My gaze focused on Deacon and the flex of his biceps as he called out for the crew to pull. Even with sweat glistening and teeth gritted, Deacon was a sight to behold. Unconsciously, I wet my lips as I continued to admire his strength and then his humility as he let go of the rope, causing the crew behind him to stumble while the teenagers' efforts faded as they achieved victory. I watched Deacon high-five a few of the kids before he strolled my way.

"The jig is up."

I turned my head to Joss with furrowed brows. "Huh?"

She stood beside me and nudged my side. "The jig is up. You and Deacon."

"What do you mean, me and Deacon? We-we—"

"…Are doing more than just co-working," Joss murmured, raising her eyebrows in response to my stare.

"Don't say anything," I whispered, as if anyone could hear us over the blaring music and the kids playing.

Joss clicked her tongue. "Come on, Lennox. You know I got your back."

Of all the crew members aside from Deacon, Joss was another I'd trust with my eyes closed. She had been genuine and supportive since I joined the team. I smiled up at her and nodded, ready to thank her before the music cut off, causing a tap and unbalanced signals that made the microphone squeal before a familiar voice filled the park.

"If we could please take a few minutes away from your fun! *Ahem* My name is Nina Franklin, and I'm the Event Coordinator for Lovey's Bay Parks and Recreation. I want to thank you for coming out to help make this effort to prepare our city for hurricane season a success!" The crowd began to clap as Deacon stood beside me, lightly brushing his index finger against my hand. I turned to him, my happiness lingering on my lips just enough for him to notice, while Nina continued speaking. "Speaking of success, we have a very special guest. He's new to Greenbrook and is seeking your help for the success of his upcoming campaign. Let's welcome Attorney Travis Beaumont to the stage and to our community!"

"What the hell?" The words escaped my gaping

mouth as I watched Travis take center stage next to Nina. He surveyed the crowd, and my heart froze when his dark eyes found me. His smile widened slightly.

"What the hell is this?" Deacon grumbled.

"Y'all know this guy?" Out of the corner of my eye, I noticed Joss glancing between me and Deacon.

Before either of us could respond, Travis began to speak. "Thank you, Lovey's Bay. It feels good to be welcomed so warmly." He fixed his gaze on me once more before sweeping over the crowd as he explained why he was there. "Lovey's Bay holds a special place in my heart because many of the people I love live here. I hope to spread the love I have for Lovey's Bay beyond the city limits and throughout the great state of Greenbrook as I prepare to run for…."

My ears started to ring as stars blurred my vision. The mild breeze did nothing to alleviate the heat flash that overwhelmed me, forcing me down into the seat behind me. I didn't need to hear any more. I had heard and understood enough to know that the one I thought I had escaped had found his way back into my world.

Deacon's presence was sensed before I heard the murmur of his voice. "You okay, Fallon?"

I squeezed my eyes shut, trying to shoo away the stars. They cleared enough for me to see Deacon looking at me with worry in his eyes. I shook my head violently, and Travis's announcement pricked my ears again, making the air around me grow thicker. "Cap, can I leave?"

Deacon's eyebrows hiked at my choice of title but relaxed as I sensed he recognized the fear I felt. He cracked, "Yeah. Let me take you—"

I raised my hand as I quickly stood up. "No. No. I'm okay."

Without hesitation, I dashed through the crowd toward my car. I was not okay. I was not fine. I was furious, frustrated, and—defeated.

———

"Why didn't you let me know Travis was here?!"

"What? Girl, I stopped giving a damn what that jerk was doing when you finally left him," Zaria said. "What do you mean he's in Greenbrook?"

I paced the fire station locker room, huffing into the speaker of my phone. "He's here! Lovey's Bay, to be exact, chasing his political dreams and terrorizing me."

"I'm sorry, Fal," Zaria said apologetically. "I truly didn't know. You know, I would've said something if I had known. Are you going to be okay? You might want to call Parris—"

"No." My stern hiss silenced Zaria. "I'm not going to keep running from Travis or turning to someone to save me. I've worked too goddamn hard for him to make me shrink myself."

"Okay, Fallon," Zaria replied, allowing me to vent my anger.

I could admit I was directing my frustrations at my best friend. It wasn't her fault. Honestly, there was no one else to blame but Travis. Among all the places he could have gone to pursue his goals, he picked the one city where I decided to start over. And what family? After all the years we were together, I've never known him to have family in Greenbrook. We hadn't even attended a family reunion here.

Puffing out my cheeks, I opened my locker and grabbed my bag before slamming it shut and saying, "Zaria, I'll call you later. I'm sorry. I know this isn't your fault. I just need some time to process everything."

"Okay, boo. Just call me."

With a quick goodbye, I ended the call and slung the strap of my bag over my shoulder. My mind was so preoccupied with getting home that I didn't notice the person I bumped into face-to-chest. They grabbed my arms to steady me, but when I saw who it was, I jerked away, freeing myself.

"So, you're actually stalking me, huh? I thought it was just a coincidence that we ended up in the same place at the same time."

"Or perhaps fate?" Travis's smirk deepened as he looked down at me.

"Bullshit," I spat, stepping back as he stepped forward. I glanced past him, regretting not taking Deacon up on his offer to escort me back. The firehouse was eerily silent with everyone at the Community Day. "What do you want, Travis?"

"Whatever happened to, "Hello. How are you doing?"" He feigned disappointment as he reached over, captured a strand of my hair, and subtly twirled it around his finger. In contrast to his touch, I swatted at his hand, zigging around him.

"I don't have time for this," I hissed.

I barely made it two steps before Travis's rough grip on my arm yanked me back, slamming my back against the wall. My breath turned to ice in my throat as my eyes landed on the familiar grimace. It was the same expression he wore just before I felt the back of his hand connect with my face once before.

Anger.

Fear.

Shock.

It all built up inside me and came out as an involuntary shaking of my body.

Travis kissed his teeth. "Tsk, tsk, tsk. I thought we learned not to sass me last time, darling."

No more than two seconds later, Travis was yanked by his collar, almost off his feet and pinned to the wall beside me. Deacon's grimace was more venomous than anything Travis could've ever managed as he stood nose-to-nose with him and sneered, "And it's clear you weren't properly taught not to put your fuckin' hands on a woman."

With malice twisting his features, Travis sneered, "Choir Boy. You're in love with her and work with her? Ha! This has gotten even be—"

The crack of Deacon's knuckles against the side of Travis's face defrosted my chilled breath as I yelped and frantically tried to pull Deacon away from him. Although he deserved it, Travis was a powerful man. Deacon proved physically stronger as the threat Travis began to pose was stifled by Deacon's relentless fist. I knew where Deacon was headed with this and what it would mean for either of us if he went through with it. My attempts to separate Deacon from Travis were met by Chief Denzel and Tevin, each grabbing hold of a side of Deacon to pull him away.

"Captain Deacon! What are you doing?!" Denzel barked, his eyes wide with bewilderment. "He's a state official!"

"Yeah, well that motherfucker is an abuser, too! I'm just showing him what it's like to fight a man instead of a woman!" Deacon bucked, but Denzel and Tevin's grip on him remained firm.

"Deacon!" My voice cracked as I scolded him. I felt exposed with Denzel and Tevin there, but now the firehouse was filled with the rest of the crew. With a heaving chest, Deacon looked at me in confusion. Stifling the urge to cry, I hissed, "That's my story to tell, and I shared it with you in complete confidence!"

"Babe…" Deacon's voice trailed off as he realized the setting we were in, and that Denzel was now looking at him with deep-set, furrowed brows, while Tevin smirked as if he had discovered the best secret. He had. With that softly spoken name of affection, Deacon exposed us.

Travis's sigh drew everyone's attention back to him as he straightened his collar. He licked at the trickle of blood trailing from his lip as he smirked smugly. "This was fun, but it's not my cup of joe." He started to walk away but paused in front of Denzel. "Chief, you'll be hearing from me about this."

When Travis left the firehouse, Denzel and Tevin let go of Deacon. The chief stood with his hands on his hips, tight lips, and a slow shake of his head, ordering, "Captain Deacon. Lennox. In my office now."

Deacon and I followed Chief Payton a short distance to his office like two teenagers in trouble. I could feel every moment Deacon glanced my way, but I kept my eyes trained ahead. My mind struggled to process the disaster that had just unfolded. I was trying not to be angry at Deacon, but he had exposed my most vulnerable spot and our relationship in front of everyone at the firehouse.

When the office door closed, the room fell into pin-drop silence until Chief Payton spoke. "Somebody tell me what's going on. No, Captain, you, the superior, explain why I had to restrain you from slaughtering a state official."

In that moment, I broke my defiance and turned my gaze to Deacon, who was looking at me with sorrow. His lips tightened before he sighed. "Out of respect for Fallon, I can't answer that openly. Just know, I didn't do it without reason. I did it to defend and protect my—"

I shook my head profusely, silencing Deacon. He looked at me, stunned, as I whispered, "No."

I could sense Denzel glancing back and forth between us, still trying to make heads or tails of the situation. "Fallon, are you okay?"

Avoiding his Chief's gaze, I looked out of the window off to the side as I answered, "I am. I was just on my way home before… Chief, is it okay for me to go home now?"

I continued to avoid Chief's eyes as his voice mellowed with concern as he said, "Of course. It's your day off."

Without waiting for any further confirmation about my departure, I turned on my heels and quickly exited his office. I wasn't quick enough, though, because moments later, I heard Deacon's footsteps approaching. His hand on my shoulders took me back to a place I had worked hard to avoid reliving. I jerked away and spun toward him. Noticing the fire-engine red of my face and my glare, Deacon raised his hands defensively.

"I-I didn't mean to…"

"What, Deacon? Scare me? Expose me? Expose us to the whole firehouse?!" I spewed, growing angrier with each scenario.

"Fallon, you know that's not what I meant to do."

"But you did!" I emphasized. "You didn't think things through, and now here we are, exposed to the world."

"Fallon, what did you want me to do? Let that man try his hand with you again?

"He wouldn't."

Deacon scoffed. "Are you sure about that? Because the way he had you pinned—"

"Stop!" I yelled, surprising myself and silencing the hum of the firehouse. I winced, realizing that I was now the one drawing attention to us. I could see them out of the corner of my eye, watching our confrontation. I shifted my position so that I could no longer see them and squared off with Deacon. "I think we've talked enough for now. You—"

"You sound like you're blaming me for this," Deacon interrupted. He stepped closer to me. "I wasn't doing anything except trying to protect you."

"I don't need saving! I don't need protection!" I hissed, throwing my hands to my sides. Tears welled in my waterline as I pointed to my chest. "I've got me. I've got me, I got me this job, and I refuse to let you or Travis take that away from me! You know that talk Travis threatened to have with the Chief? That's not a threat. That's a promise to fuck shit up for me. For you. Fire is my life! It's what I breathe! He took that away from me once, and now he's trying to do it again, thanks to you!" I sobbed as I threw my head back, completely exhausted by everything. I was tired. I was spent. Leveling my head back to center and through my blurry vision, I cried, "I knew…I knew I shouldn't have let this become a thing. I knew it would just get in the way."

Wiping my eyes, I turned and rushed out of the firehouse.

"So, how are you holding up?"

Denzel's question was loaded, yet I could only muster a single word: "Okay."

The truth was, I felt null and void. I was confused about how I ended up here again, feeling rejected by my fire company and Fallon. The solemn look on Denzel's face told me he understood the feelings I wasn't expressing.

"The only way to keep the people above me quiet was to move you to another shift. You know that, right?"

"Yeah," I replied as our waitress approached our table with our beer glasses. I picked up my dark brew and lifted it to Denzel before taking a big gulp. "You had to do what you had to do, Chief. I understand."

"Chief, man?" Denzel asked with a chuckle. "I'm on professional terms now?"

I leaned back in my chair. "I mean, Chief… Denzel… same person."

"Sounds a bit salty, Captain," Denzel replied. He rested his elbows on the table and clasped his hands together. "If my friend had told me what was going on, maybe I could've prevented some things from happening. Hell, I did. They wanted me to suspend you indefinitely."

It had been a week since the altercation at the firehouse between me and Fallon's ex, Travis. I also learned that Travis was coming into Lovey's Bay as the City Attorney, with bigger political ambitions. He was quite a big deal in the city and wasted no time exerting his influence. By the following Monday, he had reported misconduct to the Board of Fire Commissions and threatened to sue the Fire Company in retaliation for me busting his lip open. He deserved it, but the Company didn't deserve the nonsense he was threatening because of me. To appease the board and Travis, Denzel informed them that I would be put on leave for the week and then moved to another shift until an "internal investigation" was completed. That was code for Denzel coming up with a reason to get them off our backs. Although I was a little annoyed that Travis was getting somewhat of his way, I knew Denzel had my and Fallon's best interests at heart.

I groaned. "I get it, and I appreciate that, D. This situation is just wild and unnecessary. If he would've just left Fallon alone, we wouldn't be here."

"Or, had you left her alone?" Denzel asked, tilting his head. "What were you thinking? Pursuing your subordinate? C'mon, Deac."

"It wasn't even like that!" I protested, waving my hands across the table. "I met her here at that speed dating event you and Tevin convinced me to attend."

Denzel's eyebrows dipped. "Wait, so you met her before she joined the department?"

"Yes!" I nodded and then shook my head in the same breath. "By then, I was too gone. I mean, I'd only seen her that one night, but that night was…the best night I'd had in a long time."

I looked away as my mind drifted down memory lane to the night I met Fallon. It was the best night of my life. Even before I saw her, talking with her relaxed my body. She brought me peace and intrigue. By the end of our conversation, I knew I had to get to know her better; I had to see the beauty behind the voice. And when I did—by the grace of God—I couldn't stop smiling. I hadn't smiled that way in a long time. I couldn't pull away from her, from our kisses, from the warmth of her body.

"I see," Denzel responded thoughtfully. As I came back to the present moment, Denzel looked at me with one eyebrow raised. "Sounds like a good night, for sure."

I chuckled and glanced down at the fizzing drink in front of me. "It was. We tried not to go there. We really did." I looked up at him with earnest eyes. "But when something's meant to be, it always finds its way back to you."

"I get it. That's how it was with Nina and me. She tried to run away once, and then when Thandie showed up, she tried again. But somehow, we ended up back together. We've never become unglued since."

"Ya'll shit was a bit absurd," I joked, chuckling.

"Hey. Not too much on my baby." Denzel raised a hand before I grabbed it and dapped him up, signaling that everything was all love over here. "But I get it; I just wish I'd known so I could've handled things a little differently. How are things going with you two since everything?"

I released my frustration with a puff. "I haven't spoken to her since. You saw her storm out."

"Damn. I thought this would have blown over by now."

"Nah," I said, shaking my head. "It's bigger than what the eyes can see. Travis is a shitbag. Real scum at the bottom of your shoe. The type that likes to pick fights with people they think they can control."

"Did he touch her?"

I swallowed the last of my beer before slamming the glass on the table, furious at the mere thought of seeing Travis in Fallon's face that day. I narrowed my eyes at Denzel. "Out of respect for Fallon, I can't share her story. But you catch my drift, right?"

Denzel clenched his fist in his palm while resting his

elbow on the table. Nodding slowly, he gritted, "Yeah. I hear you. This motherfucka, man…"

"My sentiments exactly," I agreed, crossing my arms over my chest. I recalled that day. "I was just trying to protect her. I know Fallon is a tough cookie, but that's my Fallon, Denzel. Ain't no motherfucker gonna put his hands on her in front of me, no matter what. I'm a man of God, but I'll turn into a demon over that one."

Denzel snorted. "Your Fallon, huh? If that's true, why aren't you putting in more effort to win her back?"

Our table fell silent as the lively music and chatter of Rhythm and Brew took center stage. Glancing at my empty glass, I confessed, "I…I can't go through rejection again."

"Who said you will?" I raised my gaze to Denzel. "From what I can tell, you two have been building something really solid. You sound different when you talk about her. You sound confident. Stand by it. Get your woman back. Let her know you're not going to let a misunderstanding—or that punk Travis—keep you apart. If she's your woman, she's your woman. I'll sort out the logistics with the department. You just focus on making your relationship solid again."

FALLON

"Okay, a pitcher of sangria for you ladies and a wine glass of cranberry juice for me." Nina waddled into her living room, balancing a carafe of dark purple wine and juice in one hand and a wine glass in the other.

"Girl, I wish you would stop waddling like you're already carrying an eight-pound baby. You barely have a pooch yet," Joni teased. I giggled, silently agreeing. Nina was only about three months pregnant and had no belly to carry, yet she had already inherited the pregnant waddle.

Nina set the carafe down in front of us before carefully settling into the accent chair next to us with a huff. "Oh, leave me alone, Joni. I'm not even waddling."

"Okay, girl," Joni sang as she poured a glass for herself and then offered to pour one for me.

"Joni isn't lying," I interjected, taking a sip from my glass. "You do have a bit of a waddle, but that's cute. You deserve to waddle if you want to."

"You too?!" Nina giggled and then shrugged. "I don't do it on purpose. I think it's something that just takes over a mommy when she's expecting."

"Now, you know I'm just teasing you," Joni chimed in. "But you know your ass is a little dramatic."

"Well, I'm just gonna be dramatic for the next six months. Get used to it, Joni." Nina stuck her tongue out at Joni before giggling again. She turned her attention to me, smoothing her shirt over her belly. "How are you doing, Fallon? I heard about that fiasco at the fire department last week. Are you okay?"

My cheeks flushed as embarrassment washed over me again. "Word travels fast, doesn't it?"

"Well, I wasn't going to say anything…" Joni added. She shifted toward me and crossed her legs, glass in hand. "…but Tevin mentioned it to me, too. Girl, you dated that fine man from Community Day? What's his name…Travis?"

"Oh, God," I groaned, setting my glass on a coaster on the table and bringing my fingers to my temples. "I should've known the guys gossiped more than women."

"They do," Joni agreed.

Nina leaned in and placed her hand on my denim-covered knee. "I'm sorry; I didn't even consider that it was a private matter."

"No, it's fine," I reassured. "It's out there now. It's just… that part of my past was meant to stay in Damask."

"What? Is he stalking you or something? Because, girl, I know someone who knows someone—"

"I don't think that's necessary, Joni," Nina interjected, her eyes widening as her jaw dropped. Her shock shifted into a gentle smile as she turned her gaze back to me. "It seems like Deacon has a good handle on that."

"I didn't need him to do that, though," I protested, sinking back into the sofa. The moment replayed in my mind. "It could have cost him his job… mine…"

"It wouldn't have," Nina attempted to argue. "Denzel said it wasn't a big deal to him that you two were dating. He just wished he had known so he could have gotten ahead of all the drama Travis created afterward."

"Yes, *drama*," I emphasized. "Because of what he and Deacon did, there's drama now. There's gossip, and I'm stuck in the middle of it."

"Girl, there was already gossip about you two," Joni added. "Tevin was asking me questions months ago, and you two weren't hiding it well on the 4th of July either. We saw y'all all hugged up on the beach."

"Ugh!" I dropped my head back and groaned. "This is why I shouldn't have let this happen. I worked too hard to regain my respect as a woman and a firefighter to be tainted by gossip and drama. Travis tried to strip me of my independence when we were together, and now here I am, in a whole new city, reduced to a weak woman who needs saving by her man. Oh…and her man is the Captain. I'm sure the rumor is that I slept my way into the company, too."

"Girl, pump your brakes!" Joni said, dragging out her words. She picked up my glass and handed it to me. "Here, take a sip and relax. No one is saying or thinking any of those things."

Pouting, I took the glass to the head as Nina softly confirmed, "She's right. The only thing that was said was that Denzel stepped in because that man had his hands on you."

"Did he hit you?!" Joni hissed, rolling her neck and her eyes bulging.

Hit you…

Those two words hit me like a gut punch as the memory washed over me once more, knotting my stomach as a thick lone tear escaped from one eye and then the other. Nina and Joni gasped in unison and scrambled to either side of me, offering comfort. I squeezed my eyes shut and covered my face, embarrassed to be breaking down in front of them.

"Honey, I'm so sorry," Nina cooed, rubbing my back. "You don't need to say anything; just let it out. This is a safe space."

"Yeah, girl," Joni consoled. "You're part of the crew now. We got your back just like Deacon did. I know it's a lot, but I don't think Deacon meant any harm. Shit, I heard Deacon had that man knotted up like Martin in that episode where he fought Hitman Tommy Hearns. Remember that episode?"

I stopped sniffling and looked at Joni, just as Nina had. Joni looked between us, oblivious to what was happening. Then, we all broke into laughter. I laughed so hard that I forgot I had been crying just moments ago.

One thing we could always count on was Joni as comic relief in any situation. Our laughing session turned into a group hug, and I relaxed into it. I accepted the love Nina and Joni were giving me. It had been difficult to maintain the facade that I was okay and didn't need anyone. The truth was, I needed people. I needed friends here who would listen to me, let me cry, and hold me close, just like Nina and Joni were doing.

My newfound friend group and I talked for the rest of the afternoon. Actually, I talked, sharing about my relationship with Travis and contrasting it with my experience with Deacon. I missed Deacon so much, and I realized I had been standing in my own way, creating the distance between us right now. I just didn't know how to fix it. I actually did know how to fix it, but a part of my tough exterior wanted to keep it that way and resist seeking him out. By dusk, I felt like I needed to go home and figure out how to overcome my ego and get my man back.

"Don't be like Nina and have to go running like a track star to reconcile with your man just because a life-threatening emergency arises," Joni cautioned as she and Nina escorted me to the front door. I stepped outside and turned to see Nina giving Joni a side-eye. She noticed the gaze and reacted with a dramatic head tilt. "Don't pretend you didn't. I saw you running down the street with my own eyes."

Nina pressed her lips together. "But I got the man. You, you still have a boy toy."

"Oop!" slipped from my lips, and Joni scoffed. Before they could continue their banter, I excused myself. "Bye, ladies."

I turned around to head down the steps and bumped into Denzel. The purr of an engine made me glance past him to see Deacon's red sports car. My heart fluttered as my breath caught in my throat.

"Hey, Fallon."

"Hey, Chief. Bye, Chief," I murmured, absentmindedly waving to him as I descended the steps at a measured pace.

My stomach sank when I saw Deacon step out of his car and walk around the front. With only the dim light at the corner of Nina and Denzel's property, I could barely see Deacon at first, but as I got closer, I could make out his eyes, steady on me, soft and yearning, mirroring mine. I stopped in front of him, inches away, and looked up at him. Drawn together, our faces came close but hovered, our lips near enough that I could feel his breath.

I wanted to touch him. I wanted to kiss him. But I feared he would reject me.

"Hey," he breathed.

"Hey."

Deacon scanned my eyes and then shifted his gaze to my lips before coming back to meet my eyes. "Can we talk?"

"Yeah." I wet my bottom lip, nodding.

"Cool. Follow me to the Boardwalk?"

"Okay," my voice cracked. We stood there, searching each other's eyes, seemingly not wanting to move. I missed feeling his energy. It was filled with warmth and protection—so much love, so much of what I needed.

And then, Deacon pressed his lips against mine, softly yet firmly enough for me to feel that he needed this kiss as much as I did. I chased after his lips when he pulled away, stealing another moment of being skin-to-skin before we reluctantly separated and headed to our cars.

———

Deacon and I didn't say much as we walked hand in hand to the gated entrance. The Lovey's Bay Ferris Wheel is a city landmark known by everyone near and far. From what I've heard, it is the tallest on the East Coast, and at its highest point, it offers a stunning view of the city. As Deacon paid for our entry and guided me to our compartment, I looked forward to the view after this much-needed conversation. Once secured, Deacon and I settled in, his arm resting on the back of the seat behind me. After a few minutes, as other riders were secured, the wheel began its slow ascent into the blue-black sky. An eighties tune started to croon over the speaker, setting the perfect chill late-night ride vibe.

I glanced at Deacon, taking him in as he stared over the edge. He looked so handsome with his five o'clock shadow and perfectly groomed short coils. The veins in his biceps stood out as he rubbed his thumb and index fingers together. Sensing my gaze, Deacon turned to me.

"I'm sorry," I blurted out, scolding myself internally for rushing the apology. *Get out of your head.*

"I'm sorry, too," he replied. "I didn't think; I just acted."

"You did nothing wrong." I placed my hand on his leg and turned to look him in the eyes. "I'm not used to… this… you. I mean, someone like you."

"I'm not perfect. I'm far from perfect…"

"But you're perfect to me," I assured, my heart swelling with my words and the emotions they evoked. Deacon interlocked his fingers with mine, looking down at our hands as he caressed the back of mine with his thumb. I continued my confession. "Deacon, I came to Lovey's Bay with a frozen heart and a determination not to let anyone in, yet in no time, you broke down those walls. Over time, you warmed my heart just by being yourself. You didn't force me. You didn't try to change me. You accepted me, broken and flawed."

He looked up at me, moving his hand from mine and wiping away the tear that escaped my eye. I huffed at how emotional I had become as he confessed, "That's because you are perfect to me, too. What you think is stubbornness, I see as your strength. I love how much willpower you have. I love it when you're on your Big Mama shit, you know, bossy and leading…" I giggled at my favorite nickname he had given me. "…and what you refer to as brokenness, I consider beautiful. I love your vulnerability, too. Your vulnerability helped me to open up, allowing love back into my heart. I love you for who you are and wouldn't change you for the world."

I held the side of his face before crashing into his lips, driven by the need to feel him again. He wrapped his arms around me so tightly that it was clear he felt the same way. Our lips parted, inviting each other deeper, tongues dancing and intertwining, trying to convey how much we missed each other. The ride came to an abrupt stop at the highest point, pulling us apart to catch our breaths. I placed my hand on his chest as I pulled away enough to meet his eyes.

"I need to finish my apology. I got angry at you for trying to protect me from someone who has hurt me in the past, and that wasn't fair. I was reacting out of my own trauma from having to look out for myself for so long."

"You don't ever have to do that again," he whispered, resting his head against mine. "Look at me." I turned my eyes to his. "I love that you're strong, but you can safely take off your cape with me. Let me take care of you. Protect you. Not because you're weak, but because you deserve someone to carry the weight for you. Let me be that person, Fallon Hazel Lennox."

I didn't answer with words. I just showed him, pecking at his lips until he pulled my bottom lip into his mouth and then buried his tongue into my mouth as I released a soft moan. We stayed lip-locked and arms intertwined, binding us together for the remainder of our ride. I could be like this forever, secured and void of fear in Deacon's arms. All I felt with Deacon was unconditional love—and that's what I had for him, too.

Clear baby blue skies, a bright sun high in the sky, and the stickiness in the air made this mid-October day feel like we were retrograding back to summer. From what Deacon told me, this kind of weather wasn't unusual for October in Lovey's Bay, with warm weather often lasting until the end of October. But eighty degrees? It was too perfect of a day to pass up, especially with our schedules lining up so that we both had the day off.

"Let's go jet-skiing!" I said impulsively. I threw off the comforter covering my body and grabbed the T-shirt on the floor.

"Jet-skiing?" Deacon parroted, still lying in bed.

I tiptoed over to the window and peered out at the beach. Deacon's apartment had a better view than mine.

His unit was a few levels higher and provided an excellent perspective of the shoreline. It was still early morning, but it seemed like many shared my idea: enjoying the unseasonably warm weather as they set up their canopies and towels on the sand.

I turned on the balls of my feet, beaming as I climbed halfway onto the bed. "Yes, jet skiing. It's Wednesday, it will be eighty degrees today, and we're both off. Let's do something fun."

Deacon rolled onto his side, pulling me close as he grabbed my arm. He peppered kisses along my neck while his hand slipped under my T-shirt. "Okay. We can go after we have a little fun here."

It was tempting to stay in bed with him as I wrapped my arms around his neck, enjoying the kisses he trailed down to my chin, but I really wanted the fun in the sun more at that moment. I pulled back and gave him a quick peck before pushing away and rolling off the bed.

"We had a lot of fun last night, Daddy Deacon. Let's get out there before the day slips away from us."

With a playful groan, Deacon rolled out of bed. I left him begging for me to share the shower with him to return to my apartment. If I stayed any longer, we would be well into making fun love in the shower rather than getting ready for our fun day on the beach. Although sex with Deacon was now one of my favorite pastimes, I was determined to get out on the waters of Lovey's Bay. The spring and summer flew by so quickly that I felt like I didn't truly get the full experience of living beachside.

An hour later, Deacon and I were in our beachwear, renting jet skis at Lovey's Bay Beach. I picked an orange and black one, which matched the orange two-piece I was wearing. Deacon wasn't as particular and chose the one nearest to him.

"You don't want to coordinate?" I teased, straddling my ride.

Deacon glanced at his blue swim trunks and then at the black jetski next to him. He shrugged. "Black goes with everything."

I snickered and shook my head as Deacon climbed on. The attendant explained some rules and recommended routes to us before we started our engines and prepared for the ride. The purr of the engine quickened my heartbeat as a smile spread across my face.

Deacon moved up beside me and smacked my left cheek. "This is a different kind of horsepower than that Beemer you drive. You think you can keep up?"

I rolled my eyes as Deacon revved his engine. "Please. You should concentrate on keeping up with me."

I gunned the throttle and sped off, splashing water in Deacon's direction. I looked back and laughed as I saw the surge of water from my pull-off splash onto him, but soon enough, Deacon was right behind me and then beside me. We sliced through the waves like machetes as we zigged and zagged our way down Lovey's Bay. The sun warmed me, counterbalancing the unexpected spray of cool water that drenched me as Deacon darted in front. He glanced back, his smile shining in the sunlight, and winked.

I squinted and pressed my lips together. "Is that what we're doing?!"

I could hear his cackle as he shouted, "Just returning the favor!"

I sped up and reached Deacon's side. Just as I was about to gun it again and return the favor, I spotted a rocky cove in the distance. The water surrounding it was a beautiful sapphire, a deeper blue than the waters of Lovey's Bay. The seagulls flying and perched above it, sipping from the small waterfall cascading at the entrance of the dark cove, made it look even more magical and tempted me to explore. I pushed ahead of Deacon, waving for him to follow me. Within minutes, we were slowing down in front of the mysterious spot.

Deacon shut off his engine shortly after I did. "In all the years I've lived in Lovey's Bay, I've never seen this spot before."

"Perfect. That means we can explore it together," I said, hopping off my jet ski. The water was shallow, rising only to my waist. I waded through the water towards the hollow opening. Deacon called for me to wait for him.

At that moment, his call was merely a distant sound. As I turned my head from side to side, I felt drawn to the tranquil waterfall and the chirping birds. I took a deep breath while admiring the breathtaking rainbow reflected in the waterfall. The sun's rays danced off it and shimmered on the sparkling flecks on the rocks. My eyes brightened as I approached close enough to run my fingers over the slightly rough stones adorned with clusters of crystals.

"Only the most magical person I know could discover a hidden cove." Deacon's warm body enveloped my back as he wrapped his arms around my waist.

I snickered at the sensation of him nuzzling my neck, saying, "There's no way nobody has discovered this place.

"I don't know about anyone else, but I haven't."

"Come." I turned toward the darkened entrance, tempted to explore further. I pulled away from Deacon, letting my hand drift down to his as I linked our fingers.

Deacon halted, gripping my hand and forcing me to stop.

"Now, you know that Black folks don't explore dark places."

"Oh my, Gawd," I scoffed, tugging at his arm. I made my voice squeaky and drawled, "Not Big Daddy Deacon scared of a little ol' cave."

"I'm not afraid."

"Then c'mon. I'm sure there's nothing in there except maybe a cave monster or two." I tugged harder, giggling at my own joke and making him trudge through the small waves and the trickling waterfall. My straight hair quickly started to wave as we crossed through the water and into the cove, and I shivered as it fell onto my back. Aside from the flowing water, the cove was silent and eerily still. I squinted, trying to glimpse what lay in the depths of the darkness as I slowed to a halt, a slight fear creeping in.

Squawk!

"Oh, shit!" I stumbled back at the sound of what seemed like a bird hidden in the darkness. Almost losing my balance, I felt Deacon catch me, gripping my elbows as my body twisted toward him.

"I think you found your cave monster," Deacon teased, pointing up. I whipped my head to see a seagull perched above. My heart was still racing as I blushed and giggled in embarrassment.

I began to maneuver around Deacon as I assessed, "On that note, I think it's time for us to go."

Deacon pulled me back and into him. "No. I think we've found a nice spot to…" He pecked my lips as his hands roamed my backside. "…create a memory."

Deacon claimed my mouth before I could say anything. I had no thoughts to really protest, however. All of my thoughts were hazy with lust as his hands wasted no time traveling underneath my bikini bottoms.

His dick wasted no time steeling against my stomach either, and the feeling alone made my walls contract. As he drove his tongue down my throat, he cupped my ass with the same intensity. I loved how badly he wanted me every time, and this time was no different as my nipples hardened against his chest reactively. I slipped my hand into his swim trunks, wrapping my hand around his dick, and creamed at the feel of the veins straining against my hand.

"Ahh…" I gasped and moaned as Deacon entered a finger into my canal from behind, pushing it as deep as he could. I leaned into him, giving him deeper access, and spilled once more as his finger reached new depths.

In and out.

In and out.

He pulled his finger from me, moving them to his mouth, licking away the juices I produced for him before burying his tongue into my mouth again. Tasting myself against his tongue did something to me, expelling an energy surge through my nerves. Deacon must've felt the same because, in seconds, he was popping the strings to my bottoms. With one arm, he hoisted me up around his waist while pushing down his trunks with the other. I wrapped my legs around his waist, and in one swift rock, Deacon filled me halfway. With another rock, his girth was filling me completely.

"Mm, Deacon…"

"Mm-hmm." He hummed as he bit down on his lip,

thrusting his swollen organ in and out of me. The ridges of his veined tool against my walls sent ripples of tingles through my body, willing soft moans from me. He pulled halfway from my canal and then pushed deep again, grunting onto my lips as he stilled inside of me, "Fuck, Fallon."

I wrapped my hands around the back of his head as I pulled his bottom lip into my mouth and rocked my hips into him, encouraging him to give me what my body wanted more than anything now. Locking his mouth to mine, he palmed handfuls of my ass and pounded into me repeatedly. Unable to fight the sounds of pleasure escaping my throat, I dropped my head back and allowed them to carry through the cove, bouncing off the walls. The calming sound of the waterfall was the perfect soundtrack, relaxing my body and my walls as he drilled deeper and harder inside of me. I could hear the water crashing to the rhythm of our lovemaking, colliding with Deacon's grunts and my alternating moans and pants. The music was beautiful and erotic, heightening arousal.

Euphoric.

That was the best description for the crash of our synchronous climax.

"Deacon…Deacon…Deacon…" I moaned and repeated with each deep thrust that Deacon surged inside of me as he grunted through his own climax.

"Shit, Fallon…Goddamn….I want this forever."

"Me too. I want this forever, too," I whimpered as my

walls clenched around his dick, and another wave ran through me.

We remained locked. Our lips locked into a passionate kiss. Our bodies were locked by the way of his still-stiffened flesh. Our souls locked in with the promise of forever as we made love again.

"Hurricane Caliope is expected to make landfall as a Category 4, and as you can see, she is showing no mercy. The window for safe evacuations has narrowed to one hour, crew, and we have a foster home in the path of the direct hit that needs to be evacuated immediately. I've said enough. We've prepared for moments like this. Let's get these kids to safety!"

Chief Payton donned his water rescue helmet and quickly made his way through the crowd of firefighters. We followed his lead, looking like a bunch of highlighters in our water rescue gear. It was all hands on deck, meaning all shifts were on duty with the expectation of performing water rescues for the duration of Hurricane Caliope's time in Lovey's Bay.

This was new territory for me. Damask had never

had emergencies that required us to perform water rescues, but even though this was foreign territory, my body pumped with an adrenaline rush to take on the challenge. I fell in step with the rest of the crew, heading towards the special high-water vehicles, when I felt someone catch me by my elbow. Deacon pulled me to the side.

"You good? I know this is new for you." He looked at me with eyes that conveyed genuine concern.

I curled the corner of my lip slightly. "New scenario, but the job isn't new to me. I'm good. I'm ready for this."

"I know you're good, but this is different from last time—"

"I've been swimming my whole life. I've trained with the best deep divers. And did you forget, I'm fucking Superwoman?" I let out a short, arrogant laugh as Deacon smirked, his eyes still showing concern. I brushed my hand against his, giving it a small squeeze and reassuring him, "I'm good, Deacon. Really."

"Let's go, team!"

Denzel's last call interrupted our moment, and we hurried with the rest of the crew to our respective vehicles. I climbed into the truck with Tevin, Joss, and Farris, with Deacon at the wheel. Within seconds, we were pulling out of the station into howling winds and a heavy downpour. With each mile we drove, it felt like Deacon was in a battle for control against the wind as the truck rocked with each fierce gust. Outside the city limits, the roads darkened, and the waves seemed to crash closer than usual. When I looked out the window, I understood why the waves appeared so near. The waters of Lovey's Bay were thrashing against the storm wall.

"Naming this hurricane Caliope is diabolical," Tevin said, breaking the silence. "If I were the hurricane, I'd be mad too."

"What does that even mean?" Farris asked, frowning at Tevin. "How can a hurricane be angry? That's probably the dumbest thing you've said, Tev."

"It isn't dumb. Do you hear how this wind is howling? That's what you'd call angry."

The truck fell silent before everyone burst into laughter.

"Tev, just stop while you're ahead. Please!" Joss pleaded, clutching her stomach. "They're fittna light yo' ass up for that stupid ass analogy."

With the joke on Tevin, the truck erupted into more laughter. I chuckled quietly, but I wasn't fully engaged in what was happening. My eyes were on the house we were approaching. I widened my eyes at the sight of the lower level appearing to be underwater and then shifted my gaze to the second-level balcony, where I spotted a woman holding a child, waving us down. The handheld radio crackled, and then Denzel's voice came through.

"The water's too high for regular entry. Let's deploy the rafts and save this family."

"Got it, Chief," Deacon replied over the radio. "Alright, crew. You heard the Chief. Let's make something shake!"

As soon as the truck parked, we all hopped out and started deploying the inflatable rescue boats. I jumped in first, taking my place at the front of the boat, while Tevin and Joss climbed in after me. I was ready to wade through the water when I heard Deacon.

"I'm getting in with you all," he announced, climbing in beside me.

I looked at him with pursed lips, fully aware of what he was doing, but there was no time to address it. We started maneuvering through the crashing waves until we reached the front door, which was barely visible due to the storm surge. Naturally, I took the lead.

"Fire Department!" I called out, straining my eyes and head upwards. Through the downpour, the face of the woman from earlier appeared above us. "We're coming to get you all! How many are in the house?"

"It's me, baby girl, and two other children!" The woman called down, holding what looked like a toddler to her chest. Tevin and Joss were already working to find an entry, assessing whether the door was feasible to enter or if they should break a window. Thunder cracked above us, rattling my bones and heightening the urgency to get the family from the house immediately.

"There's no point in trying to get through that door. We just have to get up there." Deacon pointed to the balcony and rummaged through our rescue kit. Not waiting for him to find the tool he was looking for, I maneuvered to the balcony post and wrapped my right leg around it, followed by my other leg, scooting my body up.

"Fallon!" Deacon called out.

"I got this, Captain!" I shouted over my shoulder as I heaved myself up and over the balcony with all my strength.

I stumbled from the force of the wind but quickly regained my balance. I looked to my left at the mother and toddler, then to my right, spotting a teenage girl and a pre-teen standing at the balcony door. I gestured for them to join the rest of us. Soaked and shivering, I assured them, "We're going to get you all to safety."

I turned to the mother, asking her to let me take the little girl, assuring her that everyone would be fine. When she handed me the child, I turned, running into Deacon and then seeing a grappling rope flying through the air and landing at the base of the balcony. Quickly, he secured the rope again and then took the small child from my arms. Time stood still as I watched him place the child on his side, soothing her fears. In that moment, I fell deeper and harder for him. Seeing this side of him with a child made my heart and ovaries pulse.

A crack and pop echoed, and then the sky lit up again, propelling time forward at warp speed. Within a few minutes, Deacon and I worked seamlessly together: he scaled the balcony, delivering each child safely to the raft, followed by the mother, leaving me as the last to retreat. I started my descent down the rope just as a loud pop rang out and the end of a fiery power line swung towards me.

"Watch out!"

I heard a cacophony of voices yell as I released my grip from the rope to avoid being struck by the line. My descent was quick as I watched the powerline snake through the air, and soon after, I felt the impact of my body hitting the water. Unlike my last experience with water rescue, I was secured with a life jacket and buoyed to the surface, where I found Deacon fighting the current like an Olympian to reach me. Hooking his arm around my waist, he pulled me close and squared me with crazed eyes.

"You're going to be the death of me, you know that?" he huffed, clutching me tighter.

I searched his eyes with my own bewildered look, but I softened it as I found genuine fear in the depths of his gaze—the same look he gave me the first time he came to my rescue. He feared losing me, and realizing the depth of his feelings for me made me want to forget we were floating in murky hurricane water and let him have his way with me. Instead, I managed a small smile as I held onto his shoulders.

"I'm just doing my job, Captain."

He scoffed. "Yeah, well, do it a lot safer next time. I'll be damned if I lose you before… before…"

His words trailed off as the crew rowed over and began helping us onto the raft, leaving his unspoken thoughts lingering in my mind. He didn't need to finish his sentence for me to grasp what he was getting at, what he was thinking about regarding me. That thought often crossed my mind when it came to him. "It" was the thought of spending a lifetime with this man. This man who has found a way to save me from both the world and myself and carry me back to safe spaces, mentally and physically. To hear him subtly admit he was thinking about forever, too, had me in a frenzy, wondering when the thought would become a reality.

Hurricane Caliope wreaked havoc in Lovey's Bay, but it was nothing a little community effort couldn't handle. The residents of Lovey's Bay understood and took the assignment seriously, assisting with the cleanup of the residential areas. Rhythm and Brews even provided meals for families in need. Together, Fire Company 143 and the Lovey's Bay Police Department aided in the cleanup within the city limits, as well as search and rescue efforts. We were fortunate not to have many people stranded and even more grateful that the operation did not turn into a search and recovery mission. It's safe to say Lovey's Bay emerged from this disaster in moderate shape.

At the end of the second week of restoring the Bay, I had a few days off and the chance to visit my parents. Even though they didn't take a direct hit from Hurricane

Caliope, they still had some fallen trees on their property. My dad, being my dad, wanted to take care of it himself, but I convinced him to wait for my day off so I could help him and Mom. Besides, it would give me the chance to introduce my 'rents to Fallon—if she was up for it.

I was ready to introduce Fallon to my parents. We had officially been a couple since the beginning of July, but I was certain about wanting her to meet my parents from the moment she welcomed me into her world to meet her brother and mother. I knew she was the woman I wanted my parents to meet next. I felt confident about Fallon in more ways than one; all I needed now was my parents' approval—and her agreement to come with me. To my surprise, Fallon agreed with little persuasion on my part.

"I can't wait to meet the people who raised you," Fallon mused as I took the exit off the highway leading to our final destination. "I know they don't call you Deacon. I can't wait to discover what pet names they have for you."

"Oh my God," I cackled. "I don't have any wild nicknames like you…Tweety."

Fallon turned in her seat to face me, pointing her finger. "Stop. Only Parris can call me that. Ugh, I hate that nickname."

"I think it's fitting," I argued. I looked over to find her staring at me in disbelief. "You're petite and yap all the time, just like Tweety."

She gasped long and hard, and I couldn't help but burst out laughing.

"We'll find out who has the last laugh when 'Tweety' shuts her mouth and legs tonight."

I fell silent, glancing at her out of the corner of my eye. "You know I was playing."

"Mm-hmm. Whatever."

The last few minutes of the drive down the unmarked road to my parents' house were spent low-key begging and persuading Fallon not to cut me off from her goodie box. By the time I parked in the gravel driveway, I was still cut off. My parents were walking down the sidewalk when I had Fallon hugged up, peppering her with kisses.

"Deacon!" she hissed, pushing me away and straightening her unwrinkled T-shirt. She forced a smile on her face as she looked past me. I followed her gaze out the windshield to see my parents standing there. Pops wore a twisted smirk, while my mother clung to his arm with a bubbly smile. Fallon and I climbed out of the car, with me quickly trying to catch the door she had already stepped out of.

"Necking in the driveway?" My dad lifted his chin and raised an eyebrow at me.

I cleared my throat and managed a smile while Fallon scolded me under her breath. I smiled again as I took her hand, leading her to my parents. "Mom, Dad, this is Fallon…my lady."

"Well!" My mother exclaimed, her face lighting up.

She stepped away from Dad and closed the distance between us, all eyes on Fallon. "You didn't mention you were bringing someone so *beautiful*."

"Thank you." Fallon took my mom's hand and tucked her hair bashfully behind one ear.

"Fallon, huh?" Dad stepped beside Mom. With his head still slightly tilted up, he moved his gaze downward to her. A subtle smile tugged at the corners of his thick mustache as he opened his arms. "Come on in. We do hugs here."

Fallon fell into my father's embrace, her smile creating a dimple in her cheek. I had never known she had a dimple until then, and I felt a bit jealous that my father had revealed it. That jealousy faded as I realized that the meeting of the most important people in my life was going well. I expected nothing less from Reverend Nathan and First Lady Lillian Deacon. This was how they were with all new people, but this was my lady, and their warmth felt different than when meeting a new member of the congregation. After a few more moments of pleasantries, my dad was ready to get to work.

"Alright, I've got a pile of branches and limbs that we need to break down and take to the dump."

I gawked at him. "Pops, I told you I was coming. Why'd you start before me?"

"Because you know I like to get my stuff done. You like to slow-poke around."

"That's not true, Dad."

He marked me with squinted eyes and tight lips. "What happened in the spring? You came up here sulking while I did most of the gardening."

"I did not—"

"Nathan and Benji," my mother fretted. I glanced at Fallon just in time to see her smirking at the new information as she mouthed "Benji." My mother continued, "You two will never get anything done before lunch if you keep fussing over who does what. Just go and do it. Fallon, come with me to the kitchen."

"Yes, ma'am," Fallon said, following my mother toward the house. She glanced back over her shoulder. "Bye, Benji."

I half-grumbled and laughed as I shook my head, knowing this wouldn't be the last time I'd hear about it before catching up with my father. He was already making his way to the backyard. What had once been lush green trees in the backyard were now aging limbs, sparsely covered with deep shades of orange and yellow leaves. They were starting to tumble to the ground with each brisk breeze. I made a mental note to rake the leaves after we dealt with the downed branches from the storm.

"So, Fallon's your new girlfriend, huh?" Dad broke the silence with his sudden question. I glanced up from the small branches I was breaking apart. He kept breaking his branches and stuffing them into the heavy-duty trash bag.

"Yeah," I replied, standing tall. "I really like—I love her."

My confession caused him to pause, and he turned to face me. His expression was serious and unchanging as his eyebrows raised slightly before settling. "Is that so?"

I nodded, walking closer to him. "Yes. I love her, Dad. I want to marry her." I paused, recalling how I'd had this same conversation with him before. "This is different than last time, I think. I mean… I know it is." I paused again and looked down at the ground, trying to organize my thoughts. I looked at my Dad, whose gaze remained steady on me. "How did you know Mom was the one? When were you ready to propose? I'm afraid to… mess up again."

"Is that your head or your heart talking?"

My forehead creased. I was initially taken aback by his question, but then I let it settle and really thought about it. "My head. My heart says do it."

Besides the rustling of the leaves, there was silence between us once again. Oh, and the loud thud of my heart as I waited for him to give me an answer—anything that would ease my fear. I was afraid. I was afraid that I would do this, propose to Fallon, and then clam up again. One thing I knew about Fallon was that she wouldn't wait for me two years like Vanessa did, nor would I want her to. Deep down, I knew I didn't want to wait either. I knew that I would propose to her, giving her an engagement ring and a wedding ring on the same day if she'd let me. That's how badly I wanted her as my forever. Yet, fear bubbled and prickled my skin, causing me to question my readiness.

"That's the difference," he drawled. "Your mind will keep you confused and tied to all your overthinking. You know that. You know it's not God confusing you and making you fear. Silence your thoughts. Pray. And when your mind is calm, when there's nothing but the beat of your heart, feel it. If it still beats to the rhythm of your love for Fallon, if it still swells at the thought of her, if it settles in peace when you see her face…" His voice had shifted into his preacher tone before he paused. "Then that's your answer, son. That's how you'll know you're ready. Trust yourself, son."

His words alone cleared my mind, leaving only the thought of Fallon echoing. As her name resonated in my mind and filled my heart, her face emerged vividly in my memory, causing my heart to grow with love for her. I had found my answer: I was deeply in love with her. I was ready.

"So, Benjamin says you're from Damask. How are you adjusting to life in Lovey's Bay?"

"Umm, it's actually pretty good. It's much slower than Damask, but that's why I chose Lovey's Bay. A slower pace by the water—I couldn't resist it."

"Lovey's Bay is a beautiful city…"

I listened to Mrs. Deacon muse about Lovey's Bay as she waltzed around the inviting kitchen. It wasn't warm in a hot sense, but rather inviting. The walls were painted a pale yellow, radiating the same serene glow etched on her face, while the scent of cinnamon, apple, and lemon floated through the air, enhancing the atmosphere. It all conveyed sweet, loving, and wholesome family vibes.

"Yeah, Lovey's Bay is way more enjoyable than Damask on its own," I said, shifting in the wooden chair I was sitting in. "Oh, and it's better than London, too."

"London? I bet being there was fun." She settled into the seat across from me, her eyes bright and eager for me to share more. My smile hovered between indifference and disinterest as thoughts of my mother crossed my mind.

"Well…I was very young when I lived in London, so I don't have many fond memories. I just remember it always being rainy." My vision blurred as I mentally transported back to that time in my life while Mrs. Deacon waited patiently for me to continue. Her unhurried attentiveness encouraged me to share more. "I lived there with my mom. She married a man from there. I mean…it was fine, but my best memories are from when I left and moved to Damask."

"Hmm, I see," she hummed, her smile and expression still full of sincerity. "How is your mother? Is she still in London?"

"She's hell, that's what she is." That's how I wanted to respond. Instead, I pressed my lips together and let out a rough sigh as I said, "She's okay, I guess. We don't talk much. It's… kind of complicated."

I winced when I realized how much I had shared about my family life with my boyfriend's mother during our first meeting. Although it was vague, I felt my apprehension and disdain were heavy and obvious. I glanced up, hoping she wasn't looking at me as if I were a weirdo with a load of family problems. What a first impression. Instead, Mrs. Deacon slid the saucer of sliced pound cake we had prepared for dessert after lunch toward me.

"Have one with me," she suggested with a wink. "When the men come in, I can't guarantee there will be any left."

Timidly, I smiled and grabbed a slice as she pulled a folded napkin from the holder and slid it to me. I placed my slice on it, taking a small piece. The dense cake melted in my mouth, the sweetness sending a comforting tingle through me. As I pinched off a larger bite, Mrs. Deacon broke off a piece of her cake and began telling me a story, her voice steady yet pleasant.

"My mother and I used to clash something awful. It was always about something I wasn't doing right to her. She wanted me to be a nurse, while I wanted to be a teacher. She wanted me to marry Elroy, this young man I grew up with and the family adored. However, I was in love with Nathan." Her eyes grew dreamy at the mention of her husband. My heart sank at the same moment I imagined hers did. She slowly blinked out of her thoughts, returning to her original line of thinking. "When my mother started meddling in my romantic life, I declared enough was enough. It was one thing for her to try to control my career, but who I decide to share my bed with every night? No ma'am!

"It wasn't until I had Benji that I truly understood my mother and why she was so concerned about my life. I remember us butting heads once again; this time about how I was raising Benjamin. I outright asked her, "What's your deal?!" Her face scrunched as her voice rose to a level that made me sit up straight. In a calmer tone, she corrected me, "Well, I said a bit more than that, but you get the picture. A lot of what she said was nonsense, but one thing stuck with me. She said, "I just don't want you to make the same mistakes I did. I want you to be better than I was. I want you and your family to have more."

I never considered her perspective on what… what are you all calling it now? Generational trauma. I knew Mama didn't have the best life, but it wasn't bad… in my eyes. But to her, she saw it differently, which is why she was pushing so hard, and failing, to reach me. That's when I learned what grace truly meant.

Now, Mama wasn't right or perfect in how she did things, and I didn't overlook that. However, I learned not to let her ways affect me or dictate how I lived my life. It was my life. I offered her grace because she was fighting her own demons."

I rolled the small crumb I held between my fingers, letting the unexpected words of wisdom sink in. They related to my own relationship with my mother, and it was rather eerie, making me question whether Deacon shared tidbits. While my mother's antics had been very twisted and one-dimensional, I could see how she might be acting out of her own traumas. After all, she was a single mother of two before she met my stepfather. Parris and I never wanted for anything, but could I say it was easy for my mother? I couldn't. I didn't know because I hadn't walked a day in her shoes at my young age. Perhaps there was a glimmer of room for me to extend her grace and understanding, but not enough for me to overlook her outrageous perspective on my relationship with Travis.

"Thank you for sharing," I eventually said after listening to the clock on the wall tick for a moment. "I'm not sure how much grace I can show my mother…"

"Just like forgiveness, grace doesn't imply that you forget. Grace offers you an escape from the torment. It provides an understanding of what someone else might be feeling, while granting you permission to *live*…fully."

The thought of being freed from the shackles of my mother brought a relief over me, a feeling I had never experienced before. I probably would have never felt it if it weren't for the conversation with Mrs. Deacon. Somehow, this subtle message provided the healing I needed—a healing I desired.

I greeted her warm gaze with my own. "Thank you, Mrs. Deacon."

She got up from her seat and walked around the table, opening her arms wide. I stepped into her warm embrace. "Call me Mrs. Lillie… or Mom. I have a feeling you'll be around for a while."

Feeling the pavement beneath my feet felt invigorating, just like the crisp early morning air. There was a slight hint of humidity that signaled Spring was finally upon us again. "Finally" probably isn't the best word to express how I felt. Winter came and went like it was on a weekend getaway, and honestly, I was a bit melancholy to see it go. This winter holiday season was different for me. What made it different? Family.

I've always felt a sense of family with Parris and Zaria, but this year, I truly experienced what it means to be part of a family. After meeting Deacon's parents, it seemed like I was their honorary child. They welcomed me with open arms and plenty of love as if I were Deacon's other half—even though the holiday season didn't bring the gift of an engagement ring…not that I was expecting it.

I didn't give it much thought. The presumptuous notion felt like I was getting ahead of myself with my hopes. Our relationship was solid—like, throw away the key solid—so it wasn't far-fetched to think that one day we'd be married. Still, I never pushed the idea, not even in conversation. I simply enjoyed the family atmosphere throughout Thanksgiving as I helped Mrs. Lillie prepare dinner and even learned her secret recipe for sweet potato pie. Then, I loved Christmas as Deacon and I accompanied his Reverend Nathan to pick out the family Christmas tree.

Family.

It may sound strange to say, but I felt softer during this phase of my life. In the past, when I was with Travis, I acted like a "soft girl." You know, putting on a smile and making my movements delicate to please him and everyone else who mattered. After him, I became rigid and tough to protect myself from anyone's control. I didn't realize I was doing this until maybe the hundredth time Deacon showed and told me he cared about me. As he would say, "It's okay to take off the cape." Deacon made me feel safe enough to do just that. I felt secure with him, knowing that when I was ready to shed my Superwoman suit for a moment, I could depend on him to protect me and my heart. Now, instead of pretending, I was truly a soft girl—light, relaxed, and in love with life—yet still strong and ambitious in my pursuit to save lives. That was the difference with being with Deacon; he allowed me to be both soft and strong, and I loved that he offered me that on so many levels.

So, while winter is often associated with cold, dreary days, my experience was beautiful, and the chill was melted away by joy. Having never known this kind of love and happiness, I found myself wanting to savor winter a little longer, but I sensed that this season of my life wouldn't end with the change in weather.

"It feels amazing out here!" Zaria exclaimed between her steady breaths as she jogged alongside me. "The weather, the sound of the waves—I'm going to love it here!"

"I thought you loved it here since you now live closer to your BFF," I pouted, nudging her in the side. I picked up the pace slightly, avoiding her attempt to nudge me back.

"Neither of you are going to love it here if I pass out and die trying to keep up, because I'll come back and haunt your asses!" Joni yelled, huffing behind us. In a staggered motion, we came to a halt, turning to find Joni doubled over, clutching her knees. We jogged back and helped her to a nearby bench.

"Sorry, Joni," I apologized, taking a seat beside her.

I rubbed her back as she sat up straight, fixing me with narrowed eyes and pursed lips before grumbling,

"Mm-hmm. You both owe me an asiago egg and cheese bagel and a large coffee."

"You got it," Zaria promised, wrapping her arm around Joni's shoulder and giving her a squeeze.

It's safe to say I now have a solid friend group in Lovey's Bay, especially with Zaria having relocated here and Joni being more than just my nosy neighbor. It's been great to have a group of women to balance my male-dominated work life, particularly now that Zaria is part of the company. With the addition of Joni and Nina, I feel complete in my social life here.

"You know, breakfast does sound good right about now…" Zaria's words trailed off, just like her eyes. I followed her gaze, finding it fixed on the charming Chef Maxwell, standing on the front patio of Sable Pearl.

"Mm-hmm, it seems like you're trying to add some ripe eggplant to your bagel," Joni quipped, noticing where Zaria's attention settled.

Returning to the present, Zaria gawked and then giggled. "I don't know what you're talking about."

It was Joni's and my turn to pin Zaria with disbelieving stares. Catching movement in my peripheral vision, I looked up to see Chef waving Zaria over. "Looks like he knows what we're talking about."

Zaria scrunched her nose, struggling to keep her blush from spreading. She curled the ringlet at the nape of her neck with her finger as she slowly got up. "I'll be right back."

"No, you won't!" Joni and I said in unison, laughing as she jogged away.

Joni continued her ramble about breakfast, looking up the nearest diner. I listened until I felt my phone vibrate against my chest. Wiping away my perspiration, I smiled as I slid the button to answer Deacon's Facetime.

"Hey babe." I lifted my phone and angled it for a good angle.

"Big Mama." Deacon glanced down at me, flashing a big smile before returning his eyes back to the road. It was a little after nine in the morning, just after the end of his shift for the week. He flicked his eyes away from the road again, taking in my surroundings. "Out running?"

"You know it; Joni needed a break, though."

"A break?!" Deacon exclaimed, raising his voice to catch Joni's attention. With her focused on him, he joked, "The only thing Joni needs a break for is her big ol' mouth."

Joni twisted her neck, coming into the camera's view. "I know your Frankenstein monster-sized head ain't talking!"

Bubbling with laughter, I pulled the phone away from Joni, shifting my gaze between the two of them. "To your corners, you two!"

"His ass lucky he isn't here," Joni spat, shaking her fist at the camera playfully. Before turning to walk away, she announced, "I'm gonna go grab a glass of…something that says it's breakfast time but feels like happy hour at the restaurant."

"Why you gotta start stuff?" I asked playfully after Joni left.

"She knows I'm joking. It wouldn't be me if I didn't make jokes about her."

I shook my head at him, knowing it was true as he cackled. I've learned that Deacon was a jokester when it came to everyone. His laugh faded as he changed the subject. "I've got something I want to show you and get your opinion on. Do you think you can end your run a little early?"

I ogled him. "Not you trying to cut into my run time."

He shot me an apologetic smile. "I know, I know. But it's kind of time-sensitive."

My eyebrows knitted together, now curious about what this urgent matter was. I hesitated and said, "Okay… but I'm a few blocks from home."

"Near Sable Pearl?" he asked, tapping on his phone. The screen blurred as though he were using another app, and I figured he was checking my location. The screen cleared up, and he started tapping on his GPS, confirming my guess. "I'll be there in five minutes. We can take the ladies back before we head out, too."

"Wait, let me see…" I pulled up my text thread with Joni and Zaria, typing to let them know what was happening. Within seconds, they both replied, telling me to go on without them. "Okay, well, they are going to stay out here, so I guess I'll meet you—"

Before I could finish my sentence, I heard the purr of Deacon's engine. I saw his sparkling red ride gliding to a stop on the main street. I jogged over and met him as he stood at the passenger side, the door open for me. Before getting in, I craned my head back to meet his lips with mine. The feel of his lips on mine never got old.

"Hop in," Deacon said, smacking my ass as I moved to get in. I looked over at him with a smirk. His obsession with feeling on my body parts never got old, either.

Deacon and I drove about fifteen minutes toward the residential side of Lovey's Bay, engaging in small talk about his shift. The discussion about work was far less interesting than the view. We were entering a neighborhood of newly constructed family-sized homes. The houses we passed as we entered the community were completed, painted, or made of brick, while some still appeared to be under construction with unfinished driveways. As we drove further back, the homes looked less finished, including the one where we glided to a stop in front of. It only had its skeletal frame and weather barrier material in place. Sand-colored bricks lined the house, ready to be applied.

"What's this?" I asked, looking at him, confused, as he turned off the engine.

Deacon grinned at me, not offering me an explanation until he assisted me out of the car. Taking my hand, he guided me along the gravel path to the house. "What do you think about moving into a home with me?"

My jaw slacked as my eyes rounded, as I fluttered my lashes rapidly, trying to process his question. "A house?"

Deacon paused, stroking the top of my hand as his gaze lingered on me. "Yeah. Our house." I still couldn't find the words as I took in the two-story home and the base of the two-car garage. I looked back at him, my mouth opening and closing, but nothing came out. Deacon chuckled and raised a finger. "Before you respond, take a tour with me."

"Okay," I managed to say, my voice cracking.

My breath hitched as Deacon reached into his pocket, pulled out a keychain with a single key, and proceeded to unlock the front door. Then, my stomach hollowed as I took in the immaculate interior as we stepped in: hard-wood floors, a state-of-the-art chef-style kitchen with stainless steel appliances. I walked further into the home, into what would be the living room, scoping out the fire-place lined with beautiful dark brick. Immediately, my mind began to tick with ideas for making this space a home. And then, how we could gather our friends or even just me and the girls in the backyard around the firepit for wine, beer, and laughter.

I dreamed a little more as we climbed the steps to the second floor, passing by two bedrooms that I could picture… kids. Maybe a boy and a girl, hell, twins, running in and out of the rooms, their bathroom filled with rubber duckies, water toys, and little potty training seats. Then, at the end of the hall, we stepped into the master bedroom, where those children would be created. I envisioned a large canopy bed against the wall where we would make love. Hot, passionate sex where we could get as filthy as we wanted without worrying about neighbors on the other side of the wall. I imagined us getting up each morning, finding ourselves at the his-and-her sinks, brushing our teeth and getting ready for the day, or sharing intimate showers under the rainfall showerhead of the standalone shower…

"What do you think?"

Deacon's question pulled me out of my daydream, and my heart raced with excitement. I turned on the heels of my sneakers to face his hopeful expression. Taking measured steps, I closed the distance between us as he took one of my hands in each of his. I moistened my lips before sliding my hands from his and wrapping them around his neck. Rising to the balls of my feet, I pressed my lips against his.

"This is a big step, Benjamin," I uttered as I pulled back.

He chuckled. "First name basis, eh?"

"Yeah," I giggled. "You know the first name comes out when we are talking about something serious. This is serious. Like, planning a future serious."

I grazed my bottom lip with my teeth as I snickered

to myself at how I was just doing the very thing I said he was doing: planning a future. I needed to hear what he would say next to be certain we were on the same page and that I wasn't the only one planning for forever.

"I've been imagining a future with you since the moment I first saw you, Fallon. Back when I thought your name was Hazel." I snickered and shook my head at my earlier antics. "And even after discovering that was a lie, I still wanted to make forever happen with you. I'm going to make forever happen, starting with our home." He pulled back to gesture around the empty bedroom. He shrugged, raising his eyebrows. "A little out of order, but I couldn't let this house slip away. It's the last one in the neighborhood up for sale. I needed your approval for it to be our forever home so I could secure it. So…what do you think, baby?"

"A forever home." These words echoed in my head as I took a panoramic look at the room and replayed each space we walked through, my heart swelling. Coming to a stop in front of Deacon, I waved my hand around. "Go ahead and secure our forever home."

Deacon belted a laugh as he rushed toward me, scooping me into his arms and spinning me around before planting a big, wet kiss on my lips.

———

It had been a long time since we last visited Baby Dee's Barbecue. In fact, the last time we were in the building was on our first date. We've ordered delivery in the past, but tonight, after Deacon secured the house, it felt right to return to the place where it all began to celebrate.

Even with the dew point low, the small building felt sticky with humidity when we walked in, and I was grateful that I had paired a halter bodysuit with my denim jeans and jacket. I peeled off the jacket as soon as we settled at our table. A male host led us to our table, ironically the same one we had during our first visit, right off the side of the stage. A few moments later, a familiar woman greeted us.

"Oh, welcome back, Love Birds!" Our previous waitress, Niecy, lilted as she approached us. Even after a year, her warm and vibrant energy radiated just as much as her fluffy hair. She shifted her gaze between Deacon and me, asking, "What can I get you two started with?"

Knowing what we wanted, we ordered our drinks and food, and then Niecy sauntered away. Moments later, she returned with two shots of SirDavis and our favorite local beer. Deacon tapped his shot glass on the table before lifting it.

"Here's to starting our forever journey."

I beamed. "Cheers to our forever home."

We clinked our glasses and downed our shots as Niecey stepped onto the stage, tapping the microphone. "Okay, okay, settle down now!" Niecey paused, narrowing her eyes at the audience as they quieted down. Her face lit up as they complied. "We are about to kick off tonight's karaoke night with an oldie but goodie. Please welcome Deacon and…okay then…Big Mama to the stage, singing 'Through the Fire!'"

The applause around us drowned out my gasp as I realized she was calling us to the stage. Unfazed, Deacon took my hand while I protested, "Deacon! What…?"

"C'mon now, Big Mama. Since when have you shied away from a little fun?"

My mouth fell open, devoid of a rebuttal, as I peeled myself from my seat and let him drag me onto the stage while the band began to play the intro to the Chaka Khan classic. I took my place to the right of Deacon, both of us standing in front of separate microphones.

> "I look in your eyes and I can see you've
> loved so dangerously…."

Deacon crooned, slightly off pitch yet still managing to hold onto some kind of tune as he grasped the mic stand and fixed his gaze on me. He continued with the verse and then gestured for me to join in. I glanced at the screen with the scrolling lyrics and jumped in.

> "When it's this good, there's no saying
> "No…"

I cracked and harmonized as Deacon's voice faded away, giving me the stage. I giggled while the audience cheered and continued.

"I want you so I'm ready to go… Through
the fire…"

Deacon joined me in singing the chorus, and so did the crowd, which helped loosen me up. I belted out the lyrics, closing my eyes and becoming completely immersed in the music. I hadn't realized how much the song resonated with the beginning of our relationship— my timidness to fall and Deacon's persistence to go through our fiery journey for me—for us. My cheeks ached as I reflected on the past year and sang into the next verse. I was pulled out of my zone by Deacon's hand covering mine as he gently pulled me away from my mic.

"When it's this sweet, there's no saying
no…I need you so I'm ready to go…"

I jerked away, my trembling hand flying to my mouth as Deacon pulled out a felt box and dropped to one knee, revealing a blinding diamond just as the track was replaced the band at the exact moment the chorus started again. He mouthed the words. Only fragments registered as my eyes filled with tears and I processed what was happening:

> "Through the fire…to the limit…I'd
>   gladly risk it all…
> Through the fire…for a chance at
>   loving you…
> Even through the fire…"

I wiped at my eyes, clearing them and scanning Deacon for the moment to disappear. It didn't. He remained there, on his knees presenting me this ring. "What do you say, Fallon Hazel Lennox? Will you let me love you forever, through any fire, bypassing any limit?"

With shaking hands and a tremulous voice, I trilled, "Yes! Yes!"

Deacon bit down on his lip, failing to contain his excitement as he nodded and slipped the ring onto my finger before tackling me and lifting me off my feet. The crowd erupted with cheers, mixing in chants of the chorus as Deacon twirled me around and claimed my lips. Unconcerned with our audience, I deepened our kiss with a messy, passionate one of my own. The world could watch this display for all I cared. In one day, I found my forever home and my forever mate in life. All in one year. Through the fire that once was my life, I emerged like a shining phoenix. Let the world see it. Let the world see that beautiful love can come out when you go through a fire meant to destroy you.

"By the authority vested in me, I now pronounce you husband and wife. You may kiss your bride."

"Aww, shit!" I heard Joni squeal as Deacon wrapped his arm around my waist, dipping me and devouring my lips. I giggled as I kissed him back with just as much passion. The small group of witnesses clapped and cheered as Deacon brought me back up to a stand. Pecking me again, he murmured, "I always wanted to do that."

"Ladies and gentlemen, I now present to you for the first time Mr. and Mrs. Benjamin and Fallon Deacon." We turned to face our guests: Mr. and Mrs. Deacon, Zaria, Nina and Denzel, and Joni and Tevin, giving them plenty of time to snap pictures of us with Lovey's Bay as our backdrop.

A month after Deacon proposed, we decided not to waste any time and get married. Well, it was Deacon's idea. He was so ready to make me his wife, and I could admit I was ready to become his. Having a big wedding wasn't really the vision I had for myself. I wanted to marry the love of my life in an intimate ceremony with those who matter, and that's what we did. We got married in front of our family and friends—well, almost everyone. Parris and Tinsley couldn't make it to our spontaneous wedding since we decided to get married just before we left for their wedding, but we had Parris's blessing, and I was content with that. So, here we were, at Lovey's Cliff, getting married. I couldn't be happier to have married my love in the very destination we visited on our first date.

We spent a few minutes with our friends and family as they congratulated us before we had to dash to catch our flight. He was the perfect gentleman, pulling open the passenger side door to the white vintage convertible. That was my idea—no limos, just a nice ride we could zoom down the two-lane road to the airport with the top down. I smoothed my white sweetheart-neck peplum dress, grabbed the tail of my veil, and slid into the passenger seat. As Deacon rounded the car to the driver's side, I waved and blew kisses to our guests, who were watching us prepare to drive off.

"Be careful, you all," Nina called to us, wiping her tear-filled eyes. Denzel stood next to her, his hand on her round belly, gently rubbing their bundle of joy that was due any day now.

"No, don't be careful! We need you back nice and pregnant!" Joni added, tapping the air with her finger.

"I second that!" Mrs. Lillie said, giggling.

"Ma!" Deacon groaned as the engine of the car purred.

I threw my head back, laughing at everything, just as Deacon peeled away, quickly accelerating down the road. We had an hour before our flight departed, with a thirty-minute drive to the airport—assuming there was no traffic. We knew we were cutting it close by getting married so near to our departure time, but we had an affinity for thrills and high stakes. That's what I loved about Benjamin; he craved the adrenaline rush, just like me.

We reached the airport in twenty minutes, hopping out of the car after parking in the valet lane. Deacon grabbed our suitcase and then took my hand. We dashed through the airport like two excited teenagers, heading to security since we had already checked in online. Out of breath yet still buzzing from the adrenaline, Deacon and I arrived at our gate, showed our boarding passes, and then eased into a comfortable pace as we walked down the boarding hall to the plane.

"Hey, Mrs. Big Mama Deacon." As he wrapped his free arm around my waist, Deacon pulled me closer as we slowed down behind the last passengers boarding.

I chuckled at the silly mix of my nickname and my

new last name. Playing along, I said, "Hey, Mr. Daddy Deacon."

He groaned in my ear as we moved to the entrance of the airplane. "Mm, I'm gonna need you to call me that when I slide up in you later."

I giggled again like a schoolgirl as we boarded the plane and replied, "Your wish is my command."

Deacon nuzzled my neck, and I turned my head to meet his lips for a kiss.

"Welcome aboard, Newlyweds!"

I popped my eyes open mid-kiss when I heard the familiar Southern drawl. Slowly, I turned to my left and met the gaze of Captain Langston Calloway. His face lit up as he recognized me, but then fell into a slightly disappointed smile as he grasped the scenario before him.

"Langston," I greeted my smile still in place.

"Hazel. Wow, it's been... a long time." Langston glanced at me, then turned to Deacon, who I felt pulling me closer to him.

"Uh, yeah..." I said nervously at the sound of my fictitious-but-not-so-fictitious name. This was another situation I had never faced before. Much like the time I confronted the moment of truth with Deacon, I found myself in the same dilemma with Langston. I didn't owe him anything, but I was ready to let go of the last remnants of my old life. I exhaled, "...About that... my name isn't Hazel."

The captain's eyebrows knit together in confusion. Deacon stepped in to help.

"It's Mrs. Fallon Deacon," he boomed, reaching out his hand. "I'm Benjamin Deacon, her husband."

My nerves sent shockwaves through my body at Deacon's possessiveness. I liked it.

Slowly, Langston took his hand, and even more slowly, he said, "Nice to meet you. I'm—"

Deacon released his hand and dismissed his introduction. "No need to introduce yourself. I know who you are."

I turned my head to look at Deacon as the Captain asked, "Really?"

Deacon looked down at me and winked before turning back to Captain. "Yeah, you're just someone who couldn't lock it down." My jaw dropped, and I tried to stifle my shocked laughter. "Nice to meet you, Cap."

With that, Deacon grabbed my hand and led me down the aisle.

ABOUT THE AUTHOR

Danielle Brooks (born Ashley Robinson) hails from Richmond, Virginia, with a long love for writing and reading since her school-age years. Her earliest memory of writing her first "book" was as a 5th grader in a simple five-subject notebook. She later found love in poetry, only sharing it with a few friends and family and occasionally in class. In 2023, Ashley decided to follow her pursuit to become an author, taking on her alter ego, Danielle Brooks, a name that pays homage to her identity and her family lineage. She currently still lives in Richmond with her two children, a host of family, and dear friends.

http://www.daniellebrookswrites.com

https://beacons.ai/daniellebrookswrites

ALSO BY DANIELLE BROOKS

Sweet Like Sundays

Kindred Moments

<u>Lennox Protective Services Series</u>

Flight to Parris

To Parris, With Love

Midnight: A New Year's Eve Novelette

<u>Belafonte & Friends Series</u>

Just Kickin' It (Prelude)

Kenderella

Friendsgiving With The Belafontes

<u>Fire Company 143 Series</u>

Smoke Signals

Through The Fire